INTIMATE MOMENTS®

Silhouette®

671
$3.75 U.S.
$4.25 CAN.
October

esterday's
secrets...

OUR CHILD?

SALLY TYLER HAYES

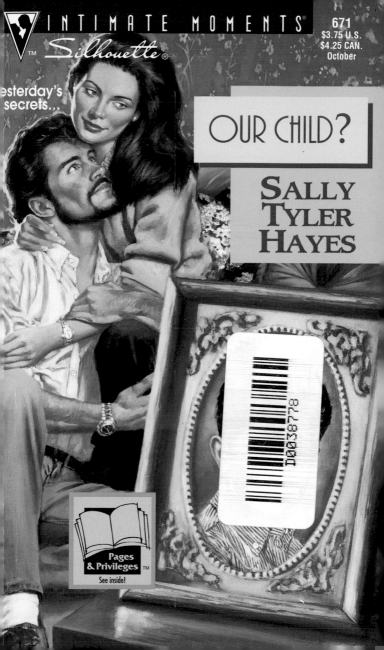

Pages
& Privileges ™

See inside!

You're About to Become a

Privileged

Woman.

INTRODUCTING

PAGES & PRIVILEGES™.

It's our way of thanking you for
buying our books at your
favorite retail store.

**Pages
& Privileges**

TM

ISBN 0-373-07671-1

9 780373 076710

50375

Enrollment Form

☐ *Yes!* I WANT TO BE A *PRIVILEGED WOMAN.*
Enclosed is one *PAGES & PRIVILEGES™* Proof of
Purchase from any Harlequin or Silhouette book currently for
sale in stores (Proofs of Purchase are found on the back pages
of books) and the store cash register receipt. Please enroll me
in *PAGES & PRIVILEGES™*. Send my Welcome Kit and FREE
Gifts -- and activate my FREE benefits -- immediately.

More great gifts and benefits to come.

NAME (please print)

ADDRESS   **APT. NO**

CITY   **STATE**   **ZIP/POSTAL CODE**

▼ DETACH HERE AND MAIL TODAY! ▼

PROOF OF PURCHASE ONLY

**NO CLUB!
NO COMMITMENT!**
*Just one purchase brings
you great Free Gifts and
Benefits!*

Please allow 6-8 weeks for delivery. Quantities are limited. We reserve the right to
substitute items. Enroll before October 31, 1995 and receive one full year of benefits.

Name of store where this book was purchased_____

Date of purchase_____

Type of store:

☐ Bookstore   ☐ Supermarket   ☐ Drugstore

☐ Dept. or discount store (e.g. K-Mart or Walmart)

☐ Other (specify)_____

Pages
& Privileges™

Which Harlequin or Silhouette series do you usually read?

Complete and mail with one Proof of Purchase and store receipt to:

U.S.: *PAGES & PRIVILEGES™*, P.O. Box 1960, Danbury, CT 06813-1960

Canada: *PAGES & PRIVILEGES™*, 49-6A The Donway West, P.O. 813,
North York, ON M3C 2E8

SIM-PP6B

Despite everything that was raging inside her head, Carolyn couldn't keep from thinking about Drew.

She was still angry at the way he'd walked away from her all those years ago, but foremost in her mind was the fact that he would somehow find out about Billy. His son. *Their* son. He would want an explanation for what she'd done, and she would never be able to make him understand.

She'd had his son without ever letting him know the child existed, without ever giving Drew the chance to have a say about what happened to the boy.

Nothing could change what she'd done. Nothing could give him back the years with Billy, and Carolyn felt sure that he would want them back.

What could possibly matter after that?

Dear Reader,

This is another spectacular month here at Silhouette Intimate Moments. You'll realize that the moment you pick up our Intimate Moments Extra title. *Her Secret, His Child,* by Paula Detmer Riggs, is exactly the sort of tour de force you've come to expect from this award-winning writer. It's far more than the story of a child whose father has never known of her existence. It's the story of a night long ago that changed the courses of three lives, leading to hard lessons about responsibility and blame, and—ultimately— to the sort of love that knows no bounds, no limitations, and will last a lifetime.

Three miniseries are on tap this month, as well. Alicia Scott's *Hiding Jessica* is the latest entrant in "The Guiness Gang," as well as a Romantic Traditions title featuring the popular story line in which the hero and heroine have to go into hiding together—where of course they find love! Merline Lovelace continues "Code Name: Danger" with *Undercover Man,* a sizzling tale proving that appearances can indeed be deceiving. Beverly Barton begins "The Protectors" with *Defending His Own,* in which the deeds of the past come back to haunt the present in unpredictable—and irresistibly romantic—ways.

In addition, Sally Tyler Hayes returns with *Our Child?* Next year look for this book's exciting sequel. Finally, welcome our Premiere author, Suzanne Sanders, with *One Forgotten Night.*

Sincerely,

Leslie Wainger
Senior Editor and Editorial Coordinator

Please address questions and book requests to:
Silhouette Reader Service
U.S.: 3010 Walden Ave., P.O. Box 1325, Buffalo, NY 14269
Canadian: P.O. Box 609, Fort Erie, Ont. L2A 5X3

OUR CHILD?

SALLY TYLER HAYES

Published by Silhouette Books

America's Publisher of Contemporary Romance

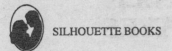

SILHOUETTE BOOKS

ISBN 0-373-07671-1

OUR CHILD?

Copyright © 1995 by Teresa Hill

Printed in U.S.A.

SALLY TYLER HAYES

lives in South Carolina with her husband, son and daughter. A former journalist for a South Carolina newspaper, she fondly remembers that her decision to write and explore the frontiers of romance came at about the same time she discovered, in junior high, that she'd never be able to join the crew of the Starship Enterprise.

Happy and proud to be a stay-home mom, she is thrilled to be living her lifelong dream of writing romances.

To the best friends a writer ever had,
the members of the GEnie Romance Exchange

Chapter 1

Little Sara Parker got away.

She was only seven, but she was fast, especially when she was scared to death. She had guts, too, because she saw her chance and she took it.

Near as the authorities could make out from what the little girl had told them, the man had stolen her off the sidewalk, a mere block from her parents' home in Russellville, Illinois, about seventy miles west of Chicago.

Four days later—she wouldn't talk about the intervening time—he'd been driving, Sara in the truck with him, then he nearly ran out of gas.

He'd stopped to get more and Sara had defied his command to stay in the cab of the pickup and keep quiet. She'd jumped off the high seat onto the parking lot, then immediately stashed herself away under a tarpaulin in the bed of another pickup, only moments before it pulled onto the rural highway.

Sara Parker saved herself.

Only trouble was, she had hidden herself away quite well in the back of that second truck, and had been too scared to move. No one noticed she was there until an hour or so had passed. The startled driver, a young boy from Bloomington, Indiana, headed for his cousin's new home on the White River to go fishing, had no idea where he'd stopped the last time; he'd been lost and looking for directions. But that must have been the place where Sara climbed into the bed of his truck.

Sara had no clue about where she'd been kept for the four days she was missing or where she'd made her escape, and so far, she hadn't been willing to talk at all about the man who'd taken her away from her poor mother and father.

Special Agent Andrew Delaney had been on the case for only three days when the girl escaped. He beat her parents to Pritchard, the little Indiana town where they'd found her, more than three hours' drive from where she'd been snatched. Drew had been the first FBI agent to speak with her.

She hadn't told him much of anything that would be useful in helping him find the man. He was tall, but then all men were to a seven-year-old girl. He smelled bad, he smoked constantly, and he'd hurt her. She wouldn't say how, but then, she didn't have to. Drew knew what bad men did to little girls.

All in all, he had next to nothing to go on in his search for the man.

Still, there'd been something about Sara that triggered some memory for him. Something about this case was so familiar, and he'd concentrated so hard on what she'd told him that he overlooked it for an entire hour and a half.

It was her clothes.

Sara Parker had been kidnapped on her way home from her best friend's house. They'd been playing in the tree house in the backyard until it turned cold on them. It was

October, so she'd been wearing a flowered pink sweater and a pair of light-colored jeans. Drew had seen some pictures taken earlier in the fall, when she was wearing the same outfit.

But when she escaped, she'd been dressed differently; in a light cotton short set more suited to summer than fall. He should have realized that earlier. That was at least part of the reason the girl had been shivering—from the cold.

Now that Drew thought about it, the clothes had seemed too big for her, too. The top had kept falling off her shoulder, and her tiny waist had been too narrow for the waistband of the shorts.

He knew those clothes.

They were red—red-and-black checked shorts with red trim, with a matching cropped top that barely covered her stomach, even if the top was much too big for her.

The answer was right in the back of his mind, hiding there in the shadows.

In an eerie premonition of what was to come, in what he could only describe as an acknowledgment that some part of his brain figured it out before the rest of him, a chill moved over him in one long wave, shaking him to the core.

Of course he knew those clothes.

He'd seen them before, on another little girl. Her parents had bought that little red suit for her one year in Texas, while visiting relatives over their Easter vacation. The little girl had worn the red suit all summer long. And one Sunday afternoon in August, after a church picnic, she'd disappeared.

It had been ten years ago.

"Carolyn! You've got to see this!"

She looked up as the door to her office, high in the corner of the old renovated house in Chicago, burst open. By the time Carolyn McKay stood up, her normally calm, cool secretary had come around to the other side of the desk and was tugging on her arm.

"Come on," Julie said. "You won't believe it."

"Okay, I'm coming."

Julie led her through the hallway and downstairs to the combination kitchen-lounge, where the whole administrative staff of Hope House, a private agency working for children's rights and safety, seemed to be gathered around the small TV set in the corner and cheering.

"Comin' through," Julie said, taking her right down front.

"What's happened?" Carolyn said. They so seldom got good news.

"They found her," Brian Wilson, the best computer expert she'd ever had the pleasure of working with, said as he threw an arm around her back and gave her a quick squeeze. "They found Sara Parker."

She gasped. Her hand came up to cover her mouth, muffling her words, as she stared at the pictures of the little girl on the tiny television screen. "Oh, thank God . . ."

Carolyn squeezed Brian back, then turned to her secretary for another celebratory hug. The administrative offices of Hope House were in an uproar. They'd been following the little girl's case for the past seventy-two hours, and most of them had expected the worst, from the information the authorities had released about her kidnapping. But it hadn't worked out that way—not this time.

"That's incredible," Carolyn said, straining to hear what the announcer was saying. "How did they find her?"

"They didn't, actually," Brian said. "She ran away when the guy stopped to get gas for his truck."

God, all kids should be so lucky—and so brave.

Carolyn felt the throbbing in her head, the churning in her stomach—which had been constant ever since they'd heard about the kidnapping—finally ease. It would be all right now. At least until the next case.

In her business, there was always another case, always another child, another set of grief-stricken parents, maybe brothers and sisters, too.

Carolyn knew all about that.

Her sister had disappeared ten years ago, and no one had ever found a trace of her or her kidnapper.

Drew Delaney sat alone at a borrowed desk in the corner of the Pritchard police station, waiting for someone at FBI headquarters to dig up the file on the ten-year-old case that continued to haunt him to this day.

He was oblivious of the constant ringing of the phone, the buzz of excited conversation around him, the curious stares of other officers, both local police and FBI. He turned his back on all that and sat facing the wall, his mind helplessly drawn back to another place, another time.

They had never found the other girl, had barely found a trace of usable evidence, not even the first good clue as to what could have happened to her.

It was even crueler than the actual death of a child, because her parents had never learned what had become of their daughter. To this day, they waited for answers. No doubt, in some corner of their minds, they still hoped for a miracle—that she was alive and well somewhere, that someday she'd find her way back to them. Some bit of irrational hope never died, making the nightmare a never-ending one.

Drew wanted answers for them, and for himself. While witnessing something as joyous as Sara Parker's tearful reunion with her parents helped ease the ache, it didn't stop it. Nothing would. Except finding the other missing child.

"Mr. Delaney?" someone called out from the front of the room.

He stood and turned around, then caught the clerk's eye. She made her way back to him, through the throng of excited, happy law-enforcement officers. They'd won one for a change, and they'd all been in this business long enough to know that they had to celebrate the victories, because the defeats were far too many, the costs much too high.

"Mr. Delaney?" she said again as she reached his corner of the room.

"Yes," he said, holding out a none-too-steady hand.

"Fax for you." She handed it over.

"Thanks," he muttered.

Drew held it facedown in his hand, waiting for the clerk to walk away. Then, once again, he turned his back on the crowded room.

It shouldn't mean so much to him—not after all this time. And it shouldn't bother him this much; he'd worked on dozens of cases like this in which they'd never found the missing children.

But that one, all those years ago, had been different. It hadn't been a case. It had been personal. Drew Delaney hadn't worked on it. He'd been a witness—one of the last people to see Annie McKay before she disappeared without a trace.

And he knew what the odds were of finding her, or finding out anything about her kidnapping, after ten years.

It would take a miracle, and Drew had been on the job long enough to know that those were few and far between. Sara Parker's escape was probably the only one he'd see for years to come. Still, holding this old picture in his hand, he couldn't help but hope.

Slowly he flipped the flimsy piece of fax paper over in his hands. It was a lousy copy of a black-and-white copy of an old color photo. The clarity was nonexistent, yet he still had to swallow hard when he saw the image. He would never forget the sight of a smiling Annie wearing that red-and-black suit; it was the image that had been reproduced thousands of times and distributed throughout the country in newspapers and broadcast on numerous television stations in hopes of finding Annie McKay.

From his shirt pocket, he took the Polaroid he'd snapped this morning of Sara Parker in that little red shorts set. He could have sworn it was a perfect match for the outfit Annie had been wearing when she disappeared—the one Annie had on in the faxed photo he now held in his other hand.

And it made sense that the red suit was too big for Sara. She was only seven, but Annie had been thirteen when she disappeared. It had been only about a hundred and twenty miles from here, across the border in Illinois, in a little town called Hope. Drew would never understand the cruel twist of fate that had bestowed that name on the town.

He'd grown up there, and he hadn't been this close to the place in years. The past four years had been spent with the FBI working on the West Coast, and before that he'd been in the army. He didn't want to get any closer to the town now, but he didn't have a choice. It was his job to track down the missing, especially the children, and Annie McKay was still missing, even if no one had been working on her case in seven or eight years.

He sat back in the swivel-based desk chair and stared at a water stain on the gray wall, near the ceiling. It had been so long ago.

Annie would have been twenty-three years old now, but in the eyes of her family, her friends, and the people who'd searched for her, she would remain forever a smiling, laughing thirteen-year-old. Annie would never grow old.

She had a sister—Carolyn, who would be twenty-seven now. Drew couldn't help but wonder if she still lived in town. He wondered if she'd married, if she had kids of her own.

Every now and then, he still let himself think about her. He wondered if she'd hated him in the end, all those years ago, wondered if she still thought of him, every now and

Our Child?

then, and what she'd do if he just showed up on her door-step.

Most of all, he wondered whether she still hated him for walking away from her so long ago.

He still hated himself for that at times.

Drew knew Sara Parker's case should take precedence over a ten-year-old kidnapping, but he couldn't help himself. As disciplined as he was, he couldn't keep his mind on Sara Parker.

He'd been there when Annie McKay disappeared. He'd searched for her himself, along with most of the people in the small town where she'd lived. For years he'd tried to somehow atone for her disappearance by trying to get girls like Sara back home, safe and sound.

And he knew that, no matter what he did today, he wouldn't stop thinking about Annie. Finally, he just gave up trying. He had a bad feeling about this. Hell, he had more than that. He had a ten-year-old photograph of a little girl who hadn't been seen in a decade, and another of one who'd disappeared four days ago, only to return in what he was sure were once Annie's clothes.

Even without that, Drew had been in the business long enough to trust his instincts. They were screaming at him right about now.

After conferring with the agent in charge at the scene, convincing himself that they had the manpower to do what they needed to do without him, he'd excused himself with a terse explanation that he had another lead. It was a long shot, but he needed to follow up on it. Then he'd promised to check in as soon as he knew something. Drew had worked with Bob Rossi long enough that he didn't have to say more than that.

Then he'd climbed into his car and headed northwest, toward a place he hadn't seen in nearly ten years.

He reasoned with his conscience, telling himself that Sara was safe now, where Annie never would be again. The authorities still owed her parents something, even if it was only a body to bury. And if Sara Parker really had been found wearing Annie's clothes, then there had to be some connection between the two cases. He had a duty to follow up on this lead.

It was difficult to go back to that town. Like stepping back in time and into someone else's skin. He'd been different here. At least, the people of Hope, Illinois, had seen him differently, and he hadn't appreciated it at all.

They'd judged him by the clothes he wore, the rundown place he called home, the mother who'd run off and the father who all too often was falling-down drunk. No one had seemed that interested in knowing *him*, because they'd thought they knew enough about Drew already.

Well, they'd been wrong, though it didn't matter much anymore. He didn't care what any of them thought.

Except, maybe, Carolyn. Because sometimes he still let himself think about her. Sometimes he imagined he caught a glimpse of her in a crowd. Sometimes he thought he smelled her perfume. Sometimes, in the night, he still reached for her, even though he hadn't touched her in years, and had never shared a bed or a whole night through with her.

Sometimes he thought about trying to find her, if for no other reason than to exorcise old ghosts, to separate the reality of Carolyn, the woman, at twenty-seven, from the memories of the girl who haunted his dreams.

But he'd never done that.

Before today, he'd have sworn he never would, because he'd decided long ago that Carolyn McKay was better off without him.

He had no trouble finding the town, despite the way the area had grown in the intervening years. There was a new, more direct road connecting it to the nearby Interstate 70, and the place was dotted with fast-food joints and gas stations.

He passed a new-car dealer, an honest-to-goodness shopping center and a big grocery store before making his way into town. Once he got within the town limits, he stopped to get gas at what used to be Eddie's Garage. In what seemed to be another lifetime, he'd worked there.

It was one of those convenience stores now—just like the ones you'd find in any city anywhere in the country. He wondered what happened to Eddie, wondered whether anyone in this town would recognize him anymore and whether he'd recognize them.

He was mildly curious about whether there was anything left of the old town he'd known. Not that he'd mourn its passing. It was just strange—like thinking of Annie being twenty-three instead of thirteen. In his mind, the town, like the girl, had never aged.

He had found the presence of mind to realize that the McKays might well have moved in the intervening years. So when he stopped for gas, he'd asked the clerk, who'd told him that they still lived on Highland Avenue.

Reluctantly he drove down the tree-lined street and parked in front of the house, one of those respectable two-story brick homes in that eminently respectable part of town. He'd been intimidated by it in his youth, but the man staring at it now found it to be smaller than he remembered, and showing definite signs of aging. The dark green paint on the trim and the shutters was peeling, the path leading to the front door was cracked. He remembered flowers—a profusion of them—in window boxes and pots on the front porch, but there were none in sight now. That was strange, he thought. It wasn't like Henry McKay to let the place go like this.

Drew opened the old ornamental iron gate, and a loud creaking sound filled the air. He wondered why someone hadn't oiled the thing, wondered why he was starting to sweat now, merely at the thought of walking into the place.

He glanced down the bare sidewalk and remembered how pretty it had been, lined with black-and-gold pansies, ones that matched the flowers in the pots on the porch. He had known from the beginning that he wouldn't fit in here.

Determined to shake off the memories, he made his way down the path toward the door and knocked.

Drew had done much harder things than this in the line of duty, so why did walking back into this house seem so difficult? Why did he dread the opening of that oversize oak door?

But it didn't open. Even after he knocked, it didn't budge. He turned to one side, noting a brown sedan in the driveway, then knocked again.

Finally, he heard footsteps coming toward the door. After what seemed like forever, it swung open.

A woman stared back at him with not a flicker of recognition in her eyes, but Drew would have known her anywhere. This was Grace McKay, Annie and Carolyn's mother. Her hair was going gray, which shouldn't have surprised him, but did. He took just a moment to survey the rest of her. She'd gained some weight, but not much. Her face had new lines running across it that seemed to have nothing to do with age and everything to do with the difficult life she'd led.

"I'm sorry," she said, quite pleasantly. She obviously didn't recognize him. "I was just watching the news. They found that little girl this morning—the one who'd been missing for four days now."

"I know," he said, before he even thought about it, then backtracked into something that wasn't quite a lie. "I was listening to the news on the radio."

"I've been so worried about her, and to have them just find her like that—it's a miracle."

"Yes, ma'am, it is," he said, feeling like a boy who was trying and failing to impress her with his good manners and his politeness.

"Now, what can I do for you?"

Drew glanced around at the porch and the path, the old houses that lined the block. It was hard to believe he'd come back here after all this time. His hand went to the outside of his jacket, where the right inside pocket was, and felt the outline of the fax paper and the photograph. For a moment, he'd forgotten where he'd put them, and he wasn't sure how to bring them out. No doubt she was going to be upset just to see him again, once she realized who he was. And once she saw the photograph—anything could happen. For a moment, he wished he hadn't come alone, or that some of her neighbors were around.

"I need to come inside for a minute, ma'am," he said, going for the case that held the credentials that identified him as a federal agent and flipping it open briefly for her to see.

"FBI?" she said, obviously taken aback at finding an agent on her doorstep.

"Yes, ma'am."

"Well . . ." She hesitated. "I guess . . . Please, come in."

He stepped into the dim entranceway, one that seemed even darker because of the sunlight he'd just left, then waited by the sofa in the living room until she invited him to sit. He chose the corner by the lamp, and he knew the moment the light hit his face, because she gasped.

"Oh, my Lord, it's you!" She sank into the chair in the opposite corner, her face deathly pale.

"Mrs. McKay, I'm sor—"

"Drew Delaney? After all this time . . ." She took a moment to gather her breath, then shook her head back and forth, as if she still couldn't believe it.

Drew didn't like the way she looked one bit. He didn't want her fainting on him, especially at the mere fact that he'd returned after nearly ten years. If that upset her this much, what would she do when he brought up Annie?

"Ma'am, is your husband home?"

She shook her head. "No."

"Could we call him? Maybe he could come, because—"

"My husband died six months ago," she said, and Drew decided that must account for the peeling paint and the absence of flowers in the front yard.

"I'm sorry to hear that," he said earnestly. Carolyn's father had been much less vocal in his dislike of Drew than her mother, and he knew Carolyn had been very close to the man.

His own father had died three years ago, and Drew hadn't even come back for the funeral. He would have felt like too much of a hypocrite. After all, they hadn't spoken in ten years.

"Look," Mrs. McKay said, gathering her strength now, "I don't know what you think you're going to accomplish by coming back here after all this time, but it's too late. Do you understand me? It's too late. Whatever you were thinking of doing, you might as well forget it, because I'll never give up my—"

Drew just pulled out the picture of Sara Parker. That left Grace McKay absolutely speechless once she caught a glimpse of it.

It wasn't the nicest thing he could have done, but he didn't want to prolong this, or to get into an argument with the woman. He definitely wasn't ever going to change her mind about him or about anything in the past. So he was going to get this over with as quickly as possible.

"I didn't come to talk about Carolyn and me." He tried to hide the anger in his voice, but he couldn't quite do it. He'd been gone for ten years, and this woman obviously still hated him—not that it mattered a damn bit anymore.

"I'm sorry, I don't know any way of making this easy for you."

She just stared at him with a look of utter disbelief. "This isn't about Bi—?" She clamped a hand over her mouth then and—if it was possible—turned even paler. The breath went out of her in a whoosh, and Drew noted that the hands she was wringing together in her lap were now shaking.

"I'm sorry," he said, searching for the all-important detachment that was so necessary to surviving things like this in his line of work.

He followed her line of vision to the end table in the corner, to the photographs in the three small brass frames. Carolyn, a shot of the teenage girl he'd known, in one frame; Annie, smiling and happy, more than ten years ago; and a photo of a little boy who looked so much like Carolyn, Drew knew he must be looking at her son.

Why did that surprise him? That Carolyn had a son? He certainly hadn't thought she'd be here waiting for him. Still, faced with the fact that there was another man in her life, that she'd had a child with him . . . it was harder than he'd imagined it would be, harder than it had a right to be.

He was finally going to see her again, and he'd do so knowing that she'd had another man's child. That shouldn't matter to him—not at all. But it did.

"Why in the world are you here?"

Grace McKay's shaky voice brought him back to the task at hand.

"Business," he said abruptly. "Official business."

He intended to look her in the eye, just once, briefly, before he flipped the photo in his hand over and got this over with. But he didn't think that would be possible now. She'd moved back in her chair, getting as far away from him as she possibly could without getting up—which would be out of the question, he was sure, because she was trembling all over now. She was having trouble catching her breath; he could hear her struggling with that now, and she had her hands up in front of her, as if to ward off an attacker. He supposed what he was about to do constituted an attack against this woman.

"About . . . Annie?"

He nodded.

"I don't want to see that," she shot back, glancing down at the picture in his hands.

"It's not Annie," he reassured her.

"I don't want to see it." She sounded close to hysteria now.

"You have to, Mrs. McKay. I need you to look at it, because I think . . . I think it has something to do with Annie. It's a picture of Sara Parker, the little girl you've been hearing about on the news. She's alive. She's going to be fine, but I need for you to look at the picture for me. It's important."

Somehow, she rose to her feet then, though Drew was sure that was a mistake.

"I don't care," she said. "I don't want to see it."

Drew backed off for a moment, rethinking the situation. He truly hadn't wanted to upset the woman, but he was trying to catch a kidnapper here. Sara Parker had gotten away, but the next little girl might not be so lucky. And who was to say whether, if someone had pushed a little harder more than ten years ago, they might not have caught that other man before he kidnapped Sara?

He had to do it. He had to make this woman help him, regardless of how much it upset her.

"I'm sorry," he said to her once more, then held the photo up in front of her.

Grace McKay gave a little cry and turned her head aside, but he watched as her eyes helplessly darted back toward the photo for a quick glance.

There was nothing upsetting about the photograph at all. It merely showed a small, thin, frightened little girl standing before the camera. She didn't even look anything like Annie. Her hair was dark, where Annie's had been blond. Her eyes were brown; Annie's had been blue. And she was six years younger than Annie had been when she disappeared. So there was nothing, nothing at all, about this picture that could have upset Grace McKay—except for the clothes.

And something had definitely upset her.

Drew felt as if a streak of sheer power, like the kind that skimmed along the electric lines outside, shot through him in that instant. He'd been right. He was certain of it now. There was definitely a link between Annie's kidnapper and Sara Parker's.

He'd just found the first good clue they'd ever had in Annie McKay's kidnapping. He was going to find out what had happened to her, finally, after all these years. And then he was going to put this whole nightmare behind him.

"Mrs. McKay?"

He looked up just in time to see her pitch forward. Her knees buckled beneath her. She nearly hit the floor before Drew could grab her. She slumped heavily against him and clutched a hand to her chest. He braced himself, then hauled her up in his arms long enough to make it to the brown flowered couch.

"My heart," she said, pressing a hand against chest. "I can't— Oh, it hurts."

"Lie still," he said, pushing her gently back against the cushions, then checking the pulse in the carotid artery in her neck. Her pulse was racing, and he heard her gasping painfully for every swift, shallow breath she took. For all the color there was in her face, she might as well have been a ghost. Drew knew enough first aid to be scared. He wondered if he'd just sent the woman into heart failure.

"I don't want to see that picture," she said weakly.

"It's all right," he said, not believing it himself, but needing to say something to try to reassure her.

It's been ten years, he wanted to tell the poor woman. Ten years, for Christ's sake. Didn't it ever get better? Hadn't any of them found a way to live with what had happened to Annie? Was he going to hurt Carolyn just as much as he'd hurt her mother, just by showing this picture and tracking down this lead?

What in hell had he started here?

He wondered, even as he picked up the phone and dialed 911. He remembered the address without any problem, and answered the dispatcher's questions as best he could while he tried to calm Mrs. McKay down.

He knew CPR, and he'd used it before. If need be, he could do it again to try to keep this poor woman alive until the ambulance arrived.

But he didn't need to do that just yet. He loosened the top two buttons of her blouse, kept one hand on the pulse at her neck, and watched her struggle for breath.

"Slowly," he told her. "Try to slow it down a little. Take deep breaths, if you can."

He was still checking to make sure Mrs. McKay's heart was beating, however rapidly, still trying to quiet her breathless ramblings about not wanting to see that picture, when he heard the ambulance pull up outside.

Drew went to the door and waved the two men inside.

"This way," he told them, stepping aside. "Her pulse is racing, and she's having trouble breathing."

"What happened?" one of the men asked as they walked across the room.

"She grabbed her chest and said it hurt."

"Okay." One of the men dropped to his knees beside the woman and opened one of his bags.

Drew stepped aside and looked away as they started working over the woman. He picked up the picture of Sara

Parker that he'd dropped when Grace McKay collapsed,
and put it back in his jacket pocket, next to the one of
Annie McKay, which surely would have upset her even
more.

Chapter 2

It didn't take the EMS workers long to decide to transport Grace McKay to the hospital. Just before they wheeled her out the door, she grabbed Drew's hand and mouthed something that sounded like "Billy."

"Who's Billy?" he said, afraid that he already knew. He must be Carolyn's son. It must be almost time for school to get out. Maybe she baby-sat for the boy. "Don't worry," he told this woman who'd hated him on sight eleven years ago. "I'll call Carolyn. We'll take care of everything."

The paramedics loaded her in the ambulance. They were getting ready to pull away from the curb when a yellow school bus came down the street.

With its brakes screeching, the bus pulled to a stop in front of the house. The doors folded open, and a little boy stepped outside.

He was long and lanky, his arms and legs seeming to be too big for the rest of his body, though he'd no doubt grow into them in time. He was wearing a pair of jeans with an oversize T-shirt and a pair of expensive black high-tops. Drew figured he had to be at least six. Maybe seven.

The boy looked at Drew, then turned to watch the ambulance heading down the street. Drew noticed with dismay that the bus driver didn't even wait to see what happened to the boy. She would have had to be blind not to see the ambulance in front of his house. He was furious that the woman had pulled away without a word. Anything could have happened to the boy, now that there was no one in the house to watch over him.

He'd have a word with the school superintendent about child safety tomorrow, but right now he had to concentrate on not scaring the boy.

He'd stopped on the sidewalk just outside the gate, and now he stood staring at the ambulance, which was disappearing from view. It was when the kid turned his face slightly to the left—to look at him without really seeming to look at him—that Drew noticed the resemblance in the kid's little turned-up nose. He'd teased Carolyn about being stuck-up, until she'd finally confessed how much she hated that nose of hers. The boy had her freckles, too, and what Drew thought would someday be a perfect match for Carolyn's hair color. For now, it was a shade or two lighter than what Drew remembered. Either that, or the sun bleached it out a little in the summer.

Damn. Here he was, face-to-face with Carolyn's child. There was no doubt in his mind.

It hurt, too, more than it should have. After all, he hadn't seen the woman in ten years. He'd walked out on her, and he'd never come back. He couldn't very well expect her to have been sitting here waiting for him all this time.

He wondered about the man she'd married, wondered if they were happy, if they had any other children. And he prayed to God that they would forever be safe and healthy.

"Is my mama all right?" A hesitant little voice pulled Drew back to the situation at hand.

"I'm sure she's fine," Drew said, still studying the boy.

"Where is she going?" the boy said, turning again to watch the ambulance, which was nearly out of sight.

"Going?" Drew said, hoping like hell he didn't have to come face-to-face with her anytime soon, yet knowing that he probably would have to do that. "Her name is Carolyn, right?"

The kid shook his head back and forth.

"Isn't this your grandmother's house?"

Again, the kid shook his head. Drew was stumped. The kid was wary of him, as well he should be, because the boy didn't know him. Obviously, someone had taught him to steer clear of strangers. Drew didn't want to do anything to discourage that. Still, what was he going to do with the kid?

"Do you live here?" he said, deciding that was as good a place to start as anywhere.

"Yes," the boy admitted.

"And you're Billy?"

"Yes."

That didn't give him any clues as to what he was facing. He would have simply explained to the boy that Mrs. McKay had made him promise to look out for him, but he hated to do that to the kid. It was too easy for grown-ups, any grown-ups, to say something like that to children and get them to go anywhere with them. He tried something else. "Billy, what are you supposed to do if you come home and no one's here?"

"Go to Mrs. Martin's house across the street."

That was good. The kid had a plan. Every kid needed a plan. "Why don't you go ahead, then? I'll watch you to make sure you get across the street in one piece."

"Okay," the boy said, obviously relieved. He turned to go.

Drew watched him run to the other house and ring the bell. He wondered who the kid could be. From what he remembered, Carolyn didn't have any close relatives in town, and obviously Billy was related to her.

He couldn't leave until the boy was safe. Then he decided he'd go inside and try to find Carolyn's number, so that he could tell her about her mother.

He stood there in the front yard, waiting for the lady across the street to answer the door. But she didn't. Billy rang the bell again and again, then finally came back across the street to stand on the sidewalk again.

"I forgot. She went to visit her grandkids," he said.

Drew watched as the boy's eyes turned all watery. He struggled not to cry, choosing to bite his lower lip instead. He had Carolyn's eyes, too, a deep, dark green.

"Okay," Drew said. "We've got a problem. What are we going to do with you?"

The boy looked at the ground, scuffed his shoes on the sidewalk and wiped away a tear. Drew thought he seemed terrified of being here alone with him.

"What's your name, son?"

"Billy."

Drew had to smile. The kid had no clue. "Billy what?"

"Billy McKay."

"I'm Drew," he said, but made no move to shake the boy's hand. He didn't want to spook him by trying to touch him. "And you know Carolyn?"

"Uh-huh."

"How do you know her?"

"She's my sister."

That took a little while for Drew to absorb. "You mean Grace McKay is your mother?"

The kid nodded. "Did the ambulance take her away?"

"Yes," Drew said.

"Is she gonna be okay?"

"I think so." He didn't have the guts to tell him anything different, not when he was so upset already.

They both just stood there and stared at each other for a minute, both of them at a loss.

Carolyn had a little brother? He supposed that was possible. He guessed her mother would be in her late forties, from what he remembered, and women were having children later and later in life now. Also, it wasn't that uncommon for people who had lost one child to have another. Some people had told him it helped to have someone else to love and to fill the time and the silence left behind, although Drew wondered where they found the courage to bring another child into this crazy, mixed-up world.

It seemed an awful risk to take—seemed they'd be scared of having someone else to lose.

It was cynical of him, but then, he'd turned into a cynical man. A cynical, solitary man. Sometimes—no, most of the time—it didn't seem so bad, having no one and nothing to lose.

He didn't have anyone at all in his life who was truly important to him. He couldn't have said he regretted that, at least not very often.

Drew felt something tugging on the jacket of his suit, looked down and saw the boy.

"I'm not supposed to talk to strangers," he said.

Drew finally smiled. "I know. That's a good rule."

"But I want to go see my mom."

"Okay, what if we call your sister? Would you like that?"

The kid hesitated and looked even more worried. "I don't know if she can come."

"Why don't we try?"

Drew turned and started up the walkway to the house. Billy lagged behind.

"Hey, mister, wait," he said. "I'm not supposed to let anyone into the house if I don't know them."

"Okay, do you know Carolyn's number?"

He shook his head.

Drew thought that was strange, but he didn't say anything. He'd thought he'd just let the kid go inside by himself and call. Carolyn could tell him that he didn't have to be afraid of Drew, then the two of them could wait there together for her to come get him.

Drew didn't like trying to talk kids around the safety rules they'd been taught. He would have just flashed his badge and told Billy it was okay to talk to him, but any two-bit crook could buy a phony badge and talk kids into just about anything. It ticked him off, and it made it next to impossible to reassure a scared child that it was all right to talk to him.

"How about this, Billy? You sit here on the porch. I'll go inside, find your sister's number, and I'll call her. We can wait out here together for her, okay?"

"Okay," the kid said, momentarily relieved. "But I don't know if she'll come."

Drew went back inside and headed for the phone. He found a cordless in the kitchen. Reading the label on the base station, he saw that Carolyn's numbers—both home and work—were programmed into the speed-dial memory. Grimly he pressed the one for her home. He sweated out five rings before he gave up on that and tried the work phone. It wasn't until the second call went through that he noticed it seemed to take forever for the phone to dial the programmed number.

He thought the woman who answered the phone said, "Hope House," but he couldn't be sure.

"Carolyn McKay?" he said, only then realizing he'd used her maiden name without even thinking about it.

But she must still be using it herself, because the woman gave him a crisp "Just a moment, sir," then put him on hold.

Hope House? The name meant something to him, but what?

He wondered where it was. From the name, he'd thought it must be somewhere in town, but now that he thought about it, there'd been too many pulses on the line when the call went through. He'd definitely called long-distance.

He wondered how far away she was, wondered if he'd be seeing her sometime today, or if she'd simply direct him to take the boy to someone else in town until she could get there.

Drew wanted to see her. He didn't think he could leave town without doing that. He didn't—

"Carolyn McKay," she said when she came on the line.

She didn't sound at all like the girl he'd known, and yet she did. Her voice was calm, cool and authoritative, maybe a bit rushed. Still, he sensed the vulnerability.

But how could he? he argued with himself. She said two little words across a hair-thin wire, the first he'd heard from her in nearly ten years, and he thought he detected something like that in her voice? He must be dreaming. It was just the past—the image that he'd always carried of her. She'd been the most vulnerable person he'd ever known. He'd come into her life at the worst possible time, and he'd hurt her.

"Hello?" she said. "Is anyone there?"

Drew couldn't help it. He wondered if she still wore her hair long and loose around her shoulders, wondered whether she still had those freckles on her nose and whether she ever let them show anymore. He wondered—

Damn. He had to pull himself together here. This wasn't the time for a trip down memory lane.

"Carolyn?" he managed to say.

"Yes." She'd gone all wary on him now. "Who is this?"

"It's Drew," he said, glad not to hear the slightest tremor in his voice.

"Drew?"

"Don't tell me you forgot," he said, thinking he might brazen his way through this.

He'd left her speechless. For a moment, he believed they'd gotten cut off, but then he detected the faint sound of her breathing on the other end of the line.

And then he found himself rushing into the business at hand, putting the past where it belonged—in the past.

"Carolyn, I'm at your mother's house. She's, uh...she had a problem this afternoon, and she's been taken to the hospital."

"A problem? What kind of a problem? Is she all right?" she said.

"I'm sorry. I don't know much. She was in a lot of pain, and it may be her heart. The paramedics took her to Hope Memorial about twenty minutes ago, and I'm here with Billy. He says he's supposed to go to a neighbor's if the house is empty, but the neighbor's away on vacation. I didn't know what else to do with him, so I called you."

He finished to dead silence on the line.

"Carolyn?" he said finally.

"Yes," she said. "I'm—I'm sorry. I'm just surprised, that's all."

"Of course," he said, rushing on. "Where are you? Do you want to come get him? Or is there someone else who can take care of him?"

"I don't know," she said. "I'm in Chicago. I could be there in about three hours, if I drive straight through and get lucky with the traffic. I don't know who else could take care of Billy. My father died six months ago, and... Drew?"

"Yes."

"Why are you there?"

She sounded terrified by the very idea, and he wondered if there was any way she could already know why he was here. He didn't see how that was possible, unless she somehow knew what he did for a living, and that seemed unlikely. And if she didn't know, he certainly didn't want to get into it with her right now, on the phone.

"I'll explain when you get here," he said.

He would explain when she got there?

Carolyn nearly dropped the phone, just thinking about what possible explanations he might have for being there.

What explanation could there possibly be?

Drew was back in Hope. He was at her parents' home, and he was with Billy.

Oh, dear God, he was with Billy.

Chapter 3

"Carolyn?"

From what seemed like a million miles away, she heard the voice. "Yes," she said, pulling the phone back to her ear.

"Did you hear what I just said?"

No, she hadn't. Not a word. She was so frightened, she'd been lost in thought, worrying about her mother and imagining the worst possible circumstances that could have brought Drew back to Hope, Illinois.

"I'm sorry," she said into the phone. "I've... I can't..." And then she simply gave up on explaining. "What were you asking me?"

"About Billy?"

"Yes," she said, starting to shake now. Hadn't he said he would explain when she got there?

"He doesn't know me. He just got off the school bus as the ambulance was leaving, and found me here. He's frightened of me. Can you talk to him? Tell him everything's all right?"

"Of course," she said, ashamed of herself now. Naturally Billy would be frightened. He knew, better than most children, how dangerous strangers could be.

She heard the sound of Drew's footsteps as he moved through the house, heard the sound of the door opening, then, from the occasional traffic sounds, realized he must have taken the cordless phone outside.

There was a long pause, then something Drew said that she couldn't make out, followed by Billy's defiant answer.

"She won't come."

And Carolyn thought he must be crying then, because she heard something that sounded like sniffling, and it wasn't coming from her. Though her eyes soon filled with tears of her own, and her blood turned to ice in her veins, she made no sound that would have given her away.

She won't come.

"Billy?" she said, though it did no good. He wasn't on the other end of the line yet.

How could he think she wouldn't come? She loved him with all her heart and soul. It was hard for her to be in Chicago, so far away from him, but it was also necessary.

She was only his sister, when she wanted to be so much more. She'd made her decision years ago, and she couldn't change her mind now—not when so many people stood to be hurt by it.

Especially Billy.

And she would not let herself hurt Billy.

But judging by what she was hearing from the other end of the phone, she'd done just that. Carolyn had never heard him speak of her with such anger in his voice.

"What do you mean, she won't come?" she heard Drew say, when she could bear to listen again.

"She never comes anymore. Ever since my dad died, she's always too busy to come and see us."

Oh, Billy, she thought helplessly. Had she really given him that impression? That she was too busy to see him?

It's not that, she wanted to tell him now. *It's not that at all.*

"She won't come," she heard him repeat defiantly.

And then, mercifully, Drew clasped his hand over the phone. At least, that was all she could figure out, because, for a while, she heard nothing from the other end.

Drew had a hard time believing what he was hearing and seeing. The boy was quite upset, and he meant every word he'd said about Carolyn.

She's always too busy to come and see us.

He'd spoken so bitterly about her. Drew couldn't reconcile the image of the uncaring sister Billy believed her to be with the reality of the girl he'd known. Carolyn had been devoted to Annie. She'd been lost without the little girl, and she'd grieved alone, for the most part, because her parents had been too caught up in their own pain to be any real help to her. That wasn't a criticism, it was merely a statement of fact. Some things were simply too overwhelming for people to handle, and Annie's disappearance had been one of those things.

He hadn't been able to handle it himself.

So, he rationalized, maybe Billy was too much for Carolyn, as well. Maybe, as she saw it, the risks were too great. Maybe loving him would be too dangerous for her to handle while she was still trying to make sense of her sister's disappearance.

Maybe he could understand.

He wondered if he could ever explain it to the boy, if he got the chance. Of course, now wasn't the time. He still had Carolyn on the line.

With his hand still pressed against the mouthpiece of the phone, hopefully blocking out the harsh words from the boy, Drew sat down on the brick steps leading up to the porch and looked the kid straight in the eye.

"Carolyn needs to talk to you, Billy," he said, in his best no-nonsense law-enforcement-officer voice.

Drew gave the boy no choice—the boy had to either hold on to the phone or let it fall to the sidewalk. Billy chose to take it.

"Say hello to her," Drew said, prompting him.

The boy sniffled once, then backhanded his wet cheeks and wiped his hand on his jeans. Finally, he brought the phone to his face. "Hello."

Their conversation was brief and stilted. Billy had nothing but *uh-huh*s to say to her. He didn't even tell her goodbye, just handed the phone back to Drew.

Drew put the receiver to his ear and heard the muffled yet unmistakable sound of Carolyn McKay weeping.

Drew was no stranger to a woman's tears, and he didn't turn to mush at the sight of a woman crying. In his business, more often than not, the women he had to deal with were upset, many of them in tears. He'd grown immune to it all over the years, and he wouldn't have thought anyone's tears could get to him so hard and so fast.

But this was Carolyn.

She was different. She made him feel as if his own heart might be weeping inside his chest. He felt the pain as if it were his own, and wished he could make it so. Once, it had been his mission in life to make her laugh, to coax just one smile onto her pretty face. It had started as a sort of penance for him—a punishment for his sins, whether real or imagined. He'd helped bring on her pain over losing Annie, so it was his duty to try to ease that pain as much as he could.

Of course, it had been more than that. She was much more to him than a girl who'd lost her sister and had no one to turn to as she tried to deal with that loss.

Once, Carolyn McKay had been everything to him.

And now she was hundreds of miles away, sobbing as softly as possible on the other end of this phone.

"Aw, Carolyn..." he said, the way he must have said her name a thousand times before, the way he must have called out to her somewhere deep in the night in the midst of some dream that would have been better off forgotten long ago.

He simply couldn't help himself. He still had dreams about her and the way things had been between them. That, in itself, was amazing, given the time that had passed and the fact that they'd had absolutely no contact in the intervening years.

"Don't cry, sweetheart," he said, the endearment slipping out as naturally as her name. Drew didn't even stop to question that. He just couldn't stand to hear her cry anymore. "He didn't mean it. I'm sure he didn't. It's probably nothing more than a misunderstanding. You'll straighten it out in no time, once you get here."

"It's not what you think," she said, her breathing settling down now, as she fought for control. "Ever since Dad died, six months ago, it's been so hard to be there. My mother and I...we haven't been getting along that well, and I've done what she asked. I've stayed away. But I never imagined Billy would think anything like that. Oh, God, Drew, I just didn't think of that."

"Carolyn, come on. It's all right. I'm sure you can explain everything to him when you get here, okay?"

"All right," she said. "I'm sorry. I'm not usually like this."

"I know."

It was a silly thing to say, but she'd seemed to need to hear it, so he'd said it. And he believed it, too. The girl he'd known would never have been too busy to make time for a little boy. He wouldn't believe the woman could be like that, either.

"So, are you coming?"

''Yes. I'll drive down. I can get anything I need when I arrive. With luck, if I beat the rush-hour traffic, I'll be there by seven.''

''And Billy's all right with that? You told him he could trust me?''

''Yes.''

''Then we'll be here waiting for you.''

And he didn't know what else to say then. Apparently, neither did she, because the conversation just died, but neither of them made any move to break the connection. Though tenuous at best, it was the only link between them in more than nine years.

So they sat there for a moment, listening to each other breathe. He tried to picture her face as it would look now, but saw nothing but the girl.

He'd loved her once. He'd lived for her.

Drew closed his eyes and tried to reach back inside himself for that feeling—of living for Carolyn, with Carolyn, within her.

She was so close now. Three measly hours and she'd be here. How would that feel—to see her again, perhaps to touch her once more?

It couldn't possibly feel the same. The years couldn't simply fall away, and yet Drew felt somehow that they had.

Three hours, she'd said. He didn't see how he could wait that long.

''I've missed you, Carolyn,'' he confessed, without one regret.

''Oh, Drew . . .'' she said, and he thought he might have set off her crying again.

''Drive safely,'' he told her.

The minute she got off the phone, Carolyn simply collapsed. The phone banged back down onto the receiver. She wasted precious energy trying to stay upright before giving in to the awful weakness invading her limbs.

It was a little better when her head came down to the top of her immaculate white desk. She had this childish urge to take her arms, her hands, and wrap them around her head, to try to block out the whole world and hide here in her nice, safe office, surrounded by people with whom she knew she was secure.

She looked at the lock on the door, the one she rarely used, and thought about turning it now, thought about locking herself away here. She could stay until the shaking stopped, until she could breathe again and felt able to cope with the task ahead of her.

But she couldn't do that. She didn't have time. Her mother was sick. That was so hard to believe. Her mother was never sick. She picked up the phone again, because she needed to call Hope Memorial Hospital, but she got sidetracked by thoughts of Drew.

Drew was waiting for her—Drew and Billy were waiting for her—and she had to get to them. Billy was frightened. No doubt, Drew was angry with her and waiting for an explanation—one she simply didn't have to give.

Her corner office, behind its locked door, looked pretty good to her now. She was still shaking, and she wasn't certain she was getting enough air into her lungs to satisfy her. She wasn't sure when either one of those nervous reactions would subside.

She hadn't been this out of control for years, and she couldn't help it.

Carolyn looked down at the notepad in front of her. Sometime during their conversation, Drew had given her the phone number for the hospital, and she'd scribbled it on the pad.

It was so hard to believe—Drew was there.

He was waiting for her.

God, had he really said he'd missed her?

Nearly ten years and not a word from him, yet now he was back. How could that be? People just didn't drop out of the sky and land in Hope, Illinois. He had a purpose in coming back, and she was afraid she knew exactly what that purpose was.

He must be looking for someone—and it wasn't her.

He was after her son—their son. A miracle, in the form of a child.

The boy the whole world thought of as her little brother.

He'd never understand what she'd done, especially when she didn't even understand it all herself anymore. Carolyn argued back and forth that way with herself as she drove through the steadily falling rain that had dogged her all the way from the outskirts of Chicago.

Once she'd pulled herself together, she'd quickly called the hospital to check on her mother's condition—stable, though they weren't sure exactly what was wrong with her. Then she'd given a hasty explanation to her secretary and gotten in her car, beating the worst of the afternoon traffic.

It wasn't that much of a drive, three hours in most cases, yet she'd rarely made the trip in the past six months. She had been busy. Purposely, she kept very busy. The schedule suited her, for it left little time for anything else. But that certainly wasn't the reason she'd seldom made it back to Hope lately.

She'd gone often before her father died, even though the trip had been quite painful for her. The house, in many ways, remained a kind of shrine to Annie, who'd been gone for ten years now. Her room was still intact, waiting for a little girl who no longer existed. Her pictures still hung on the wall, and that alone would have been enough to keep Carolyn away from the house.

She had her own pictures of Annie, which she kept hidden away in the back of a drawer and took out only once in a while, only when she thought she could handle it. But to just glance up at the living room wall and see Annie's face, day after day, with no warning and no time to prepare? Carolyn couldn't take that. She wasn't sure how her mother could do that, either.

And, if Annie's memory wasn't enough, there was Billy, and her memories of Drew. The three of them gave her more than enough reason to stay away, and somehow her recollections of them all had gotten hopelessly intertwined in her mind. Carolyn couldn't separate the memories of one from another.

She'd adored Annie, and she'd lost her. She'd loved Drew, the way she hadn't loved another man since, and he'd left her. Carolyn had tried hard to guard her heart against loving Billy, because she'd feared he was lost to her before he had ever been born.

Of course, she hadn't really been able to do that. Billy had found his own very special place in her heart, and she loved him. She loved him too much. More than she had a right to. And she wanted things from him that she couldn't have. She wanted to give him everything—all the love she had to give. But she wasn't free to do that.

For all he and the rest of the world knew, she was nothing more than his older sister. That was all she'd thought she'd ever be—until her father died.

That had truly shaken her. Besides missing him terribly herself, for he'd been a wonderful father, she'd grieved for Billy and the loss he'd suffered.

When she, at seventeen, had made the difficult decision to give her baby to her parents to raise as their own, she'd known very clearly what she wanted for him. A loving father, a caring mother, a strong family—strong despite the tragedy they'd experienced.

Her parents had married young, as soon as her mother got out of high school, and they'd had her right away. Her mother had been only thirty-seven years old, her father forty, when Billy was born, and both of them had been in good health.

Carolyn had felt sure that they'd be there to raise him to adulthood. And she had to admit they'd needed Billy so much after losing Annie. Billy had been their miracle, their reason for getting up in the morning, for putting a smile on their faces, for going on living. They'd devoted themselves to him, and Billy had flourished under all that love.

If nothing else, she could reassure Drew with that. Their son had lived a wonderful, safe, happy life. She'd done that one thing right; she'd made sure Billy had all those things.

But her father's sudden death, from an aneurysm, had been a shock to them all. And it had created anew this terrible yearning inside Carolyn, one that she'd fought for the past nine years and successfully kept at bay, the yearning to be more to Billy than just a sister.

Of course, she couldn't do that. She'd made her decision endless years ago, and she couldn't go back on it now. It wouldn't be fair to anyone—least of all to Billy.

But she couldn't help how she felt. She'd tried simply to bring the subject out into the open for discussion with her mother about five months ago, but the woman had hit the ceiling. Things had been strained between them ever since. Carolyn knew her mother felt threatened by her feelings for Billy, knew that it must be incredibly hard for Grace to think about losing Billy so soon after losing her husband.

But Carolyn didn't see it that way. She didn't understand why her mother thought she had to lose a child in order for Carolyn to gain one. Surely there was enough time and love for both of them to share him. Carolyn didn't want to take anything away from Billy. She wanted very much to give things back to him—his sense of security, for one thing.

But she hadn't been able to explain that to her mother yet, and she'd followed Grace's wishes and kept her distance these past few months in hopes that the older woman would calm down and see things more clearly.

And now her mother was ill? She couldn't let herself think of all that might mean. Carolyn and Grace had their problems—what mother and daughter didn't? But she truly loved her mother, and she couldn't imagine losing her. Nor could she imagine what it would do to Billy.

Of course, while all this was raging inside her head, she also kept thinking of Drew.

She was still angry at the way he'd walked away from her all those years ago, but foremost in her mind was the fact that he'd somehow found out about Billy. He'd want an explanation for what she'd done; he would insist on that. And she'd never be able to make him understand.

She could beg and plead and cry, if she sank so low that she reached that point, but it wouldn't make any difference. It wouldn't change anything. It wouldn't give him back the years with Billy, if he regretted the loss of those years and wanted them back. And Carolyn felt sure that he would.

He would be furious. But, somehow, she would have to get around his anger. She had to make him see this whole thing from her point of view.

It wasn't as if she didn't hate herself for what she'd done—but it was a futile exercise. She couldn't change the decisions she'd made in her life. She couldn't explain the things that had happened, or find any useful purpose in them all. And she had no insights that had ever allowed her to accept it all with grace, as a better woman might have done.

She'd had Drew Delaney's son, without ever letting him know the child existed, and she'd given up that child without ever giving Drew the chance to have a say about what happened to the boy.

It was the irrefutable truth.

What could possibly matter so much after that?

Chapter 4

She'd braced herself to drive down that familiar street, to walk into that house and see them—and it had all been for nothing.

They weren't there.

Instead, she found a note in what had to be Drew's handwriting. That alone shook her, holding something that he'd written. She'd waited years for just a letter from him—something, anything, to explain why he'd simply disappeared from Hope. And she'd gotten nothing. He'd never written a word. Now, he'd been in her parents' house. He'd been there when the ambulance took her mother away and when the school bus dropped Billy off. It was all so strange and so hard to believe.

Billy had gotten upset, he told her in the note. He'd wanted to see his mother, and Drew had decided to take him to the hospital for a visit while they waited for Carolyn to arrive. She wondered if the two of them were still at the hospital, wondered where she'd rather face them—here in the house, by herself, or in a hospital full of strangers.

Carolyn leaned against the living room wall for a moment, her eyes carefully downcast so that she could avoid seeing any of the pictures—either those of Annie or the ones of Billy. She concentrated hard on trying to stop shaking. She had spells like this, when she simply couldn't stop shaking. Her therapist would probably have some two-hundred-dollar word for it, but she simply called them spells. The past caught up with her sometimes, and when it happened she couldn't do anything but shake.

She'd had them since the age of seventeen, since Annie had disappeared, since the time she'd faced the fact that Annie wasn't ever coming back. And she tried not to make a big thing out of them. Everyone had problems, some worse than others. People coped in different ways. Some drank. Some smoked. Carolyn got the shakes every now and then. It didn't sound so bad when she thought of it that way.

But she'd have to control it now. Billy didn't need to see her this upset. And Drew? She suspected it wouldn't matter that much to him. No doubt he'd be too angry to care about her own problems, because she'd taken his son from him.

In that instant, Carolyn knew she had no time to waste. She'd much rather find them at the hospital than here at home. Strangers were definitely preferable to the privacy of these walls.

She gave herself the luxury of a few deep breaths, now that the worst of the shakes had passed, then walked back out the door. Hope Memorial was only ten minutes away. Sooner than she would have liked, she was walking down a hallway at the hospital, following the instructions the receptionist had given her to help her find her mother's room.

She couldn't imagine her mother suffering a heart attack at forty-seven. Her mother was never sick.

She rounded the last corner, found room 203, then quickly scanned the corridor for any sign of Drew or Billy. She nearly missed them. Just when she'd decided to turn and go into the room, she caught the sound of Drew's voice coming from a room down the hall.

Her head whirled around, her gaze zeroing in on a room about ten feet away and to the right. Room 203, her mother's room, was just to the left, and she thought about slipping in there, taking the coward's way out—but Drew's voice was so compelling. He was right here, right on the other side of that wall, and she hadn't seen him in so long.

Even though she dreaded what was sure to take place between them, she wanted to see him so badly.

Still, she should have waited. She should have headed back down the hall and hidden herself away, just for a few moments, and she would have, if she'd thought it would do any good.

But it wouldn't. No amount of time would have allowed her to prepare for this moment. There was no way to be prepared. It was an unmanageable situation. She'd been involved in too many of them not to recognize that.

She wondered if he'd hate her for what she'd done, even as she took that first step toward him.

Carolyn was careful to stop just outside the open door, which was marked Family Waiting Room. Not wanting to draw attention to herself just yet, she somehow managed to keep silent. But it was hard. It was incredible and exhilarating and frightening—all at the same time. The emotions rolled over her, like waves breaking over her head, choking her.

Clamping a hand over her mouth, she drank in the sight of the two of them, together for the first time.

Drew had his back to her, and he was down on one knee so that he could look Billy in the eye. She took a moment to study them both. Carolyn couldn't tell much about how

Drew looked now, except that his hair was now short, but still full of those small, tight curls, and he still had a beard.

Billy had Drew's hair, even had it styled in nearly the same way; curling waves of golden brown, clipped close to his head and brushed back from his face. Billy's was lighter, but time would change that. Someday it would be as dark and brown as Drew's was.

Her son had his walk, too, that loose swaying of his backside and those long legs. She'd tried not to notice over the years, tried not to search through her mind for memories of Drew with which to compare him, but it was one of those inevitable things. It could not be avoided. They were father and son. Naturally, they were alike in so many ways.

Billy got up from the chair, and Carolyn quickly stepped sideways, hiding herself behind the doorway, buying herself a few more moments to herself. Billy seemed so much taller now. The last time she'd seen him had been three months ago, when she'd come here to try to talk to her mother. He seemed to have grown so much in just a few months. The time just flew by—another month, another season, another year of his life that she'd missed. He seemed so grown-up now, she could hardly believe it.

Carolyn was bracing herself for the walk through that door when she realized Billy was becoming upset. Drew held him by the arms when the boy tried to pull away.

"Wait a minute," he said. "What's wrong? What are you so afraid of?"

"She's going to die," Billy said, his lower lip trembling now. "My mama's going to die."

Carolyn once again had to press a hand over her mouth to stay silent. Could that be true? Was the situation much more serious than the nurse had led her to believe when she called to check on her mother's condition?

"No, she's not," she heard Drew tell Billy. "She's just had a rough time of it since your father died, and she hasn't been taking care of herself the way she should. But that's all it is, Billy.''

The child just shook his head defiantly. "She's going to die, just like my dad, and then I won't have anybody."

Carolyn should have spoken up then. She should have been the one to take him in her arms and promise him that he'd never be alone in this world, but it was Drew who was there instead.

Drew, already on his knees in front of Billy, hauled him up against his chest and held him there, despite the resistance Billy put up. He held on to him until he wasn't fighting anymore, until Billy's head came down to Drew's shoulder, his arms closed around Drew's neck, and sobs shook his whole body.

It should be me, Carolyn thought. *I should be holding on to Billy that way. He should have come to me, and I should have been there for him.*

Instead, she stood alone in the doorway. With her back rigid, the breath frozen in her lungs, her arms wrapped around her own waist, she tried to hold herself together with nothing but the memory of what it had felt like to be in Drew's arms. He'd held her just like that, so many times.

It should have been me, she'd told him, so many years ago. *I should have been the one who was walking by myself that day. I should have been the one who was taken.*

Annie should still be here.

Somehow, everything in her whole life had started and ended with Annie's disappearance.

Drew had heard it all from her, many times before. He'd understood, and he'd tried to comfort her, to help her make sense of it all as well as two teenagers could understand something that left adults absolutely baffled.

She'd lost Annie. She'd lost Drew and their son.

Oh, God. What a mess.

From inside the tiny waiting room, she heard Billy call out. "Carolyn's mad at us, and I don't think she loves us anymore," he said. "I heard her and mom yelling at each other the last time she was here. She's selfish and mean. I heard my mom tell her so. And she won't come."

Drew yelled at him then. "Billy! That's enough."

"I'm telling you, she's not coming."

"She's right over there," Drew said, settling that whole argument, leaving both her and Billy speechless.

Carolyn stared from one of them to the other. Drew let go of Billy, stood and turned around to face her. By the way he was looking at her, as if he would have done anything to have kept her from overhearing those words, she decided he must pity her. That fact, and nothing but that, was what she needed to hold herself together. It was by sheer force of will that she kept her tears from falling. Her shoulders didn't sag, and her chin went up another fraction. She would not have Drew feeling sorry for her because of the mess she'd created.

Billy didn't say anything. If he could tell how much he'd upset her, he didn't seem to care, because he stood defiantly by Drew's side.

She wanted to go to him then, wanted to wrap her arms around him and never let go.

Her son thought she didn't care about him. He thought she couldn't even spare a day or so here and there to come to see him. He seemed to honestly believe that the only mother he'd ever known was going to die and leave him all alone in this world. He had no idea how wrong he was.

"Billy..." she began, but she couldn't get anything else out.

He turned to face her, obviously uneasy about having been overheard. His lower lip was trembling, and his face was streaked with the remains of his tears.

Carolyn felt his pain like a dagger shoved into her chest. She would have done anything in this world to keep from hurting him, even if it meant hurting herself. And he didn't seem to understand that at all. She didn't see how she could explain it to him, either.

He hesitated for a minute. She held out her arms to him in a silent invitation as she watched him wavering. Then he brushed right past her.

"I'm going to see my mom," he told Drew, pointedly ignoring her as he walked out the door and into the room across the hall.

Carolyn watched him go. She stood there in the hallway as the door to her mother's room slowly slid shut behind Billy. She stood there trembling, her stomach in knots, not knowing what to do next.

Drew was watching her; she felt that so clearly, though she had her back turned to him now. He was waiting, and she had to turn around and do something, tell him something, yet she had no idea what. She'd never find the words. She'd never make him understand. And right now she was too worried about Billy to even try.

"I'm going to go talk to Billy," she said, without turning around to face him. But Drew would have none of that. He took her by the arm and turned her around, pulled her into the room with him and closed the door.

"I have to talk to him," she said. "I have to explain. I have to go to him, and—"

"In a minute," he said, quite calmly, quite gently. "First I think you'd better sit down, before you fall down."

"I . . ." She didn't know what to make of that. Her eyes darted around the room, taking in the beat-up old couch, the uncomfortable plastic chairs, the magazines scattered across the end tables, the emptiness. Mostly the emptiness. She was alone here with him, when she'd so hoped for the presence of strangers to act as a buffer between them.

Carolyn shook her head sadly. Her tears lay heavily in her eyes, still threatening to overflow, and she wished she'd been the one to end up standing against the wall, the way he was, instead of here in the middle of the room, with nothing to lean on, nothing to hold her up. Because he was right. She might well fall flat on her face.

"Drew, it's not usually like this between us," she had to tell him. "Things have just been so difficult . . . since my father died. I had no idea Billy was so angry at me."

As he watched her struggling with her composure, watched her literally swaying on her feet, Drew didn't know where he'd find it in his heart to tell her what had brought him back to Hope, or about the role he'd played in her mother's collapse. There'd be time for that later, when she was up to hearing it.

Right now, he didn't think Carolyn could take much more. Hell, he wasn't sure he could.

He was having trouble believing he was finally in the same room with her. She looked just the way he remembered her, beautiful, endearing, and heartbreakingly vulnerable—such a dangerous combination.

Drew wasn't sure what had happened between Carolyn and her mother and her brother, but he'd seen right away that it had left her as torn up as he'd ever seen her. She looked almost as upset as she'd been when Annie disappeared.

He'd tried to comfort her then, to ease the guilt she carried, even as he tried to ease his own. He'd held her so many nights when she sobbed her heart out, and he wanted to do that for her right now.

"Carolyn," he said, taking a first step toward her, wanting to erase all the years between them with just one embrace.

She stepped back, alarm showing clearly on her face.

"It's all right," he said, reaching for her hand, taking it in his and drawing her closer with it. Gently, the way he might have approached a frightened kitten that had been backed into a corner, he stroked his fingers over the back of her hand.

"I..." She stared down at their intertwined hands, as if she couldn't believe he was touching her, then looked into his eyes. "I messed it all up, Drew."

He'd held her so many times, Drew told himself. How much could one more time matter in the scheme of things? Carolyn was hurt and upset. She needed someone, and he was here. How many others had he held on to for a moment, just because they were upset and he was there? Countless numbers. It didn't mean anything. At least, it didn't have to.

He'd done it so many times for strangers. Surely he could do it for Carolyn, as well.

Drew wrapped both his hands around the one of hers that he'd managed to get hold of before she turned all skittish and shy on him. Her hand was soft and small, cold to the touch, and there was a fine trembling within her that went all the way down to her fingertips.

What in the world had happened to her? She seemed as vulnerable as ever, and he couldn't stand that idea. He'd believed her whole life would have come together after he left—that the healing would have started, that she'd be whole and happy by now.

He'd thought all he had to do was leave....

"I'm sorry," she said, choking back the distress that threatened to overtake her, trying to pull her hand away from his. "I just... I can't believe what a mess I've made of all this."

But Drew wasn't ready to let go of her, not just yet. It had been too long since they'd been together for him to give her up so fast. He took another step closer. One hand continued to hold hers, while the other slid along her forearm to her elbow. He cupped it in his hands.

Her eyes, huge and rounded now, fringed with smoky brown lashes spiked together by her tears, locked on his.

Clearly, she'd been so distressed before that she didn't realize how close he'd gotten to her. The breath stuck in her throat, the fine trembling that was coursing through her body not so fine anymore. He'd been right; she might fall if she didn't sit down soon.

"Carolyn," he whispered, hating to break the silence, hating to end the spell they were caught up in. "It's going to be all right."

And he smiled at her then, because he wanted to reassure her, not frighten her.

Why would she be so frightened of him, anyway? He didn't have time to stop and figure it out. He took the hand that he still held and pressed it to his chest.

She swallowed hard and made one last attempt to step away from him.

Clearly, she wasn't used to having anyone see her this way. He'd have bet money that she didn't have anyone to hold her when she cried, either, and he couldn't have said whether that made him happy or sad.

He would make *her* sad, though. The reason he'd come back to town—the matching clothes, the other little girl who'd disappeared, yet been found safe and sound—it would take her back in time, to the worst days of her life. He was going to hurt her, and he didn't want to. But his job meant he would. It was a commitment he'd made when he was put on Sara Parker's case. It wasn't enough just to have the child back. He had to find the man who'd taken her, and when he did that he might finally figure out what had happened to poor little Annie McKay.

All of that was going to be hard as hell on Carolyn, and if he could help her now, if he could hold her and make her feel a little bit better about whatever combination of things was tearing her up inside, he'd do it. He owed her that much.

And besides, he wanted to hold her so bad, he'd have cut off his right arm for the privilege.

Ten years gone by, thousands of miles—and despite it all, he just wanted to hold her so much. It was staggering how much he wanted that simple connection with her one more time.

"C'mere, sweetheart." He folded her into his arms, easing her toward him, inch by torturous inch, until the wonderful, familiar weight of her body settled against his.

She resisted right up until the end. Her back was ramrod-straight, her head was held high and proud, and the look in her eyes was telling him that he'd caught her by surprise and frightened her at the same time.

"What are you so afraid of?" he asked.

She opened her mouth, then paused, as if she didn't know what to say. Finally she just shook her head as her eyes flooded with tears once again.

"Carolyn?" He was intrigued now.

"You're not . . . mad at me?" she said.

"Mad? Why would I be mad?" He couldn't imagine.

And then, with a little gasp, she just melted against him. All the fight went out of her, and she turned boneless in his arms. He guided her head down to his chest and held it there with his hand in her soft hair, his chin resting on the top of her head. Her breasts were pressed against his chest, her arms were anchored around his waist and holding on for dear life.

He remembered now how this had felt. He remembered everything about holding her and trying to comfort her the best he knew how. He remembered the way she'd had of making him feel like a man, the way she'd clung to him as if he were the only solid thing in her world.

"Let it go, sweetheart. Let it all out," he said, and she finally started to cry.

For Carolyn, being in Drew's arms was like coming home. Of course, she couldn't know if the similarity was exactly true, because she didn't have a home. She had a house. An apartment, really, one that might as well be empty, for all the care and effort she'd put into trying to make it a home. She had a few friends she seldom saw, lots of business associates who were dear to her, yet carefully kept at a distance when it came to her private life.

She had a mother she hadn't seen in months—all because of some destructive mixture of guilt and anger over things Carolyn could not change. She had a son who didn't know she was his mother and probably never would know, a father she wanted to believe was in heaven now and felt no pain, no emptiness, no sense of loss. And she had a sister who might as well have vanished into thin air.

That was it—the sum total of her personal life.

She didn't remember the last time she'd given in to the luxury of letting go like this and crying her eyes out. And she couldn't remember the last time anyone had been around to witness it, much less wrap her up in his big, strong arms and hold her the way Drew was.

He wasn't even mad at her, and that was an absolute impossibility. She'd known he would be furious, and justly so, she thought. But he wasn't. He was tender and kind, warm and strong, incredibly handsome and so achingly familiar.

This couldn't be real. She knew that, even as she clung to him, much too long after her tears had stopped falling.

He said he'd missed her. Imagine that... He'd told her everything would be all right, and she loved him just for saying it, even if there was no way it could be true. But she'd needed so much to hear it, and he must have known that. Somehow, he'd always known what she needed.

"Oh, Drew..." she said, then felt the touch of his hand in her hair turn into a caress instead. He threaded his fingers through the strands, then brought a handful up to his nose and drew in the smell of them, then kissed them softly.

She couldn't do anything but shiver at the incredibly intimate gesture.

"I've missed you so much," he said, and it was so sweet to hear it, despite the obvious questions his admission automatically brought to mind.

Why had he left?

Why had he stayed away?

In this instant, she didn't care. She was just so happy to have him back. Even if it didn't last, even once the past interfered, she would savor this precious moment with him.

He was so warm and so solid, the feel of him so familiar, it overwhelmed her and it made her so hopeful.

Maybe the world wasn't falling apart. Maybe he would stay. Maybe she'd find a way to trust someone again, to believe that not everyone would either walk out on her or be snatched away. Maybe they could find a way to be together—her and Drew and Billy.

Oh, God. Billy.

He was so upset and worried. She had to find him. She had to explain.

Abruptly she pushed him away, then backed away herself. The three steps she took seemed like a mile, but she managed to take them, then hold her hands up in front of her to keep him from closing the distance again.

"Wait a minute...." Drew protested.

"Billy," she reminded him. "I have to find Billy."

"In a minute," he said. "I want to know about you. Are you all right?"

"Yes." She actually managed to sound halfway convincing. "I am now."

Carolyn's face flooded with heat at all that confession implied. Now that he'd held her so tenderly in his arms and she'd bawled her eyes out, she was all right.

But she had to get back on solid ground. She wasn't seventeen years old anymore, and Drew wasn't her savior.

She was on her own now. She'd made this mess. She'd have to try to sort it out as best she could.

"Are you sure?" he asked, and it was only then that she realized she was swaying on her feet.

She supposed that was better than leaning over her desk or against the wall, shaking like a leaf, but it still left a lot to be desired.

"I'll be fine," she said. "I'm not usually like this, really. I'm usually...."

Cool, calm, quiet.

Unemotional?

She liked that word. She'd strive to attain that state of mind. It didn't sound nearly so bad as the truth—that she'd simply shriveled up inside herself, to the point that nothing and no one mattered to her that much.

She was utterly and absolutely alone in this world, by her own choice.

It was safer that way.

It was manageable.

It was difficult and lonely as hell, but that was her life, her right, her choice.

At least it had been until now. Now Drew Delaney was back. He'd held her in his arms, stroked her hair, caught it to his lips and kissed it tenderly—and she wanted him.

It was next to impossible, but she wanted him.

"Oh, Drew." She sighed again. It was impossible. Then she ducked her head, sidestepped her way around him and said, "I have to go find Billy."

Chapter 5

Carolyn walked out of the waiting room and didn't let herself look back. She couldn't begin to explain what had just happened in there, and she honestly couldn't even think about it right now. She had other things to do that had to take precedence over Drew Delaney's return.

She looked up to find an old family friend, Dr. Benjamin Moore, coming out of her mother's room, and she took a deep, hopefully steadying breath.

She couldn't help but wonder if he'd seen Drew and recognized him, then put everything together. Dr. Moore, the family's doctor for three decades or so, was one of the very few people in town who knew Grace McKay hadn't given birth to the child she called her son.

"Carolyn," he said, a smile on his kind, well-lined face, something harder to read in his eyes. "I'm glad you're here. I need to talk to you."

One telltale glance at the waiting room—no doubt at Drew, standing in the doorway behind her—and the doctor told her all she needed to know. He'd definitely put everything together, and that was going to complicate things greatly.

Not that he would tell anyone. Carolyn was sure he wouldn't.

That wasn't what was uppermost in Carolyn's mind right now. It was the fact that Dr. Moore had easily put father and son together.

How many more people in town had already done the same? And how long before the whole thing got back to Billy?

"Billy," she said to the doctor, seeing a way out of this awkwardness, at least for a moment. She needed it, to collect herself and try to find a way to, at best, muddle through this. "First, I need to check on Billy."

"He's fine. Worried, but other than that, fine. He's watching some kids' show on the television in there, and your mother's sleeping. I decided that more than anything she needed rest, and I've sedated her."

"Do you know what's wrong with her yet? Drew said he thought it was her heart."

He took her by the elbow and turned her toward the waiting room she'd just left. "Why don't you come and sit down with me for a few minutes?"

Carolyn felt the tension in her escalate one more step, to the point where it was certainly near the limit that she could endure. How much worse could this get?

She walked with the doctor into the waiting room. Drew was still there, and she felt compelled to introduce the two of them.

"We've met," Dr. Moore said, when she started to make the introductions. "Mr. Delaney was telling me about the discussion he and your mother were having when she collapsed."

Carolyn sat down hard on the worse-for-wear tweed sofa. The two men took chairs on either side of her. She couldn't look at Drew. She simply couldn't find it in her to face him right now, and she could only imagine the kind of discussion he and her mother had been having. It left her no doubts about the fact that Dr. Moore knew exactly what was going on.

"I'm sorry, Carolyn," Drew said. "I never meant for anything like this to happen."

She nodded in his direction, her eyes glued to the floor, surprised that he would apologize, all things considered. She'd certainly never thought he'd meant to upset her mother so much that she landed in the hospital. "We don't need to get into this now, all right? We will, just not now. All right?"

"Of course," he said.

Thank God for small mercies, Carolyn thought, then turned to the doctor. "How is she?"

"Well, she didn't have a heart attack," he said.

"You're sure?"

"Ruling that out is the easy part. When the heart is damaged, there are certain enzymes that spill into the blood from the damaged heart muscle, and they're easily detected in blood tests. We didn't find any of those in your mother's blood."

"So what was it?" Carolyn asked.

"I honestly don't know yet. I've ordered some more tests for tomorrow, and we should know more then."

"That's it?" Carolyn said. There had to be more than that. She had to be able to tell Billy something.

"It may be nothing more than severe stress—some sort of panic attack. That would account for her heart racing, for the shortness of breath, as she got more agitated, even the pain in her chest. It's not uncommon for people to think they're having a heart attack under those conditions. For now, it's best that she rest, so I sedated her. She'll probably sleep through until morning, and then we'll run some more tests."

"Just stress?" Carolyn was so relieved.

"Now, I don't want you to get the wrong impression," Dr. Moore said. "Stress can do incredible things to people. Her heart rate was dangerously high, as was her blood pressure."

"Is it serious? Is it a life-threatening thing?" Carolyn asked.

"Anytime your heart rate is that high, it's serious." The doctor held up his hands to silence her. "But we don't know what the cause was. The first thing I need to do is run some tests to rule out other physical problems. We'll know more tomorrow, so let's just leave it at that. Anything else I could tell you would be sheer speculation and probably only frighten you needlessly."

She nodded and didn't press further.

"Now, I have to go," the doctor said. "If you want to see your mother, that's fine. But, as I said, she's not going to wake up until tomorrow morning, so you might as well take Billy and go on home."

"You'll call us, if there's any...change?"

"Of course. Leave your number with the nurses." He rose to go, then turned back to Drew. "Whatever you need from Grace is going to have to wait. She's not up to dealing with this right now. She might not be for a while."

Drew nodded. "I'll see if Carolyn and I can't handle it by ourselves."

Carolyn closed her eyes and looked away. She and Drew couldn't settle anything without her mother. No doubt he wanted Billy, whether to simply see him on a regular basis or, God forbid, to try for custody—it didn't matter. They couldn't settle anything among themselves, because Carolyn didn't have any rights where Billy was concerned. She'd given those up a very long time ago.

Drew must have known she had nearly reached the limit of what she could endure, because he suggested that they all get out of the hospital and go back to her parents' house.

"I want to see my mother first, just for a minute," she said, still not looking at him.

"Billy's in there," he reminded her.

She crossed her arms in front of her and shook her head. Billy. Her mother. Drew. No matter where she turned, it just got worse. Drew must have seen the despair in her face, and amazingly, despite all that she'd done to him, he still had the capacity to be kind to her. It amazed her.

He walked over to the sofa where she sat, and stood beside her. One hand went to her back, making small circles there, his touch steadying her, his warmth creeping into her.

She fought it with all she had, but the invitation was too much to pass up. He was right there, so solid and so big, so willing to comfort her in any way he could.

That part still amazed her—that he cared enough to want to comfort her, when she was the one who'd kept this awful secret from him.

But she knew what was facing her when they got home. She had to try to explain things to Billy, and then she had to explain them to Drew.

How in the world would she ever be able to explain what she'd done to Drew?

Her head came down despairingly as she struggled for control. Drew took a little step closer, and before she knew what was happening, her face was pressed against one of his thighs. The hand at her back went to her hair, holding her close against him.

"We'll deal with it, Carolyn. We'll get through it all. I promise you we will."

A few moments later, Carolyn watched, in something of a daze, as Drew crossed the hallway to her mother's room. She heard him lure Billy out with the promise of a soda and a discussion about what kind of take-out food they were going to order for dinner, then left her for a few minutes alone with her mother.

Carolyn entered the room and noted how a cardiac monitor displayed the now-regular, if slightly fast, beating of her mother's heart. Grace had an IV in her left arm, but that was the extent of the equipment hooked up to her. Her face was terribly pale, and the lines around her eyes were deeper than Carolyn remembered. And she looked so frail. Somehow, *frail* was one word she'd never associated with her mother. Even after Annie had disappeared, even after her father had died.

Maybe it was simply age, Carolyn thought. Although her mother was only forty-seven.

She reached out to take her hand. Finding it cool to the touch, she tried to warm it between her own hands.

Grace McKay was a good mother. She expected a lot from her children. She wouldn't tolerate back talk or misbehavior, but she was strong and loving and steadfast. Billy had been happy with her. He'd been safe and happy and healthy.

What more could a mother want for her child? Carolyn had pondered over that question day after day.

Through her work at Hope House, she saw the runaways, the teen prostitutes, the drug addicts, the hopelessly inadequate and terribly young teenage mothers. After seeing the way some children turned out these days, it seemed selfish of her to want more than to know her son was healthy and happy and safe.

But she did.

She wanted much more than that.

She wanted him back.

Feeling absolutely overwhelmed, she lowered her head to rest atop her mother's hand, clasped within the warmth of her own, and considered offering up a prayer, though she wasn't sure there was anyone out there to hear it. It came out as nothing more than an incoherent plea for help—for herself, her mother, her son, and his father.

Billy and Drew decided on carryout pizza for dinner, and Carolyn was grateful to Drew for going to pick it up himself so that she could have a few minutes alone with Billy. She didn't want to have her talk with him with Drew listening in.

She didn't try saying anything to him in the car. Once they got to the house, he headed straight for his room. She gave herself five minutes to formulate some kind of plan for what she would say to him, then followed him.

Billy's room was cram-packed with everything an eight-year-old boy could possibly want. An antique electric train set, a skateboard, a computer, an electronic keyboard. She hated to admit that she'd bought all of these and more. She couldn't seem to resist the urge to buy him presents. Right now, he was sprawled out on the floor, in front of the controls to the video game set she'd bought him two Christmases ago. The screen of the TV to which it was attached was alive with color and a flurry of movement as he tried to escape from some evil villain's spaceship.

"Billy?" she said between blasts of super laser torpedoes.

He didn't answer.

Carolyn turned off the TV, earning herself a look of pure venom. She winced and tried to tell herself that mothers endured things like this all the time, so she ought to be able to take a few without falling apart.

Still, she couldn't escape the doubts. What if he found out what she'd done one day, and he hated her for it? How could she endure that? How could she explain?

What if Drew made her tell Billy? He might well insist on that very thing tonight, when he returned. How would she handle that?

She looked down at her little boy, his defiance fading, his doubts setting in. He was so much like Drew sometimes, she couldn't understand how the whole world didn't know whose child he really was. It was so clear to her in the shape of his body, the slim hips, the long legs, the lanky arms that would be thick with muscles someday.

Billy walked over to his dresser and picked up a small picture of her and Annie when they had been close to his age, and bent his head over it. Carolyn tried not to wince at the image of her sweet-spirited, smiling sister.

"Do you think Annie's in heaven?" Billy asked, throwing her totally off-balance.

Carolyn gave herself a moment to take that in and think about it. What did she really believe? That Annie was dead? Most certainly. That she would go to heaven? Definitely. That there truly was a heaven? A God who let innocent children suffer so? That was where her doubts and her anger started.

"I think—" she chose her words carefully "—that Annie would definitely have gone to heaven."

"And my dad?"

"Yes," Carolyn said, unable to figure out where this was leading.

"Do you think Mama wants to go to heaven, too?" He had his back to her now, but she knew from his tone of voice that they were close to the crux of the problem.

"Someday," Carolyn said.

"But she misses them both so much. She's told me so, and I thought, maybe she misses them so much she's decided she wants to go to heaven now, so she could be with them."

"Oh, Billy." Carolyn sat down on the edge of his bed, close to him, but not touching him. She was suddenly afraid of touching him. Once she got him in her arms, how would she ever let go? "She would never leave you, Billy, not voluntarily, anyway. She loves you so much."

"But she loved them, too. And my dad loved me, but he's there now. So Mama might go too, right?"

Carolyn wanted to make blind reassurances to him that he'd never lose the woman he called his mother, but you couldn't do that to a little boy who'd lost the man he thought of as his father a mere six months before.

"I know you're frightened," she said, feeling totally inadequate explaining things to him that she could never begin to understand herself. "I'm frightened, too, Billy. But I talked to the doctor, and he thinks he can make her better. He's running some tests tomorrow, and after that, he thinks he'll understand what happened to her and how to fix it."

"Really?" he asked, smothering a sob with the back of his hand.

"Really," Carolyn replied.

"Is she going to wake up tomorrow?"

"Yes. The only reason she was asleep tonight was because the doctor gave her some medicine to help her rest."

"Honest?"

"Honest."

"I was scared when she wouldn't wake up." He'd made a quarter turn to the side now, so she could see the tear tracks on his face, the stubborn set of his jaw that showed he was still not ready to forgive her.

"It scared me, too," Carolyn said.

"And if she never woke up..." He lost it then. His precious little face crinkled up in a superhuman effort to hold it back, but he lost it. Billy started sobbing. Stubbornly he stayed where he was, in the middle of the room, neither inviting nor rejecting her touch. His back rigid, his eyes overflowing, he haltingly told her the rest. "If she never woke up... I don't know... What would happen to me?"

Carolyn dropped to her knees in front of him, then, amazingly, found herself having to look up at him from this height. It was amazing how fast he'd grown. Surely it hadn't been that long ago that she could do this and be at eye level with him.

"Billy?" She took his hand and made herself smile back at him instead of crying. "If anything ever happened to Mama, you'd have me."

He practically snarled at her through his tears, the little boy inside him warring with the little man who wouldn't wear his heart on his sleeve.

"You haven't even been here lately," he sobbed, the hurt coming through now, rather than the anger.

"Not because I haven't wanted to be here."

"You're a grown-up, and grown-ups can do anything they want."

"Oh, Billy, you've got a lot to learn about being a grown-up. I most definitely cannot do whatever I want."

"Maybe," he conceded, "but if you wanted to be here, you could have."

Carolyn wanted to be as honest with him as possible. But she couldn't tell him everything. Not tonight. And she didn't think she could ever tell him about this awful tug-of-war she felt caught in with her mother. She loved the woman, but she envied her, as well. Grace McKay had Billy. Carolyn didn't think she ever would. She didn't have the right, not after all these years. She knew that, but it didn't stop the yearning for him.

No doubt her mother felt threatened by Carolyn's feelings, and she was very vulnerable at this point in her life, so soon after losing her husband. Her mother hadn't actually ordered Carolyn to stay away, but it had been clear she wouldn't be welcomed, either.

She couldn't explain any of that to Billy.

Carolyn sighed as she stared at him. "I love you very much, Billy."

That touched a nerve. He started to say something right away, but got all choked up instead, which made him mad all over again.

"I'm sorry I hurt your feelings because I haven't been here as much as I should have these last few months. I never thought you'd think that you couldn't count on me, or that I didn't care about you anymore."

He shrugged it off, as if it meant nothing to him. Eight-year-old boys were like that at times, especially when they were trying hard to live up to someone's idea of what a man should or shouldn't do. Crying, hugging, talking about their feelings, all were right up there at the top of the list of things *not* to do. Carolyn knew that. It was the only reason she didn't have him in her arms right now.

She settled for wiping one little curl off his forehead and felt rewarded when he didn't pull back. "And if you ever need me, I'll be here for you, Billy. You won't ever have to be all alone in this world."

Drew brought back pizza, and they ate it. They called the hospital once more, to find Grace McKay's condition unchanged, and then Carolyn put Billy to bed.

She walked back into the living room, found it empty but the front door open, then walked out onto the front porch.

Drew was standing in the shadows by one of the support columns, smoking a cigarette, the end glowing a bright reddish orange in the darkness.

"Going to lecture me about my nasty habits?" he said easily.

"No," she said, trying not to concentrate too hard on how incredible he looked now that she had a moment to study him.

She'd always known he'd make a handsome man someday, but she hadn't been prepared for this. He still had the mustache and the beard, but they were slim and trim these days, framing his face in a very elegant way. And his hair was still as thick, still curly, but he wore it fairly short and brushed back from his face. He had on a sleek, dark suit, instead of the jeans, boots and black leather jacket that had once made him look so dangerous on his motorcycle.

But she still remembered the bike, remembered hanging on to him as they sped through the streets. She remembered it all so well, and seeing him now seemed to have brought all these old adolescent feelings roaring back to life inside her. The excitement, the magic, the intensity of falling in love for the first time. It all came back so vividly now.

She couldn't help but let her eyes trail over that tall, sleek body of his, encased in that formfitting dark brown suit. She knew the shoulders were broad, the arms strong and muscular, the hands gentle.

If she closed her eyes, she could remember the feel of his body lying atop hers. She could feel the fine sheen of sweat on his back, the slightly rough feel of his thighs intertwined with hers, the intensity of the look in his beautiful brown eyes as they'd stared down at her.

Once, he'd meant the whole world to her. He'd been the only thing in her universe that was safe and solid and sure. And then he'd left her, devastated her, at the time when she needed him most.

If only he'd stayed.

She'd thought about it again and again, playing endless fantasy games with herself. Her and Drew and Billy together in a million different places throughout the years, so happy they could hardly stand it.

She'd imagined it so many times, and now, here they were, together—except it wasn't anything like her dreams.

"Old Mrs. Watson still on the corner?" he asked, the cigarette glowing bright as he took a drag.

Carolyn turned toward the brick house on the left. "Of course." Some things never changed.

"She's watching us," he said, obviously amused. "I'd forgotten that—the way people in little towns think it's their right to know everything about everyone else's business. Wonder if she's figured out who I am yet.''

''If she hasn't, she will soon enough. She won't give up until she knows. Besides, I'm sure some people recognized you at the hospital this afternoon, and Mrs. Watson has connections all over town.''

Carolyn was already resigned to the fact that they'd be the talk of the town by morning.

Drew finished the cigarette and disposed of it in the empty soda can he'd set on the porch railing. He picked it up now and turned toward her, then replaced the can and gave her a look that could have melted butter. Though he was two whole steps away, she could feel the power he still had over her. She was aware of him with every fiber of her being. She wondered if he could possibly feel that, too.

It amazed her. Her whole carefully constructed life was falling apart around her, and all she wanted to do was stand on the porch in the darkness and marvel at how wonderful it was to see him again.

He took one more step toward her, his face bathed in shadows, making it impossible to tell anything about his expression. Yet she knew he was looking at her. She could feel it. And she thought he must have smiled, and somewhere in her short-circuiting brain she knew that couldn't be right, that it didn't fit at all with the reason he'd come back here.

It had to be Billy. He must know, and he should be angry. God knew he had the right.

But he was smiling at her. She was certain of it now that he'd come one more step closer. She could reach out and touch him if she wanted. She could walk right into his arms, and he'd hold her there. Somehow, she knew that too, and it simply didn't fit.

He gave her a look of pure mischief that would have made the devil proud, then glanced back over his shoulder toward Mrs. Watson.

"Want to really make her day?"

And then his lips came down toward hers.

"Drew?" She was surprised, a little amused.

He caught her in his arms and lowered her into an elaborately theatrical dip, then brought his head down until his lips were half an inch from hers. She could just imagine what it would look like from Mrs. Watson's vantage point. Laughter bubbled up inside her as he brought her upright again.

She was still giggling, feeling almost giddy, as well, and utterly caught up in this magic moment with him, when she caught him staring at her again.

"What?" she said.

He shook his head and sighed. "You know, there was a time in my life when I would have given anything to see you smile or to hear you laugh like that. There was a time when I lived to make you happy."

And then she knew that he hadn't staged this scene for Mrs. Watson's benefit. He'd done it for her, just as he had done things for her so often all those years ago. When the whole world looked bleak and cold and unforgiving, Drew could make it seem like springtime. He had the gift, and he lavished it upon her.

"I lived to see you smile," he said soberly, his head bent downward, his hand catching the end of her hair in his fingertips, then lingering beside her shoulder at the spot where he'd captured it. "I didn't even know how much I'd missed you, Carolyn. Not until I finally saw you again. It was hell being away from you all these years."

Carolyn was stunned, the breath simply leaving her body, and the energy, as well. She felt like a rag doll, boneless, bloodless, ready to bend or break at his will.

It wasn't supposed to be like this. It wasn't supposed to feel so good or so right, not after all this time, and especially not after the way things had ended between them.

Something wasn't right about this, and now that she had a moment to think about it, it was starting to scare her a little.

As she'd told herself earlier, when she'd talked to him on the phone, people just didn't drop out of the sky and land in Hope, Illinois. He was back for a reason. And if it wasn't Billy, then what had brought him here?

"Say something," he said softly. His voice, coming to her through the darkness and the silence—the smoothness of it, the deep pitch, the sweet familiarity—sent shivers of anticipation down her spine.

"What do you want me to say?" She chose her words carefully now, as the uncertainty took over.

He shrugged, glanced around the porch, looked down the block, then back at her. "I thought you might hate me now. Lord knows you have the right. At the least, I was sure you'd be angry at me, if you still gave me a thought at all."

The knots in Carolyn's stomach, the ones that had finally eased when they found that little girl in Indiana, were coming back now. Stress always hit her there, with her insides twisting upon themselves. And she was happy for the darkness and the things he couldn't see.

If he knew about Billy, he'd have to be angry at her. But he wasn't. He was wondering why she wasn't angry at him.

But she didn't want to think about that, not if she could help it. She wanted to go on with this conversation. She wanted to hear the part where he told her he still thought about her sometimes, that he missed her and was glad to see her again. Those were some of the sweetest words she'd ever heard, ranking right up there with Billy telling her that he loved her.

"Carolyn?" His hand slid down from her shoulder, along her arm, to cup her elbow. "Tell me you don't hate me."

She shivered again, and he must have felt it, must have attributed it to the cold, because he slowly pulled her forward, stopping just shy of having her in his arms.

"I did for a while," she admitted, having to try hard to concentrate on what they were talking about. A woman shouldn't have to think when she was this close to a man like Drew. "But I had a lot of good memories of you, too, and I didn't want to lose them. I wanted to hold on to the good times. I needed to, and I couldn't quite do that and hate you at the same time. So I let it go."

It sounded lame, even to her, but that was what had happened. It hadn't been Drew's fault their whole world got turned upside down after Annie disappeared, and if that had never happened, who was to say what would have become of her and Drew? She tried not to even let herself get angry about it anymore, because it served no purpose. The past was an unforgiving place, and she had no intentions of living there.

"And now?" His other arm came up to take her hand in his. He held it for a moment, then slid his hand along her forearm to her elbow. With her very nearly in his arms again, he stopped and waited.

What did she feel right now? Giddy, almost drunk on the sight of him and the sound of his voice, warmed from the heat coming off him, and so very hopeful.

It was like stepping back in time, like waking up and finding that the past ten years had been nothing but a bad dream. He could still be in love with her, she in love with him. She could never have given up Billy. He could still be this tiny creature nestled safe and sound inside her body.

What did she feel right now? "Oh, Drew. I couldn't begin to explain it to you."

"Try," he said coaxingly, his voice as soft and smooth as warmed honey.

"I can't believe you're back. I . . ."

She paused. She'd been so happy, so thrown off-balance by this whole thing and his behavior, that she'd forgotten to be scared. And she had good reason to be scared.

Except he wasn't angry at her—not at all—and that didn't fit. She'd missed something here, something vital. And she couldn't ignore that any longer.

"Drew, why did you come back?"

Chapter 6

He went absolutely still, the magical mood broken as effectively as if someone had doused them with ice water. She heard him sigh once, felt him staring at her through the darkness.

"You don't know?" he said, his arms dropping to his sides.

She shook her head, certain now that she didn't want to know.

"I thought..." He turned aside and swore softly. "When the doctor was talking to you, when he told you I was with your mother when she collapsed, you acted like you knew why. I just assumed that he'd told you."

Carolyn had no idea what Drew was saying or why he was here, but she was certain of one thing—he wasn't mad at her. He never had been. If anything, he was apologetic about whatever had caused him to return to this town. And whatever it was that had brought him here, it wasn't Billy.

Thank God, she thought, relief overwhelming her. It

wasn't Billy. He didn't know. For a moment, she forgot everything else. Drew didn't know!

But this also presented her with a whole host of other problems—such as how she was going to tell him, and when. And what would her mother say? What would Grace do? What if Drew insisted on telling Billy? Her mind was racing through a whole new set of questions with no answers.

"You really don't know?" he asked.

Again, she could only shake her head. Again, the warning bells were going off inside her head. Something was very wrong here.

Drew caught her in his arms this time and held her so tight she could barely breathe. He took his hand and pushed her face down against his shoulder. He was trembling, too; she could feel it now.

"You're scaring me, Drew."

He only held her tighter.

"Sweetheart, I'm so sorry."

He was acting as if he were about to tell her she'd lost her best friend in the world, but that wasn't possible. Her father had died months ago. Billy was in the house, asleep. Her mother was resting comfortably; they'd called to check on her half an hour ago. And Drew was holding her in his arms. There simply wasn't anyone else in her life who was really important to her.

Except Annie.

She couldn't say where the thought came from. It just hit her like a ton of bricks. She was sure she would have fallen flat on her face if Drew hadn't been holding her so tightly.

Annie.

This had to be about Annie.

"They found her body?" she said, in a daze, not even saying her sister's name aloud.

It wouldn't be so bad, she argued with herself. Not after all this time. Annie was lost to them already. She always had been, from the day she disappeared. Carolyn knew that. She'd fought for years to accept that.

Annie wasn't ever coming back. And there would be some relief in having a body to bury, in maybe finding out after all this time what had happened to her. Perhaps even, if they were lucky, finding the person responsible and putting him behind bars, so that he wouldn't do to anyone else what he'd done to Annie and the whole McKay family.

"They found her, didn't they?"

"No." He whispered it against her ear. Maybe he'd been telling her that the whole time, and she'd simply been unable to hear him. He gave her a little kiss in the spot right beside her ear, as he whispered it again and again.

It took a while for it to sink in. When her mother collapsed earlier, she'd been with Drew. What had he told her?

"I don't... I don't understand," Carolyn managed to say.

He was scaring her, and she knew that she must be scaring him, as well, with her reaction. She felt curiously detached from her body, so it was no wonder she could barely stand, no wonder he was so worried about holding her up.

"I don't—" She had to stop to breathe. Why was it so hard to breathe? They were on the porch; she remembered that much. It was dark and cold. No wonder she was tingling. It was cold, and nosy old Mrs. Watson was watching them, and Drew had claimed that he still missed her.

It had been magic.

Pure magic.

And it had turned to this.

It was like that day so long ago, when Annie had disappeared.

Through the fog that had filled her soul, she heard Drew calling to her.

Annie, she thought. He was trying to tell her about Annie, and she didn't want to hear it.

After all this time, after asking God to please just let them find her, to let them finally know for certain, Carolyn found that she didn't actually want to know.

Suddenly, she became aware of Drew's hand on the side of her face, of the way he'd forced her to look up at him and brought his head down to hers.

"Carolyn." She watched his lips move, and read the words coming from them. "Listen to me."

But she didn't want to listen. She wanted to hide. Carolyn McKay, all grown up, all too familiar with the ways of the world and injustices committed against even the most vulnerable of children, wanted to hide her head in the sand and pretend that none of this was happening.

"Don't tell me," she pleaded.

"Shh ... just listen. We didn't find her body."

Carolyn made a desperate grab for air, the blood rushing to her head, the porch starting to revolve in tight little circles. "You didn't?"

"No."

"Oh, thank God."

He gave her a minute to absorb that. She tried to take it in, amazed at the enormousness of her relief, amazed at the power this still had to hurt her.

Ten years had passed, and for a moment, the feelings that came at her were so strong, it felt the way it had the first day, the first hour, even.

And then it hit her. If it wasn't Annie's body that they'd found, and if this wasn't about Billy, then what?

"What?" She said it aloud this time.

"I think I found the clothes she was wearing when she disappeared."

* * *

Reality slowly came back to her. The roaring in her ears receded. The frightening void that had engulfed her, the tunnel vision that had allowed her to see only her sister's face, was lessening. Night sounds—the crickets humming, the occasional blast of a car stereo as it passed by on the street—came back to her. She felt the natural coolness of the late-October evening, and not the chill of fear. And Drew. She was with Drew on the porch, and he was the only reason she was still standing.

"Her clothes?" she said, at first able only to repeat what he'd already told her. "I think I need to sit down."

"Let's go inside." He let go of her slowly and opened the door for her to pass through.

The living room was dark, save for the lamp on the table in the corner. Carolyn sat down on the big, overstuffed sofa. Helplessly she felt her eyes drawn to the pictures spotlit by the lamp. Annie smiled back at her with all the warmth and innocence of a thirteen-year-old. Billy, in the photo beside Annie's, smiled, as well.

Carolyn looked away, only then realizing that Drew was right in front of her. He'd sat on the edge of the coffee table, which put him at eye level with her. His hands closed around hers, and his face wasn't more than a foot away from hers now.

"Annie's clothes," he said slowly, giving her time to take it in. "The shorts set with the red-and-black checked pattern, the one she brought back from Texas. You remember?"

Carolyn nodded. "She wore it to the picnic that day." God, that awful day.

"Yes, I remembered it from the picture of her we put on the fliers, and the ones the police gave the press."

"You found the red suit?" Carolyn shook her head in disbelief. It was so hard to comprehend. They'd found it, after all this time?

When Annie disappeared, she'd been walking down the road from the city park to their house, three blocks away. She'd been going to retrieve the loaves of fresh bread her mother had baked for a town picnic, the bread Carolyn had been supposed to get. As the investigators soon realized, either Annie had taken a shortcut through the woods or someone had lured her into them. It was as if the woods had swallowed her whole.

The police had found a print or two from a nondescript tennis shoe, size twelve and a half wide. They'd found Carolyn's mother's house keys in the dirt along the path through the woods, but no sign of Annie. There had never been the slightest trace of her outside those woods—until now.

"It's been ten years, Drew."

"I know. It's crazy. The whole thing is crazy, but I swear they're Annie's clothes."

"My mother didn't know for sure?"

"We never got that far," he said. "As soon as she found out I was here about Annie, she just lost it."

Carolyn paused for a moment, knowing the next questions she had to ask, not sure she was up to hearing the answers. Drew sat in front of her, holding her hands, just as he'd held on to her long into the lonely nights after Annie disappeared.

Back then, it had been as if her whole world had been turned upside down in an instant. She'd known that everything had changed. Annie wasn't coming back, not ever, and certainly not after ten long years.

"She's dead," Carolyn said, absolutely certain of it.

Drew was obviously at a loss. "We don't know that. There's nothing about the clothes . . . to indicate that."

"Ten years," Carolyn argued. "No one disappears for ten years and then comes back, especially not a child. She was probably dead the day she disappeared."

He didn't say anything then.

"You know it as well as I do, Drew. I've known it for years, so... it shouldn't be this hard to handle what's happened now. I mean, it's nothing but a shirt and a pair of shorts, but I'm falling to pieces here, even though I know she's dead and gone...."

Carolyn stopped, to breathe and to think. Her words were coming out too fast, her voice was breaking up, the hysteria deep inside her was pushing its way to the surface.

"I know she's dead," she said calmly, once she could.

"Maybe," Drew conceded. "But it would be something to know for sure, wouldn't it? Wouldn't that help? To know what happened to her? Maybe even to catch the bastard who did it? To at least make sure he doesn't do it to anyone else?"

"Yes." Carolyn looked down at their intertwined hands and was grateful that he was still hanging on to her. She was feeling a little saner, a little more capable, than before. There were things that had to be done, and it looked as if she was the one who would have to handle them. Her mother was in no shape to do it herself. "Where did you find the clothes?"

"Sara Parker—"

"The little girl who was kidnapped?" Carolyn interrupted, recognizing the name immediately, recognizing the significance of finding a link between Annie's kidnapping and that of another little girl.

Drew nodded. "She was wearing them when she escaped."

And that changed everything, as Carolyn saw it. That suggested there was some pattern to this man's actions. That Annie's kidnapping hadn't been some isolated incident, or the work of someone who was merely passing through the area. That obviously, since Sara Parker had been found across the state line and to the south, the man was still in the area. That Sara Parker might know something that could lead them to Annie's kidnapper—and to the answers of questions that haunted Carolyn and her mother to this day.

"It's so hard to believe," Carolyn said.

"I know." He was rubbing his hands against hers now, massaging them a little, trying to warm them, or to get the blood pumping down into them again.

Carolyn still couldn't believe he was here after all this time. She still—

"Drew, what do you have to do with Sara Parker's kidnapping case?"

"I'm with the FBI now. I do a lot of work in child abductions."

As did Carolyn, and she had to wonder if he did it for the same reasons she did. "Still trying to exorcise an old ghost?"

Suddenly he wouldn't meet her eyes. "Maybe. And you?"

Touché, she thought. Carolyn shook her head noncommittally. "It's all just so crazy."

"I know, sweetheart. It's a damned crazy world out there."

"So what do we do now?" She pulled her hands from his and, because she so desperately needed to think straight, because that was difficult enough even without being this close to him, she stood up and walked to the window.

"I have a picture of Sara wearing the red suit. And if you think they're Annie's clothes, I'll get on the phone and have one of the agents bring the clothes here for you to look at more closely."

Carolyn felt a chill shoot through her. To see them was bad enough. But to touch them? To hold them in her hands? "Why would the guy still hang on to her clothes after all this time?"

"I don't know, Carolyn. I haven't had time to even try to figure it out. I've spent the last three days and nights looking for Sara Parker. I saw her this morning, and I knew there was something about her that was familiar. As soon as I figured it out, I was on my way here. And things have been crazy ever since."

"I know," she said, feeling nauseous. "If he took her clothes..."

Drew seemed to understand what she was implying. "It doesn't mean anything," he told her.

She didn't argue with him. There was no point. He worked with missing children; he knew as well as she did the kind of things that happened to them once they disappeared.

"Carolyn, either the guy lives in a very remote area or he has a hideout of some sort where he takes the kids."

"Kids?" she said. "How many are we talking about?"

"I'm not sure. But these guys don't stop at two kids. Especially not ten years apart. If he's been in the area all this time, we're going to find out about others."

Yes, she was certain he was right. The statistics her own organization had gathered estimated that the average child sex offender had more than one hundred victims—an astonishing number, until you realized how hard it was for a child to tell someone about being victimized, how hard a charge it was for most adults to believe and how difficult it was to prove. Even if all those things worked together and someone got convicted, the justice system didn't always manage to keep them in jail, and that was a fact that made Carolyn furious.

She understood the system all too well. She fought this battle every day. One of the most important parts of her job was acting as a lobbyist for children's rights, particularly in the area of changing the laws to protect children.

It didn't seem like that should be much of a fight—getting people to protect children—but she could attest to the fact that it was.

Carolyn looked up at Drew then. He worked for the FBI, finding missing children. She didn't want to think what that implied. Old ghosts, old guilt, things that they should have put behind them long ago—these still lingered, and still carried within them the power to hurt. Drew was absolutely right. It was one damned crazy world they lived in.

"We'll check the records as best we can tomorrow," he said. "If the guy was smart, he'd have realized he'd be harder to find if he crossed all sorts of jurisdictional lines, hoping that no one would ever put together the pattern."

"But kidnapping is a federal offense," she said.

"Of course, but unless there's some evidence that a child has actually been kidnapped, the Bureau wouldn't get involved. At least not right away. The reports would come in as a missing child, and the local authorities would handle them initially," he explained. "So, if this guy's smart, if he's somewhere nearby and he's been going after kids for the past ten years, he might have taken them from that state, plus Illinois, Ohio, Kentucky, Missouri, maybe Tennessee and West Virginia. Who knows."

"We can help you there," Carolyn told him, amazed that her own organization might be able to aid in finding her sister's abductor. "Among other things, Hope House is a clearinghouse for information in the region, including reports on child abductions."

"Hope House. Of course. I should have put it together when I called you there. I've only been in Chicago for a few months now, but I've heard of the group. The Bureau people speak highly of your organization—when you're not embarrassing them, of course."

"Only with good cause," Carolyn stated. "We do our best."

"So do we."

"Of course, it isn't enough. Sometimes I think no matter how much we do, it won't be enough."

"As long as you don't stop trying," he said, then seemed to regret it.

Instantly she was reminded of the fact that *he'd* simply given up on them when she needed him most. It wasn't working out, he'd told her during those last moments they spent together. By the time she knew what he planned to do, it had been too late. He'd already enlisted in the army. He'd presented her with a fait accompli, and hardly any time to even say goodbye.

Of course, that hadn't kept her from literally begging him to stay. And *that* hadn't kept him from leaving.

"Carolyn..." he began. The deep timbre of his voice, the way he drew out her name, letting it linger on his lips— it all told her he'd managed to read her thoughts much more easily than he should have, that he was ready to get into things they had no business discussing tonight.

"So," she said, jumping in before he could finish, "what do you think? About Sara and Annie?"

There was an awkward moment of silence, while he no doubt thought about challenging her on the abrupt shift, but he let it pass.

"There are a lot of wooded areas in southern Indiana and Illinois, not far from where we found Sara. If Annie's clothes were there, then Annie was likely there at some point herself. And for Sara to show up wearing Annie's old clothes tells me Sara must have been in the same place."

Carolyn had to agree with him. She heard him coming up behind her, but he stopped before he was close enough to touch her again.

"We could find her," he said. "We could find Annie and the man who did this to her. This little girl, Sara, could lead us to both of them."

Drew turned Carolyn to face him. There was compassion in the look he gave her, and determination, as well. "I'm sorry. I know this is going to be difficult. I know it's painful, but if there's a chance of finding out about Annie and finding the man who took Sara, I'm going to push as hard as I can to do it. I can't do anything less."

Carolyn nodded, her gaze finally landing on the square of paper in his left hand, her heart leaping at the sight of what must be the picture of Sara Parker in those clothes. Suddenly she felt as unsteady as she had that moment on the porch when she realized this was all about Annie.

"Show it to me," she said, before the feeling got any worse and she lost her nerve.

She closed her eyes to give him time. When she opened them again, she found herself staring at a Polaroid of a small, dark-eyed, dark-haired girl who seemed to be trying as hard as she could to shrink away from the camera.

"She looks scared to death."

Drew shrugged. "She's a tough little kid. She was doing all right until I tried to take her picture. I think the flash blinded her for a moment and scared her all over again."

"It's hard to tell... about the clothes, at least from the picture. They look the same, but I can't be sure."

He tucked the picture into the inside pocket of his jacket. "I'll call and have them brought here before they go to the lab in Chicago."

He turned to go into the kitchen. Carolyn's entire body sagged like a balloon leaking air. There was a small upholstered chair to the right of the window, and she managed to make it there just as every bit of energy and self-control she possessed drained out of her. Sitting down weakly, leaning her head back against the chair, she thought about all that this terrible day had brought her, all that she had left to face tomorrow and the next day and the day after.

Her sister. Her sweet, innocent little sister. At one time, she would have sworn it would be a relief simply to know for sure that she was gone. But now, Carolyn had her doubts.

Her mother? What in the world was wrong with her mother? And what would that do to Billy?

Billy. Drew's son.

Would she tell Drew? Should she? Would it only hurt him to know? Would he insist on telling Billy? Even fight her mother for custody? And what would that do to Billy?

She had to do what was right. But at the moment, she had no idea what "right" was.

Chapter 7

Drew put down the phone in Grace McKay's kitchen. He'd checked with Bob Rossi, who was still in the little town where they'd found Sara Parker. The agents had gotten little useful information from the girl about where she'd been held for the past week. They would try to get more once they had a psychiatrist to help them.

So far, Sara's description of the man—tall, white, middle-aged, with a killer nicotine habit—would fit about a quarter of the population. Interestingly, though the man had taken her clothes away from her and given her the red shorts set to wear, she hadn't been molested, at least not as far as the doctors who had examined her could tell. No doubt Carolyn would be relieved to hear that. There wasn't a mark on her except for some bruising on her upper arms, no doubt where the man had grabbed her, and some rope burns on her ankles where he'd tied her feet.

So, if he wasn't some kind of pedophile, what was he? Why did he like to snatch little girls?

Despite all the talk of child abductions in this country, there were actually relatively few children snatched by strangers and either killed or simply never seen again. Oh, it happened, but children were much more likely—in fact more than a thousand times more likely—to be kidnapped by a parent or relative. That was relatively common. Stranger abductions of children were much more rare, coming at the rate of a little less than one child a day for the entire country.

Drew thought of the numbers, thought of the odds that on that day ten years ago, Annie had been the *one*.

He paced back and forth in the kitchen, hardly believing that he was actually in this house again, in this town, involved once again with this woman he'd once loved. And he'd hurt her just by being here. He'd always known he would do just that if he ever came back.

He and Carolyn had fallen in love in the midst of her sister's disappearance, and at its best their relationship had been bittersweet. At its worst, it had been riddled with guilt that they were so happy with each other while Annie was simply gone, that while they sneaked off for a few stolen moments together, Annie had disappeared.

Drew had thought at first that the experience would bring them closer together, but it hadn't worked out like that. Carolyn had seemed to withdraw from him. Sometimes, he'd thought she blamed him. Other times, she seemed to blame herself. Eventually, she'd been racked with guilt every time they were together. Instead of getting better, it had only gotten worse.

It had hurt him, and it had angered him. And he hadn't been able to handle it.

Now that he'd seen Carolyn again, now that he'd touched her, held her in his arms, the pain was almost unbearable. The enormity of what he'd lost was staggering to him.

He'd been alone for a long time, so long that he'd forgotten what it was like to want a woman so much. He'd regretted leaving her, almost from the first, but he hadn't known how to fix it. Besides, by then he'd already enlisted in the army, and you just couldn't tell them you'd changed your mind and wanted to go home.

By the time he got out, having amazingly managed to earn a college degree while serving his time and working in army intelligence, one of his former superiors had gone to work for the FBI, and he'd recruited Drew to join him there. Once he found the special task force that worked on child kidnapping cases, he'd been sure that he'd found what he was meant to do with his life.

Looking back on it now, he experienced his first doubts about his choice.

Carolyn had seen right through him. He was still, in some irrational way, trying to make up for what had happened to Annie. Ten years later, he was still haunted by it.

And so was she.

That was the hardest part. Carolyn was in the same shape. He knew about her group—an incredibly loud, aggressive, well-funded barracuda of an organization that expected, either by force of public opinion or by sheer staying power and perseverance, to change the laws in this country to protect the children.

Idealistic? He was cynical enough to say that they were, but he was still glad. Somebody had to fight the idealistic fight. While laws simply weren't enough, they provided one hell of a start.

The group had money, computer links, and a lot less concern for jurisdiction than any law-enforcement group he knew. They cared about solving cases, not which agency actually cracked them.

No doubt if he hadn't been on the West Coast for the past four years, he'd have known much more about the group, and he'd most likely have run into Carolyn at some point while working on a case.

He wondered what it would have been like—to see her again under any circumstances but these. He wondered if—

"Drew?" Carolyn called from the living room.

Recognizing the urgency in her voice, he was there in an instant. He found her sitting on the sofa with the phone receiver still in her hand and her face as pale as the white of the walls.

"What is it?" He sat down beside her and turned sideways to face her.

"My aunt Ellen called. She heard about my mother, and she wanted to know if there was anything she could do. Then she asked what had upset her so much, and I told her about the clothes."

"Isn't she the one in Texas?"

"She used to live there. She's in St. Louis now, but she was the one we went to visit that year, when we bought Annie the red shorts set. Aunt Ellen remembered, because my parents bought Annie's at the same time she bought her daughter one. They matched, and they had trouble keeping them straight during the trip, so my mother and Aunt Ellen put the girls' initials on the tags of their shirts."

"Bingo," he said.

Pale, but composed, she nodded. "We can figure it out now. If those are Annie's clothes, they'll have her initials on the tag."

He thought about taking her into his arms then, but he wasn't sure he could stop with just that. And now wasn't the time. They had Annie to find. Carolyn's mother was in the hospital, and little Billy was scared.

Now definitely wasn't the time. Besides, they had a lot to settle between them first. He had to somehow explain to her why he'd left and how much he'd regretted it, then hope she could forgive him for it—before they could start again.

He desperately needed to believe that they could start again.

Drew decided to stay where he was.

"One thing at a time," he told her. "We'll get the clothes, look for the initials, and if they're Annie's, we'll find the man who took her."

He glanced at his watch, because he couldn't just sit there and stare at the heartbroken look on her face any longer. It was nearly eleven. He was exhausted, but he didn't want to leave.

"Are you and Billy going to be all right here?" he asked, looking for a reason to stay.

"Of course."

"Did this town ever get a decent motel? Or am I going to be staying at that dump on the south side of town?"

"There's a bed-and-breakfast downtown. It's the old Williams place, on Main."

He gave a look of disgust. "Frilly sheets, little scented things in the drawers to make my clothes smell like lilacs or something? Tea and those little cakes in the afternoon?"

"I wouldn't know. I've never stayed there. But you're welcome to stay here, if you want. I stay in my old bedroom upstairs, next to Billy's, and there's a guest room downstairs that's always made up."

He wondered if she realized he'd been fishing for an invitation, even though he couldn't be clear on the reason why. Part of him was a little concerned, even if it was totally irrational. The man who'd taken Annie was still out there somewhere. He had to know by now that they'd found Sara Parker, and surely he remembered what she'd been wearing when she escaped. Drew still had to work under the assumption that the guy had known Annie somehow when he snatched her.

It was crazy to think that the guy might come back here for some reason, but Drew was more than a little irrational about this case.

And he didn't want to leave Carolyn, not yet. He'd just found her again. They'd forged some fragile bond in the brief hours they'd been together today, and he didn't want to risk losing that.

She was overwhelmed today. Scared, tired, worn-out, and all those things must have made it easier for her to accept him, even to lean on him a little. He was willing to bet that would all have changed by tomorrow. A little rest, a chance to think things through, and he would guess she'd try as hard as she could to put a little distance between them.

He didn't want to give her the chance.

"You don't mind if I stay?" he asked, wondering if she saw right through him.

He thought she must. Either that, or she had some disturbing thoughts of her own, because she finally had a little color in her cheeks.

"Not at all. In fact, I was just thinking—if something happened to my mother in the middle of the night, and I needed to get to the hospital, I'd hate to have to get Billy out of bed and take him with me. He's upset enough as it is."

"Okay," he said, telling himself that this was what he wanted, after all. And he'd already resigned himself to spending the whole night through dreaming of her, no matter where he slept. "Let me just get my bag out of the car."

He turned and started searching his pockets for a cigarette—his fifth of the day. He had it lit and in his mouth by the time he closed the front door behind him. Force of habit had him checking the street up and down before he stepped off the porch.

Funny, he'd been a million miles away from this place for what seemed like forever, yet he could still come back and have his whole past seem so close he could reach out and touch it. He could close his eyes and look around and feel as if he'd never left.

He wondered what in the world would have happened if he'd never left.

Would he and Carolyn be married by now? Have children by now? Would they have found a way to forget about Annie and be happy?

He was angry at himself for even wondering. After all, it did no good. Regrets were the most useless things in the world. They changed nothing.

Drew grabbed his bag out of the trunk, and a fresh suit hanging from a hook in the back of the car. And all the while, regrets bombarded him with a relentlessness that set him on edge.

He didn't have any business spending the night in this house, with Carolyn upstairs. But he was going to do it anyway.

And maybe tomorrow they'd have some answers. Maybe she'd listen while he tried to explain, and maybe, just maybe, she'd understand something that he'd never truly understood himself.

How in the world he'd ever managed to leave her—and to stay away for so long.

Drew was pulling out his shaving kit and storing it in the bathroom when he heard Carolyn come back downstairs. Moving back to the guest room, he took off the jacket to his suit and hung it in the closet, then removed his tie and laid it across the bureau.

She shouldn't have come back downstairs.

He stood absolutely still and listened as she moved through the house, turning off lights and flicking the locks into place. Finally, she stood at the doorway to the bed-room.

This day, and all the ones that had come before it, had started to take their toll on him. Once he started on a case, once a child went missing and there seemed a valid reason to hope the child was still alive, he barely slept, seldom ate. He lived and breathed the case, his world narrowing down to nothing but the investigation and the reward at the end. He'd been on Sara's case for seventy-two hours before they found her, and he'd come straight here after that.

He was bone-deep tired, frustrated that they had so lit-tle information on Sara Parker's kidnapper, both hopeful and frightened that he was now working on Annie Mc-Kay's decade-old disappearance.

He should be asleep before he hit the bed, but he doubted he would be. One thing about being too tired—he couldn't summon up the self-discipline it took to keep his mind off Carolyn, especially when they were alone late at night in a room that happened to contain a bed.

Though he knew better, he once again let himself take a long, hard look at her. She had on sleek fitted trousers that showed off her longs legs and her trim hips. Her sweater was incredibly soft—he knew that from when he'd held her earlier—and it was a pale cream color that did wonders for her fair skin and her dark eyes. She wore her long hair pulled back from her face, and she had dainty little gold hoops in her ears. Overall, the picture was one of simple elegance, and right now she was making his blood boil.

"I just wanted to see if you needed anything before I went upstairs."

He smiled, despite the tightening in his chest that made it difficult to breathe. Ten years' worth of need, of lone-liness and memories and dreams, welled up inside him.

He needed *her*. Desperately.

Drew stood in front of Carolyn, his need warring with his sense of right and wrong. She was exhausted, too. Her mother was in the hospital, her little brother was upstairs asleep, and they were in her parents' house. It wasn't the time or the place for the kind of discussion they needed to have. Of course, his mind wasn't on talking right now, anyway, which was no surprise.

It had been years since he'd been this close to her, and right now it felt as if he might not get such an opportunity again. Few knew better than he and Carolyn that life had a way of throwing the unexplainable at you, the unmanageable, unchangeable. How everything could shift in an instant, and reality as you knew it could simply disappear.

He might not get another chance. At least he could touch her one more time.

Drew crossed the floor in a second and took her by the arms. "I need to kiss you, Carolyn. I need a whole hell of a lot more than that, but I think I could get by on a kiss. And once I do that, I think you'd better turn around, go upstairs and forget about coming back down tonight."

She gave a little sound of surprise. He watched as the pulse point in her neck began to speed up, and thought about covering it with his mouth. But he'd set his terms. One kiss. Surely he was strong enough to stop at that.

When she didn't protest, he settled her close against him, then closer still, until she was flush against him from head to toe. Her arms came around him, urging him nearer. Her eyes locked on his.

He thought about telling her how much he'd missed her, how empty the years had been, how empty his bed had been. But it didn't seem like the kind of talk a man had with a woman when he was allowing himself nothing more—at the moment—than a single kiss good-night.

And it was absolutely unbelievable how much he wanted this kiss.

He backed off a fraction of an inch, just for a second, when his self-control threatened to desert him altogether.

"I've dreamed of you," he told her, unable to help himself. "I've spent night after night alone in hotels, so exhausted I couldn't even tell you which state I was in, not really caring, knowing I needed to get up in a few hours, and still not able to forget your face or the way you felt in my arms."

He tucked her head against his heart and kissed her hair while he thought about saying more.

"I should have never left you. I'll regret it until the day I die. You've got to believe that, Carolyn."

When she didn't answer, his hand went to the side of her face to turn it up toward him, and he detected a telltale trail of moisture on her cheek.

He'd made her cry. Again.

This time, he kissed the tears away, one by one. "Till the day I die," he said, his lips against her soft, wet cheeks. "Do you believe me?"

"Yes."

He decided to go for broke. "Gonna give me a chance to make it up to you?"

"Yes, if you want it."

"Sweetheart, I definitely want it."

His body turning into a throbbing mass of need, his arms locked around her, his senses overwhelmed by the feel and smell and taste of her, he fought for control.

Suddenly, a real kiss seemed much too dangerous a thing to undertake.

He'd overstepped the emotional boundaries he'd set for them, and now that he'd done that, there was no telling what else might happen.

Suddenly, he felt as if he had about as much control as a teenager, felt as eager as one, too. God knew he hadn't wanted a woman like this since he'd been nineteen years old and aching for Carolyn.

"You need to go upstairs, Carolyn," he said, with the last shreds of his self-control. "Hurry."

And she did.

Chapter 8

She still hadn't gotten her kiss.

It was noon. Her mother had been awake, though groggy, when they went to see her this morning, and that had frightened Billy. Carolyn had calmed him down as best she could, then talked him into going to school for the afternoon—with the lure of the annual class Halloween party that afternoon as the major inducement—because she didn't want him to be frightened any more than he already was by the sight of her mother in this hospital.

She'd spoken with her mother's doctor, who remained optimistic that Grace McKay's condition had to do with stress, rather than a physical problem with her heart. She'd welcomed her aunt Ellen, who'd arrived unexpectedly around midday, because she was worried about both Grace and Carolyn herself. She'd run into some old friends from high school and friends of her mother's—putting them off as best she could when they asked why she was in town, why Drew Delaney was in town, and exactly what his car had been doing outside her mother's house all night long.

She'd barely seen Drew. He was already showered and dressed when she'd awoken. And he'd been on the phone all morning, no doubt arranging for someone to bring those clothes here for her to identify. Carolyn put Drew in touch with Hope House's computer expert, and the two of them had started a search through the data banks for any other cases that might be linked to Annie's. She'd left Drew at the house, without a word passing between them about what had happened last night before they went to their separate beds.

With her life in such total chaos, Carolyn couldn't understand where she found the time to think of anything as trivial as a kiss she'd never received. But she did. She sat in the waiting area across from her mother's hospital room, trying to keep her head down or her face turned away so that she wouldn't be recognized by anyone she knew and be asked the inevitable questions that would follow. And she thought of Drew and the kiss he'd promised her.

She thought about the child they'd shared in the smallest of ways—and in none of the ways that really mattered. Should she tell him? Would it only hurt him more to know? Would he, in turn, whether from anger or haste or an honest desire to be a father to his son, end up hurting Billy in some way? It would have to hurt Billy to discover he'd been lied to all these years, that the parents he'd known and loved from the time he was a baby hadn't been his real parents.

And, selfishly, Carolyn wondered if Billy would come to hate her.

Carolyn couldn't even plead ignorance. She'd made a conscious decision to give up her son. But Drew never had.

"Carolyn?"

Startled, she looked up to see that her aunt had returned.

"I'm sorry, dear. I didn't mean to frighten you."

Carolyn shook her head. "I was just thinking."

"I got us some decent coffee from that little café around the corner, and some sandwiches." She handed Carolyn a cup, then set her own down on the table and opened up a brown bag she'd tucked into her purse. "Any word?"

"No, not yet," Carolyn said, sipping the coffee. She took the sandwich her aunt offered, placed it on her lap. She couldn't even think about food right now. "They're still running tests."

"I'm sure she's going to be fine, dear. Your mother's a very strong woman. Think of how much she's endured in her lifetime."

"I know, Aunt Ellen. It's just that it hasn't been that long since Daddy died, and to have this thing with Annie coming so close on top of it… I have to wonder how much she can take. And I hate to see what this is doing to Billy. He's—"

She broke off when Drew came strolling into the waiting area. His gaze locked on to hers, and for a moment her thoughts ran back in time, to the night before, when she'd felt how much he wanted her, felt the emotions warring inside him. She'd thought that he might actually tell her he loved her still, she'd imagined what it would be like to hear that again, maybe even to let herself believe it.

It would be something to hold on to in the days ahead, when everything was sure to turn crazy. She'd held on to Drew's love before, and it had gotten her through a lot.

"Hello," she heard Drew say, as he held out his hand to the woman beside her.

"I'm Carolyn's aunt, Ellen Monroe."

The two were shaking hands before Carolyn even realized how rude she was being. "I'm sorry," she said. "I…I guess I'm a little distracted today. Aunt Ellen, this is Drew Delaney."

"I'm the one who's sorry," her aunt said. "I know I should have remembered your name, because your face looks so familiar, but I just can't place it."

Drew didn't say anything, though his curiosity was clearly aroused.

It was all Carolyn could do to stand there and remain silent while she watched and waited for ten years' worth of lies to dissolve in front of her eyes.

"I don't believe we've met," Drew said. "Unless you used to live here?"

"No, I never did. My sister moved here when her late husband got a job here, just before Carolyn was born," Ellen said, clearly as puzzled as Drew. "You used to live here?"

"Ten years ago," he said.

Carolyn fought to keep the terror she was feeling from showing on her face.

She should have told him last night, when she had the chance. Either then, or ten years ago, when she gave birth to his child.

"Oh." The little sound her aunt made spoke volumes to Carolyn, who shot her a pleading look.

"Drew's with the FBI," she managed to say in a somewhat steady voice. "He's the one who picked up on the link between the other little girl's kidnapping and Annie's. He recognized the clothes."

"Oh," her aunt said again.

"Are they here yet?" Carolyn, desperate to change the subject, said to Drew.

"What?" he asked, obviously aware that there were things going on in this room that he didn't understand.

"The clothes? Did they come yet?"

"Yes." He gave her the strangest look, then held up his briefcase. "That's why I'm here."

That was all the excuse Carolyn needed. She no longer had to hide the fear that threatened to overwhelm her. "I want to get this over with as soon as possible."

"Are you sure?" He put his hand on her arm, perhaps because he realized she could fall over at any moment. Her legs felt like rubber and she had to get him away from her aunt before Ellen said any more.

"I'm sure. Is there somewhere we can go, besides here?"

"Of course," he offered.

"Aunt Ellen, you'll stay here, in case there's any news about Mom?"

"Yes, dear," she said, but her eyes told Carolyn something quite different.

He's the one, isn't he?

Carolyn nodded. Then she turned and headed for the door, pausing only when Drew didn't immediately follow her. He stood in the middle of the room, looking from Carolyn to her aunt, then back again. Finally, he turned to Ellen and once again held out his hand. "It's been a pleasure meeting you," he said.

When she didn't add anything else, he walked across the room to Carolyn and put his hand at the small of her back, and they started walking down the hallway.

Carolyn was still worried that they were going to run into someone else who'd recognize him, someone who knew Billy and would put two and two together.

"I took a room at that bed-and-breakfast you mentioned," Drew said. "It's only three blocks from here. We could talk there, if you like?"

"You can stay at the house again, tonight. We have the room," Carolyn said.

"I'm not sure that's a good idea."

Carolyn thought of the sexual tension that had flared between them last evening. Maybe it wasn't such a good idea for Drew to be sleeping so close by. "All right. We can go to your room at the inn."

"How's your mother?"

"They're still doing tests."

The elevator doors closed, giving them a moment of privacy. Drew stepped closer, pulling her against his side, reassuring her with his touch. "Did your mother remember talking to me yesterday?"

"I think so. She wouldn't talk about it. Or... actually, she wouldn't let me talk about Annie. But I think she remembers."

"Want to tell me what was going on back there with your aunt?"

Carolyn shivered, but not from the cold. "I will," she said, committing herself to getting the truth out. "Just... not now. Not here. All right?"

The elevator doors opened, revealing a crowd that parted to let them make their way out. Thankfully, amazingly, she didn't recognize anyone.

"This way," Drew said, leading her out the side entrance and into the sunshine.

They walked briskly through the clear but cool day, toward two of the grimmest tasks Carolyn had ever faced. Wordlessly they made their way inside the stately old house of white stone, up the winding staircase and into Drew's quarters.

She was studying the contents of the room—a huge antique four-poster bed, a comfortable-looking sofa done in a bright floral print, fresh flowers on the bureau, bright sunshine streaming in through the long, flowing lace curtains—when she heard the lock click shut and turned to face Drew.

"I didn't think you'd want to be disturbed," he said as he stood by the door.

She shook her head. "I just... I need to get this over with."

"Sit down," he said, motioning toward the couch.

She sat with her hands clenched in her lap and her eyes closed. "First," she said, "would you kiss me? Just once?"

"Carolyn, you don't—"

"Please. Just once."

It was a ridiculous request, considering why they'd come here and what she had to do. And she was definitely stalling, even though she claimed to want this over with as quickly as possible. But she needed him right now. She needed to be in his arms, to feel close to him, one more time, before it all dissolved away.

"Just once," she repeated, afraid to even open her eyes.

Carolyn felt the couch give with his weight beside her, felt him haul her into his arms and, when that wasn't enough—when they still weren't close enough—lift her up and sit her on his lap. Drew leaned back into the corner of the sofa, his arms pulling her head down to the hollow between his neck and his shoulders. He squeezed her tight, his heat soaking into the chill that seemed to go all the way down to her bones. His breath was warm against her cheek, and his hands tenderly stroked through her long hair.

She waited for the touch of his lips against hers, but it didn't come. Instead, they settled high on her cheek, next to her ear.

"Sweetheart," he whispered against her skin, "you don't have to look at anything. Do you understand that? I already looked myself."

"You did?"

He nodded. "I would have told you at the hospital, but I didn't want to do it with a bunch of people around."

"And they're Annie's clothes, aren't they?"

"Yes."

Carolyn hadn't even realized her tears were falling again. She hadn't been sure she had any left to cry, but they just poured out of her now, and Drew wiped them away.

"I found the initials," he said. "They're faded, but they're there."

He held her tighter then. For a moment, she would have sworn he was the only thing holding her together.

He'd found Annie's clothes. He'd found a link between her and another little girl, who'd gotten away.

Why couldn't Annie have gotten away?

"I still miss her," Carolyn said. "When I come home, I still go and sit in her room at night and imagine that she's going to come running through that door, still thirteen years old."

Drew just held on to her. It was the most amazing feeling in the world. She felt safe and secure and—did she dare think it?—loved. And even that, even after all this time, seemed traitorous to her lost little sister.

"She was my best friend," Carolyn said. "And she never should have disappeared. It shouldn't have happened to her. It should have been me."

"No," Drew said. "I'm not going to let you do this to yourself."

"I sent her there," Carolyn said. "I was supposed to be the one to go back to the house, because my mother asked me to go, but I sent Annie instead. Don't you see? It should have been me. I should have—"

And then she couldn't talk through her tears any longer. She couldn't remember the last time the guilt had come on strong enough that it seemed capable of driving a hole through her heart this way.

She didn't remember the last time anyone had been willing to listen to her talk this way about the little sister she'd lost. She couldn't remember when she'd last felt comfortable enough with someone to show what Annie's disappearance had done to her, what it still did to her today.

Drew understood. He'd been there. He'd lived through it with her, and it was different, sharing these old feelings with him, from the way it had been to tell them to someone who hadn't ever known Annie or loved her.

She cried until she felt drained of all emotion and all energy. Cried until that blessed feeling of being washed clean inside came over her.

And he held her through it all. He didn't try to stop her or rush her. He simply accepted what she was feeling, and let her get it out.

"I'm here," he said, when the sobbing subsided.

He kissed her hair, kissed her wet cheeks, and Carolyn found herself wanting more than anything to press her lips against his and lose herself in the magic of his touch.

It was still magical. It was still there between them, this connection, this attraction. It was still there—and likely still as doomed as ever.

She watched as the world seemed to slow down around them, as she could see only him, feel only the warmth of his touch and, for an instant, think only of him.

There hadn't been anyone else, not in all these years, who managed to touch her heart the way he had. From time to time she'd tried, in desperation, to feel just a little of what she'd felt for him with someone else, but it had never happened. She wondered now if it ever would, wondered why it should be this way. Why she was destined to feel like this only with Drew, when she didn't see how they could ever make things work between them.

Still, in this moment when there was nothing in the world but the two of them, she wanted him. She wanted him so much, and she was tempted to take what he was offering her, with no word to him about what she'd done, and no thought to the future.

After all, she hadn't seen him in ten agonizingly long years. Surely it wouldn't be so bad to take one night, out of ten years of lonely nights, to be with him.

He would likely hate her before morning, anyway, because she had to tell him. She'd been living on borrowed time ever since he'd come back. She didn't think she would get another chance to tell him herself before someone else put the pieces together and let the truth slip out. And she knew that the news had to come from her. In the back of her mind, she thought that might count for something—that she'd chosen to tell him rather than let him find out from someone else.

Carolyn watched, fascinated, as his face came down to hers. His lips closed over hers, and she felt as if she'd opened up her soul to him. As if she could simply let go of the years of loneliness and longing now, because he was finally her with her.

"I don't know how I ever stayed away," he took the time to say, before kissing her again.

"I wish you hadn't," she said, perilously close to tears again.

She wanted to hang on to him, wanted to hold back the hands of time and give the two of them just a few moments together.

She hadn't realized how much she missed him, how much she needed him, how terribly lonely she'd been without him.

The kiss was devastating, turning her bones to mush, her resolve to sheer indecision. Her body, which might as well have been in some sort of deep freeze for the past ten years, had come roaring back to life, the feeling overloading her ability to think and reason.

She was vaguely aware that his hands had come up to her face again, that his lips had left hers again, and then she felt the tears. He'd found them before she realized they were there, and now he followed the tracks of her tears with the side of his thumb.

"It won't always be like this," he said, and she thought he meant it as a promise to her, but, of course, he didn't know everything yet. Otherwise, he wouldn't make promises like that.

Carolyn closed her eyes and kissed him again, urgently this time, wishing she could sink back into the wonderful oblivion of his touch and forget everything else.

He kissed her back, just once, so hard and fast that the blood went pounding through her heart. And then he pulled back and it was all over.

"I'm sorry," she said, unable to figure out exactly what she was sorriest about. The list seemed endless.

"Why?"

"Because...because I'm so afraid that I'll never get to be with you again like this, that I'll never feel like this again. And I don't see how I can get through the rest of my life without any of that."

"Why won't you ever be with me again like this?"

Hastily she dried the rest of her tears and put a little distance between them. Time for the hard part. Time for her confession. God help her, it was time to own up to the mistakes she'd made all those years ago.

"Oh, Drew..." She barely managed to get the words out. "I'm so afraid."

"Why? Because of Annie? Because of something that happened ten years ago, when we were just kids? You're going to let that ruin everything between us, all over again?"

"Not just that."

"Then what?"

She felt sick to her stomach then. There it was, the perfect opening. And she didn't see how she could take it. Her courage had totally deserted her.

"Ok, let's go down the list," he said. "Annie's disappearance. Why does that still have to be between us? How can you let it? Because it won't bring her back. And you can't believe that she'd want her disappearance to keep us apart."

"It should have been me," she said, knowing she'd said it before, knowing how truly irrational her feelings about this were. "My mother sent *me* back to the house, and I'm the one who sent Annie instead."

"So do you blame your mother, too? Or the town, for having a picnic that day? Or whoever turned that day in August into a town holiday and scheduled a picnic celebration?" Drew asked. "You don't blame them, do you?"

"No."

"Do you blame me? I'm the one who wanted to be with you. I'm the one your parents didn't want you to see."

"No, I never blamed you."

"Carolyn, you couldn't stand to have me touch you after she left. You didn't even want to be in the same room with me. Did you think I couldn't see that? Or that I didn't understand why?"

Drew knew he had to be careful. He had to watch that the memories that had been dragged up, and the emotions that went along with them, didn't choke him.

They hadn't done anything so terribly wrong, anything that hundreds of thousands of kids didn't do every day. There'd been this town picnic. He'd missed Carolyn. Her parents hadn't wanted her to see him, because they didn't approve of him. He'd been a little too rough, and his family had been too poor and his father too big a drinker, for him to be associating with their daughter. But that hadn't stopped them from sneaking off to see each other. After all, they'd been in love.

He'd seen her at the picnic, but stayed out of sight because he didn't want her parents to see him. When she left to walk the three blocks from the park to her house to get the fresh-baked bread her mother had left at home, Drew had followed. He'd caught up with her as she left the park, and suggested that they find someplace where they could be alone for a while.

Carolyn had agreed. And Annie had shown up just then. She'd been a beautiful child, just starting to grow a little taller, still tomboyishly thin, her long, pale blond hair shining in the sunlight. She'd liked Drew, even though she knew her parents didn't. She'd promised not to tell her parents that she'd seen Carolyn and Drew together. And Annie had been the one who ended up going back to the house to get the bread for her mother.

Carolyn had asked Annie to do that, after Drew pressured her into sneaking away from the picnic with him.

They'd been necking behind a huge old tree at the edge of the park while that man snatched Annie.

Drew would never forget the way her mother had questioned Carolyn, the way Carolyn had broken down and sobbed when it became clear that her sister was nowhere to be found.

Day after agonizing day had gone by, with no word, no clue. The days had turned into weeks, the hopes fading away with each day that passed. Carolyn hadn't been able to look at him. She hadn't let him touch her for the longest time. She'd simply withdrawn from him and from everything else.

He knew now that some people dealt with grief that way; that otherwise stable marriages dissolved under the stress of the disappearance of a child. They'd just been two teenagers in love. Carolyn had been seventeen, Drew nearly nineteen. It was no wonder that Annie's disappearance had torn them apart.

Of course, he could have stayed. He could have waited it out. Eventually they might have overcome the grief and guilt. But he hadn't stuck around to see that happen. He'd gotten angry and impatient and scared, because he hadn't been able to find a way to make things better for Carolyn, no matter how hard he tried.

And if he'd failed her then, when she needed him more than she ever had, he was sure to fail her again. At least that was what he'd thought back then.

He'd gotten angry one night. Drew had always hated Hope, Illinois, and without Carolyn, there had been nothing there for him. He'd enlisted in the army a few months after Annie disappeared.

He'd come to Carolyn's house one night and boldly knocked on the front door, enraging her mother in the process, and calmly told Carolyn that he was leaving. He could have asked her to write, to call, to wait for him. But he hadn't.

He'd been tired of shouldering the blame for something that wasn't his fault, tired of trying to make it better for Carolyn and failing miserably.

He'd just walked away and left her.

She'd cried. She'd asked him not to leave her. She'd said she needed him, but he'd thought that more than anything she needed to forget about him and all the guilt she'd come to associate with their relationship. But he hadn't told her that. He'd said that he couldn't help her any more than he already had and he couldn't take the guilt any longer.

He'd never come back. He'd been tempted, but he'd stayed away—another mistake to add to his list. He recognized them so clearly now. He should never have left. And even then, even if he'd had to go, he should never have stayed away from her, because he had this sneaking suspicion that he was still in love with her.

It sounded crazy, after all these years, when he'd spent not even twenty-four hours with her in the past ten years, but that was how he felt.

Still, there was so much between them. Annie's disappearance still being the biggest obstacle, his own desertion weighing in as a strong second.

Yet he couldn't deny how strong his feelings were for her. He was shaking, caught up in the past, still angry about it, still resentful about what had happened. But he hoped that they could overcome all that now, because he desperately wanted another chance with her. The knowledge simply burst forth from somewhere deep inside him, leaving him a little dazed but feeling more alive than he had in years.

He'd spent too much time needing Carolyn and denying that need or trying to simply kill it off, too much time telling himself that it was too late for them and that he couldn't change what he'd done any more than he could bring Annie McKay back.

And then, amazing as it was, Annie had been the one to bring him back.

Drew wasn't a religious man, but he had the oddest feeling that he needed to thank her for that, that she was somehow watching over them all and had brought him home again. Crazy as it sounded, he offered her his silent thanks for drawing him back to this little town.

"Carolyn?" She was still in his arms, and he wanted never to let go of her. He kissed her hair, dried her tears, and wondered what he could do to make her smile for him now.

"I didn't blame you," she said shakily. "I blamed myself. Not you."

"Sweetheart, you didn't want to be with me after Annie disappeared. You didn't want me touching you, couldn't stand me kissing you."

"Because I felt too guilty. Before, I wanted you so much that nothing else mattered. I would have done anything to be with you that day, and if I hadn't felt that way, if I'd been thinking about anything or anyone more than I'd been thinking about being with you, this might never have happened. Annie might still be here."

"No," he told her. "If there hadn't been some sick man out there who liked little girls, Annie would still be here. If he hadn't decided to come to Hope on that day ten years ago, Annie would still be here. If Annie hadn't caught his eye somehow, she would still be here. Or if someone like me had been doing their job a little better, and caught the son of a bitch long before he ever turned to Annie, she'd still be here. That's why stuff like this happens. Not because two teenagers wanted to spend ten minutes alone together.

"You know it's true," he told her. "You work with missing kids. You know there are always a million little things that any number of people could have done differently to change everything—to make the difference in any one child's life. It only takes a split second for everything to change. And once it does, nothing can turn things back to the way they used to be."

"I do know that," she finally admitted. "In my head, yes, I know it. But my heart—I can't convince myself of that in my heart. She was my sister. She looked up to me. She thought I was perfect, and that I had all the answers, but I didn't."

He looked down into her tearstained face, the despair there enough to break his heart all over again, if it hadn't been broken so irrevocably the day he'd left her ten years ago. "None of us is perfect, Carolyn. Thankfully, none of us is held to that high a standard."

"I know it's irrational, Drew. Believe me, I know that. But it doesn't change how I feel."

"Look at me, Carolyn." He pulled back just enough that she could look him in the eye. "It's not your fault. And you know that. It was that man who took her—it was his fault, and I'm going to find him. I'm going to find out what he did to Annie, and then I'm going to be damned lucky if I don't kill the guy myself."

She paled at that, and he took a moment to try to calm down. "I've spent ten years of my life trying to make up for this," he said, when he could speak more calmly. "I feel sick inside every time I hear about another child who's missing. I feel it in my gut, every minute we're looking, every minute some creep gets a little farther away from us with some little kid. I do that day in and day out, week after week, year after year, because I'm still trying to make up for what happened to Annie.''

He didn't like admitting that to her. He didn't like admitting it to himself. It was as irrational as the way she blamed herself, but it was all he knew. Punishment or penance, he couldn't be sure which. He only knew that the job satisfied some deep-seated need in him, in a way nothing else did. In much the same way being with her, holding her in his arms again, satisfied him on the most basic level.

He wouldn't think about all that he'd lost when he gave her up so long ago. He wouldn't rage at the injustice that both of them were still trying to somehow make up for.

He'd thought her guilt was tied up with him and with their relationship, that she was punishing herself and him by denying them any chance at happiness. That the guilt had twisted things so badly in her mind that she didn't think they deserved to be happy because Annie was gone.

And he'd thought that by leaving her, he could somehow take away the guilt, as well.

But now he knew. He'd left for nothing. He hadn't spared her anything at all. If anything, he'd probably made things worse by walking out on her.

How would he ever explain that to her? How would he make her understand something he couldn't understand himself? He didn't know, but he'd find a way. He'd make a second chance for them.

"Carolyn," he began, "I told you last night that I never should have left you, that I'll regret it till the day I die. Do you believe that?"

"Yes," she said, hesitant now.

"Do you think you can ever forgive me for that?"

"Oh, Drew..." She looked scared now, and he wondered if he was pushing too hard, too fast.

"I want us to have another chance. Last night, you said you could give that to me."

"I—"

"Speechless? I love leaving my women speechless."

She almost smiled then, and he knew how much she needed to. But it did bring up a terrible thought. There weren't any other women in his life. There hadn't been for a long time. He was too busy, and honestly not that interested. But he'd never even asked if there was a man in her life. Just because she still used her maiden name and there was no ring on her finger, that didn't mean she was free.

"There isn't anyone else, is there?" he asked, when she still looked worried.

"No, it's not that."

"Then what? I know my timing's lousy, but I can't help it. I can't wait, when I don't know how long it's going to take before things get back to normal."

She hesitated, composed now, but still obviously frightened. Of him? Surely not. Of being involved with anyone? He could understand her being apprehensive, but that wasn't what he was seeing here. It was out-and-out fear. God knew he'd seen that emotion often enough to recognize it.

Why would she be so frightened?

He wanted to make her smile again, wanted to wrap his arms around her and keep her safe from anything and everything in this world that had the power to hurt her. He wanted her in his bed and in his life, forever. He would not leave Hope again without her.

Drew waited a minute as the realizations clicked into place inside him. It felt...right. It felt as if everything were right with his world—a crazy sentiment, in the midst of all this insanity. But that was how it felt. He was with Carolyn again, and he wasn't ever going to let her go.

This was what he'd been waiting for, what he'd been missing his whole life. This would make him complete and whole and happy. Carolyn. Somehow, it had always been Carolyn. He was so relieved to finally admit it to himself.

Now to convince her of that. He chose his words carefully, not wanting to frighten her, and careful not to belittle the things standing in their way. He knew there were many obstacles, but they could overcome all of them. Nothing would stop him from making it happen.

"It won't always be like this," he told her. "I'm going to find out what happened to Annie, and we're going to let go of all the guilt and the anger. It's time, Carolyn. We don't need to be beating ourselves up over this anymore. And we can't let it keep us apart any longer."

"It's not that simple," she said.

"It is. It's in the past, and no matter what we do, we can't change it. And you can't tell me that you're willing to give up on us again because of what happened to Annie."

Carolyn sighed wearily. The past, she thought. Unchangeable as something set in stone, and all-powerful. He understood that, and he was asking her not to let it stand in their way. But how would he feel when he was the one who had to do the forgetting and the forgiving? When he had to understand that some decisions, once made, could not be undone? Would he be able to put the past behind them?

She was almost certain the man was about to tell her he was still in love with her, and she couldn't let him. As much as she longed to hear the words from him again, she couldn't let him say them now. Not when he still didn't know.

She knew. She felt the love in him, knew she was this close to getting him back, only to lose him all over again. But she couldn't think of that now. Not now. There was no time, and it would only make this more difficult.

"Drew, it's not just Annie," she said, turning her back to him and searching for strength. "God knows I still feel guilty about what happened to her, but she's not the only thing standing between us right now."

Chapter 9

Drew had a sixth sense about bad news. He would have called it a premonition, if he believed in such things. But then, the label wasn't that important; it was the feeling that mattered. He knew now that something very bad was about to happen.

He took hold of Carolyn's shoulder, turned her around to face him again, and he saw it right away.

Guilt. He could read it as clearly on some people's faces as he could a sign on the side of the road. The woman looked guilty as hell, and that simply didn't make any sense. What could she possibly have to feel guilty about?

"There's no other man?" he asked, wanting to get that out of the way right now.

"Not the kind you think."

"You're not involved with anyone? In love with anyone? Sleeping with anyone?" Irrationally, he felt murderous at the possibility, though he had no right to do so.

"No."

"Then what?" he said, waiting to be blindsided.

"There are things I haven't told you, things I should have told you years ago."

"Okay," he replied, wondering how people felt when they turned around on the street and found a car barreling toward them. In that instant before they were sent flying through the air, did they have the time to think the situation through? How it would feel? How badly it would hurt? What they could do to stop it?

"Carolyn, you're frightening me." And he wasn't a man who was easily scared.

She looked like a woman whose heart had been recently broken. Clearly, the wound was still fresh. He watched while she gathered herself together.

"I need to tell you about what happened after you left," she said finally.

He braced himself even more, if that was possible. He deserved this, he reminded himself. He'd left her, and he deserved to hear about the pain that desertion had caused her. But that wasn't all there was to this. He was certain of it.

"Tell me," he insisted. He could take it.

"I . . . I thought I was going to die. I think I could have died, happily, for a long time afterward. This town, the house, the pictures on the walls of Annie, and the pictures in my mind of you and I—" She just shook her head. "The memories were everywhere. Sometimes at night, I'd swear that once I stopped crying, I could hear my mother crying in Annie's room and my father sobbing in their bedroom. Our house was the most awful place in the world.

"I want you to understand how they were—my parents, I mean. They were devastated. Annie was such a joy to them. She was like sunshine, she just lit up the room. And the way she laughed . . . I'll never forget her laughter.

"Anyway, when she was gone, once we all accepted the fact that she wasn't coming back, it was like no one would ever smile again. No one would laugh. I didn't see how we were going to go on, because there just wasn't any reason to."

Drew suddenly felt sick to his stomach. "Are you trying to tell me that you tried to kill yourself?"

"No," she said tentatively, "although there were times when I wished God would just take me, when I tried to tell him to bring back Annie and take me instead."

"Carolyn . . ." he began, but she stopped him by laying a hand on his arm.

"That's not what this is about," she said. "I want—no, I need—for you to understand what it was like here. I don't know how we all survived it, how we got through the days. They all just blurred together after a while, and nothing mattered. Not anything.

"And then Billy came along." She shook her head in wonder, obviously going back in time to those days. "It was like a miracle. We weren't sure of that at first, and we were all so scared of caring about someone else. We knew there just weren't any guarantees in life. One day, you have someone. The next, you don't. It's so different once you understand that. It's so much harder to love someone, knowing how easily and how quickly you could lose them.

"Anyway, we were scared about Billy, but he turned out to be the best thing that could have happened to us. He gave us all a reason to keep going, and eventually he taught us how to laugh again and to smile and to look forward to each day.

"You have to understand that, Drew. Without him, I don't think we would have survived. My parents . . . Billy meant the world to them. And when you left, I thought that you just didn't love me anymore. That you never had. That whatever was between us just hadn't meant that much to you."

"That's not true," he said.

"I know. Now, I see that so clearly. I think I have for years. But then, I didn't. I was just so hurt and so scared and so alone . . .

"Oh." She paused, clearly lost. "Where was I?"

Drew shook his head.

"I'm not making much sense, am I?"

"No."

She nodded. She'd already known that.

"Carolyn, whatever it is, you can tell me."

"I just thought, if you understood the way it was back then, that you might be able to see the rest of it the way I did. I regret losing you, but I can't regret what I did. I've watched, over the years, and I know how much they needed Billy, and he's been happy with them, Drew. I know it looks bad now, but it's only been this way since my father died. Other than these past six months, Billy's been happy and safe and loved.

"I couldn't have asked for more than that for him, and you have to understand. At least, I thought you'd understand a little . . . I thought that would mean something to you.

"I did the best thing that I knew to do. And you can't ask me to be sorry for that or for him, but I'm so sorry for you . . . for what I did to you."

"Carolyn, you're not making any sense."

"Billy," she said. "It's about Billy. He's ours. At least, he was ours."

"Our child?" he said incredulously.

She nodded.

"You're telling me that we have a child?"

"We did. He's theirs now. My parents."

Drew wasn't sure exactly what he said then, or what he did. But he could hear her voice. It seemed to be coming to him from so far away.

"I'm sorry," she said. "Drew, I'm so sorry."

* * *

Drew didn't exactly know how he felt. He was surprised, and people so seldom surprised him. He usually knew what they were going to do or what they were going to say. It came from years on the job, years of watching people and understanding what made them tick.

But this? This had come out of nowhere.

Because it was so ingrained in him to analyze each and every piece of information he received, to try to figure out in hindsight what he'd missed along the way in any investigation, and where he'd gone wrong, he ran through the clues he'd missed from the beginning. Besides, that kept him from thinking about the real issue here. He forced it out of his head for another moment.

When he came here, to Grace McKay's home, she'd said some strange things to him, something about knowing why he was here. Yes, he could see it now. She'd acted as if she already knew why he'd come back. But she couldn't have known he'd come about Annie. So she must have thought he'd come because he'd found out about Billy.

And the doctor, the man who'd been the family doctor for years, had acted strangely, too. He'd have to have known all along that Grace McKay hadn't given birth to her child. And Drew would have bet the man had put everything together when he returned.

Carolyn, too, had seemed so frightened at first, almost afraid of him, even, before he told her about Annie. He remembered now, and saw it for what it was; she'd actually been shocked when she found out he wasn't here about Billy.

He should have seen her reaction for what it was. Carolyn wouldn't be afraid of him. Angry at him, maybe, unsettled by his unexpected return, apprehensive, perhaps, but not afraid. He'd never given her reason to be afraid of him. He wouldn't do that now, though the temptation to give in to the rage that he felt was overwhelming.

She was still here...still in the same room with him. She was sitting on the corner of the couch, her tears dry now, as she waited for him to say something.

God, what could he say?

He stood at the window and looked out at the main road of this town he had come to hate more than any other—and had missed more than it seemed possible.

He'd missed Carolyn, too, but he'd never even had a chance to miss their son, because he hadn't known about him. His son.

Drew slammed his fist against the windowsill. He heard Carolyn gasp as the window rattled, though it didn't break. He felt a little better for having tried to drive his hand into the wooden casing around the window, and considered doing it again. It might feel even better the second time. And it might help dissipate some of the all-consuming rage he felt at this moment.

Curiously, Drew realized, he wasn't that angry at Carolyn. It was life that had him so enraged. It was the circumstances that had led her to make the decision she'd made.

If he believed there truly was a God, he'd be cursing him right now. How could he play with people's lives this way? How could he let evil, such as the man who'd taken Annie, exist in this world to hurt little children and mess up so many lives in the aftermath?

It made no sense. There was simply no logic to it. And Drew still wanted the world to make some sense at times, feeling he was owed that, at least.

Otherwise, he had to accept the fact that random acts of violence were simply that—random, careless acts. That at any moment he could get his brains blown out, or could crash his car into a concrete wall or drive it over the side of a mountain, and that there was nothing he could do about it. That he had no control over this world in which he was living, even over his own life. And he just couldn't accept that.

Show me the purpose in this, he railed to the sky outside his window. *Make sense of this for me.*

He dared anyone to do so.

Once more, because he had all this energy that he had to expend, he slammed his hand against the windowsill.

He turned toward the door without looking at Carolyn. "I have to go," he said, latching on to the job that had been his life for years now. It was certainly easier to deal with than reality at this moment.

"Drew?"

"There's a psychiatrist coming in from Chicago to be with Sara Parker while we question her tonight. It's to be at one of the field offices in Indiana, and I'm going to be there. I've got to ask Sara about the clothes, and about Annie."

He gathered up his briefcase, his jacket, the keys to his rental car and to the room, and headed for the door. Carolyn hadn't moved, and he . . . he just didn't care at the moment. He didn't have anything he could say to her right now about the things that were uppermost in his mind, and she'd just have to understand that. He had enough to do, trying to understand himself.

But first, he had a job to do.

"I'm going to find out what happened to Annie," he told her. "The rest of this will have to wait until then."

"Drew." She came to stand in front of him. He thought for a moment that she might ask him not to go. That she might even beg him. She'd done that once before, and he hadn't listened.

"I have to go," he told her, and walked out the door.

* * *

Carolyn wasn't sure how long she sat in Drew's room. She didn't want to lift her hand to look at her wristwatch, because she was afraid if she moved, she'd fall apart.

Drew had simply left the room. He hadn't said that he hated her, that he'd never forgive her, that he wished he'd known . . . anything like that.

And he hadn't given her any indication of what he was going to do, now that he knew about Billy.

Carolyn didn't want to think of the possibilities. She didn't want to acknowledge the fact that there was a real chance Billy would be hurt.

She and Drew had never talked about having children. They hadn't gotten to the point in their relationship where they daydreamed about being married and raising a family of their own. She didn't even know if he had any desire to be married, let alone have children.

Yet they'd had a child.

Once upon a time.

But they didn't anymore.

She had to make him understand that they didn't have any rights to Billy. They couldn't take him away from the person who'd been caring for him and demand to have him back.

Children belonged to the people who loved them and cared for them, not the ones who happened to have given birth to them.

Yet it was true that she'd never given Drew a choice or a say in the matter.

Drew had rights; if he insisted, he could exercise them in the courts. She would have to convince him not to.

While she was at it, maybe she could convince him not to hate her, as well.

Carolyn finally risked moving enough to check her watch. It was ten to three. Time to go get Billy from school. If she left now, she could catch him before he got on the bus, then take him to the hospital to see *his mother*. And then she needed to explain to her mother what she'd done.

Billy told Carolyn that he'd had a good afternoon at school. He'd enjoyed the Halloween party and gotten lots of candy. Carolyn was glad she'd insisted that he go, because he'd needed to get away from the hospital for a while.

She'd checked on her mother's condition by phone before she left, and been told she was awake and alert, so she and Billy went straight to the hospital. He was eager to see his mother, and Carolyn was afraid that if she didn't force herself to tell her mother what she'd done this afternoon, she might lose her nerve.

It wasn't going to be pretty. And she'd have to clear the situation with Grace's doctor first. But her mother had to be told.

Because Carolyn had no idea what Drew was going to do next, and they had to be prepared.

It occurred to her now, after she'd panicked and told him, that he had far more legal rights to Billy than she did. Hope House did a lot of work on children's rights, on the laws affecting children and on court precedences. Lately, courts had again and again reaffirmed the rights of biological fathers in cases of adoption.

Carolyn had relinquished all rights to her son at his birth. She'd simply signed them away. Drew had not. He'd never been told the child existed, and that gave him incredible power in the courts—if he decided to press the issue that way.

She looked over at Billy, who was happily digging into his bag of Halloween treats, and saw again how very much he looked like his father.

She didn't think Drew would hurt him like that, not once he'd had a chance to calm down and to think things through. But right now, when he was so angry, she wasn't sure.

"Billy," she said to the boy, trying to keep that quavering tone out of her voice, "I love you very much."

He barely glanced up from the candy bag. "Love you, too, Carolyn."

They arrived at the hospital shortly, then took the elevator up to Grace McKay's room. Billy paused in the doorway and called softly, "Mom?"

Grace was lying on the bed, dozing, but she woke up right away and turned to him with a smile. "Billy!" She threw her arms open wide, and Billy ran to her.

He loved her so much. Carolyn reassured herself of that right then. Billy had a good life with the parents she'd given him. Drew would have to understand that.

She watched as her mother caught Billy close and squeezed him tight. Above the boy's head, Grace McKay looked at her daughter, and the smile faded. Uncertainty, maybe even fear, replaced the joy.

Carolyn looked away then. When she couldn't be sure she could control her own emotions, she backed out of the room and went across the hall. Thankfully, she found the waiting room empty. She went inside and closed the door behind her, then tried to block out the image of her mother's face. Her own mother was afraid of her. She was afraid of what Carolyn was going to do.

It was the stuff of nightmares, and she didn't have anyone she could talk to about this. Drew was furious with her, and her mother...this whole mess was pulling the two of them apart.

Carolyn's aunt walked into the waiting room about fifteen minutes later. She graciously offered to take Billy home, and didn't ask any questions that Carolyn didn't want to answer. All Carolyn had to say was that she needed to talk to her mother, and Aunt Ellen understood.

She knocked quickly on her mother's hospital room door and then went in. As she'd noticed before, her mother seemed to have aged overnight. The tiny lines around the corners of her eyes and her lips were more pronounced. The gray in her hair seemed to stand out more than usual, and she still had a fragile air about her that Carolyn found frightening. She'd hoped that her mother's appearance was temporary, that it would disappear after a day of rest, but it hadn't.

The doctor had assured her that all his tests had found nothing physically wrong with Grace. But emotionally she was exhausted. He'd warned Carolyn to be careful, but she didn't see how she could avoid telling her that Drew now knew everything.

"Well, come on over here and tell me what you've done, Carolyn," her mother said, making her feel as if she were eight years old.

"You went and told him, didn't you?" Grace stated, saving Carolyn from having to say it herself. "God help us all."

"I had to," she replied, wishing that she was a little girl again, that she could pour out her troubles to a mother who would make everything all better. "He and Billy look exactly alike. Dr. Moore saw it. Aunt Ellen saw it. It was only a matter of time before someone else saw it and said something to him, or until he figured it out himself."

"What did he say?" the older woman asked matter-of-factly, clearly in control again.

Carolyn shrugged helplessly and looked away, glad to see this take-charge side of her mother coming back again, but wishing the reemergance of her mother's true disposition could have held off a little longer.

"Carolyn?" Grace said, prodding her.

"He was stunned. He was angry. He . . ."

"And what's he going to do?"

Carolyn swallowed hard. "I don't know."

"He can't have Billy," her mother said, sounding amazingly strong for someone who'd been rushed to the hospital just a day before. "He can't come back here after ten years and take Billy away from me."

"We never gave him a chance all those years ago." Carolyn was defending Drew, and maybe trying to defend herself, as well. "He never had a choice in the first place."

"He can't take Billy."

"It was wrong," Carolyn said. "What we did to him was wrong."

"We did what was best for Billy," her mother insisted.

"I believe that, and I think we can make Drew understand that, but that still doesn't make what we did to him right." Or what we did to me, she considered, though she didn't voice it out loud.

She thought again of that awful day when her mother had suggested this way out for her, when Carolyn had known for certain how much her mother wanted and needed Billy.

Carolyn had needed him, too, even if she was a seventeen-year-old scared to death at the thought of being responsible for another person's life. What if she messed up? What if he got hurt? Or lost? She couldn't even face that possibility.

She'd jumped at the idea of giving Billy to her parents to raise. It would mean that she could still see him. She'd always know that he was okay. She could still hold him in her arms to reassure herself of that. It hadn't sounded nearly as difficult as giving him up to some strangers.

And it had been the right thing to do for Billy at the time. But what about now? she wanted to ask her mother. Looking down at the older woman, who was still uncharacteristically fragile looking and plainly weakened by this ordeal, Carolyn decided this wasn't the time to take this argument any further. Particularly when they had so many other things to deal with.

"I don't know how to tell you the rest of it," Carolyn said, wishing she knew what her mother remembered and what she didn't about the events that had led up to her attack. "Drew . . . he thinks there's a chance that whoever took that little girl from Chicago last weekend could be the same man who took Annie."

Sara Parker was still in southern Indiana, near where she'd been found. She was leaving for her home tonight. But first, a child psychiatrist who frequently worked with the police and the FBI on cases such as this had come from Chicago to talk to her about what happened to her. They hoped that keeping her in the area would help her to remember.

Drew had to be there while they questioned the girl. This was his job, something he could finally understand. The criminals, the victims, their families—the things that happened to them seldom made sense, but his job did. He found the kids, and he caught the bad guys. It was wonderfully simple, all-absorbing; it was often mentally and physically exhausting, as well, but he didn't care.

He threw himself into his work, because then he didn't have time to think about what Carolyn had told him or to begin to imagine what he was going to do.

Drew arrived at the hospital room where Sara had been kept overnight for observation, just in time for the session with the psychiatrist to begin. He had already met Dr. Nicholas Garrett, and he was glad the man was here to help them. The psychiatrist was kind, soft-spoken, low-key, and he started by talking about nothing more than the kinds of dolls Sara liked to play with and her favorite TV shows.

Sara looked almost normal today. She sat cross-legged on the hospital bed, wearing Cinderella PJs. She held a ragged-looking doll in her lap, and one of Sara's tiny hands was swallowed by that of her mother. Slowly, carefully, she answered all the questions Dr. Garrett put to her, all the time keeping her eyes steadily on his.

She remembered more now than she had before, although she said she'd seen little and hadn't recognized anything about the place where she was kept. The bad man had pulled his truck to a stop beside her as she walked along the street. He'd told her that her house had caught on fire, and that she couldn't go home. He'd offered to take her to her mother and father, and he'd had a fireman's helmet lying on the front seat of his truck and been wearing what looked to her like a fireman's coat. She'd gone willingly, without making a sound, and he'd let her wear the fire helmet.

Just great, Drew thought. The firemen taught kids not to be afraid of going with them while they wore their oxygen masks and fireproof suits if their houses ever caught on fire. And now he needed to tell kids not to trust strangers with fire helmets who told them their houses had burned to the ground. They should be careful about people who looked like policemen and told them their parents had been hurt in a car accident, and nice-looking strangers who claimed to have lost their puppies, too. That was another favorite they used. "Little girl, I've lost my puppy, and I was wondering if you could help me find it." Off went the kid into the woods with a total stranger.

It made Drew sick.

He sat there in silence while Sara told them that the man had soon blindfolded her, tied her hands and feet and tossed her in the back seat, under a blanket. She couldn't remember how long they'd driven, because she'd cried herself to sleep. They'd spent the night somewhere—she didn't know where. She'd just slept and slept. Obviously the man had drugged her.

She didn't know where he'd taken her next, or when, but it had been dark when they got there. She remembered what had sounded like the interior of a cabin.

Sara had thrown up on the man when he told her that her parents were dead, that they weren't ever coming back, that he'd be her father from now on. And the next day, before he could hurt her too badly, something had frightened him. There'd been a loud noise—like the sound of a firecracker.

"Hunters?" Drew mouthed the word to his boss, Bob Rossi, who was standing across the room.

It was a logical assumption, if they'd been off in the woods at some cabin used for hunting and fishing. And that kind of place would certainly provide the man with the privacy he needed.

Sara continued her story. The noise had seemed to scare the man as much as it did her, and they'd left the place quickly. This time he hadn't taken the time to tie her up. They'd driven for hours, until the man cursed and screamed as he beat on the dashboard of the truck. He'd been nearly out of gas. She wasn't sure where they were then, but he'd found this country store in an isolated area. And when he went in to pay, she'd slipped out of the truck and into the back of another one and the vehicle had taken off before the mean man came back outside the store.

She'd tried not to look at the man, because he'd frightened her. He wasn't anyone she knew. At least she didn't remember him.

Her description of him was vague to the point that it might as well have been nonexistent. He was Caucasian, older than her father, who was twenty-seven but looked ancient these days. He had dark, short hair. She hadn't looked at his eyes, had no idea of their color. He was a little overweight and smoked a lot of cigarettes.

Dr. Garrett conferred with Bob Rossi, Drew and the two other agents in the room. He told them that he didn't think they were going to get anything else out of Sara today regarding the man who'd taken her. Finally, it was Drew's turn.

"Hi, Sara," he said, trying not to look grim. He didn't want to frighten her. "Remember me? I'm Drew."

She nodded. "I found my mommy again."

"I know." He actually managed to smile. "I told you that you'd find her."

"I want to go home now," Sara said. "My mommy promised, if I talked to this nice man, I could go home."

"Just another minute," he told her.

He started running a hand over the various pockets in his jacket and his shirt, until he found the imprint of the Polaroid of her he'd taken and the one he had of Annie in the little red suit. He was more nervous than he remembered being on any other job.

Of course, he'd never worked on a case where he'd known the victim, and that, he saw, changed everything. He wanted to solve every case on which he worked, but this one—he needed to solve this one. He was desperate to do so, and this little girl's memories were essential to him.

"We just need one more thing," he said. "About the clothes? The ones you were wearing when you got away? Where did you get them, Sara?"

She looked confused for a minute.

Drew pulled out the picture, selecting the one of her first. "These," he said. "Remember, Sara? It's important. Where did you get them?"

She glanced at the picture and quickly turned away. Obviously she didn't like looking at it. "The man . . . the bad man."

"He gave them to you?"

She nodded.

Drew thought he was going to choke before he got through this interview. He wanted to know why. Why would this man give her these particular clothes? Did they hold some significance for him? Some memory he had of Annie?

But he was afraid to ask, because he didn't want to ask Sara why the man had taken the clothes she was wearing or what he'd tried to do to her afterward.

The doctors who'd examined her said she hadn't been raped, and the only bruises they'd found on her were on her upper arms, no doubt from being held against her will. But that didn't mean much. There were all kinds of ways a man could hurt a little girl, and not all of them left bruises.

Drew backed up. Sara said the bad man had given her the clothes. That was a starting point. He would go from there. "When did he give you the clothes? At the cabin... the place where you heard the firecrackers?"

She nodded. Dr. Garrett looked nervous. Drew realized he was in dangerous territory.

"Did he say why he wanted you to wear those clothes?" Drew asked, holding his breath.

Sara shook her head. "No."

Drew pulled out the other picture, and when Sara turned away without even looking at it, he moved it around until it came into her line of vision, even though she obviously didn't want to see. Dr. Garrett rose to stand behind him, no doubt ready to cut him off, but he put up a hand to tell him to back away.

"This is a friend of mine," he told Sara, fighting to keep his voice steady. "This is a little girl named Annie, and I've been looking for her for a long time. She disappeared many years ago, and she had a little red suit just like the one this man gave you to wear."

Sara said nothing, but she was visibly upset. Drew felt his opportunity slipping away from him, and he wanted to scream at the injustice of it.

"Sara, did he say anything to you about Annie? Did he tell you where he got the clothes? Or why he kept them? Or why he wanted you to wear them?"

She started to cry then. Her lower lip quivered, and then the tears began to fall.

She knew something. She knew something she wasn't telling him, something she was afraid to tell him. And he couldn't make her.

Her mother gathered her close in her arms, burying Sara's face against her chest and covering the little girl's ears with her hands. She looked at Drew as if he were lower than pond scum.

"That's enough," Dr. Garrett said, pulling him back.

He had to fight to make himself turn and go. God alone knew when he'd get another chance to talk to Sara. She was the only person who could help him figure out what had happened ten years ago and how it was connected to her disappearance.

Moving on sheer force of will alone, he made it to the door. It was killing him to walk away when he knew he was so close, but he made himself do it.

"Hey, mister?" he heard a tiny little voice say from behind him.

He whirled around, hope surging within him. "Yes?"

Sara peeked out from the curve of her mother's protective embrace. "The other little girl—?"

"Annie." He was barely able to say the name.

Sara looked pained when she heard it. "Did she ever get back home again?"

Drew took the innocent question like a kick in the gut. He couldn't believe how hard it was for him to admit this, even after all these years, couldn't believe how much it still hurt.

He looked at Sara Parker, her eyes locked on his, her tears not quite dry. He watched her, safe in her mother's embrace, ready for her trip home, and he thought of Annie.

"Not yet, Sara." He had to stop and clear his throat. "She hasn't made it home yet."

Chapter 10

It was late when Drew returned. The bed-and-breakfast was dark, but one of the keys he'd been given opened the front door. The agent in him wondered how many other such keys had been given out, how many were ever returned and who could get into this house at any time if they wanted. But the man simply didn't care about any of that right then.

He was going to his room. Then he was going to do his damnedest to forget everything that had happened to him since he'd come back to this town. He still couldn't believe someone had the nerve to name this place Hope.

Hopeless, they should have called it.

It was simply hopeless.

Sara Parker had summed it all up with her innocent question about Annie.

Did she ever get back home again?

And what had he said? *Not yet.*

Who was he kidding? It had been ten damn years. Annie McKay wasn't ever coming back home again. Why had he ever thought she would, or that anything he could do now would somehow make a difference about what had happened all those years ago?

Had he thought he could simply erase everything that had gone on in the past ten years? Had he thought he could go back in time, pick up where he'd left off with Carolyn and relive those years he'd spent without her?

He was crazy. This whole situation had made him crazy ten years ago, and it was still doing that to him, even now.

It was the past, he told himself sternly, and he could not change it.

Nothing that happened now, nothing he did to find out what happened to Annie, could change all that had gone on since she'd disappeared.

He and Carolyn had a son, and he'd never even seen him until a day and a half ago. Billy had lived the first eight years of his life without Drew, and he might live the rest of it, as well, without ever knowing Drew was his father.

Drew thought about turning around and going back outside, maybe going for a long, mind-numbing run through the darkened streets, or just walking and never stopping.

He took a minute to assess the situation. It was nearly midnight. He was exhausted, and he honestly believed that he could have walked to the next county and still not be able to clear his head.

In the meantime, he found himself at the door to his room. He went inside and not bothering to flick on the light, threw his coat across the chair, took off his shoes and socks, then headed for the bathroom.

It was a telling indication of how caught up in the past he was that he'd spent at least forty-five seconds in the room before he realized there was someone else inside already.

Carolyn was in the corner, curled up in the big, wing chair.

He uttered a single, blasphemous curse, louder than he intended. It seemed to reverberate around the room for an eternity, and had her nearly jumping out of the chair.

Drew turned his back, not wanting to see what the day had cost her, not wanting her to see what it had done to him.

"I don't have anything to say to you tonight," he told her, his tone dead even. The furor of his emotions had left him drained and empty.

And then he headed for the bathroom and closed the door behind him. He brushed his teeth, washed his face, then started pacing while he waited for the sound of the door closing behind her. The only problem was, the bathroom was too damned small for walking, and he could have sworn, from what he heard and what he sensed, that she hadn't budged from the chair.

He could not deal with this tonight. Grimly he turned to the door, wrenched it open and stalked back out. He didn't care to make any explanations to anyone tonight—least of all her.

And he didn't owe her any, dammit.

She might feel she owed him some more, but he wasn't interested in hearing them.

"Not tonight, Carolyn," he said when he saw that he was right. She hadn't budged yet.

Drew looked longingly at the wall he'd nearly put his fist through, at the glass he couldn't afford to break. He wasn't a violent man, but he certainly felt like one tonight.

"What do you want from me?" he asked, unable to think of any other way to get her to leave. "What?"

It didn't mean he'd answer her, but maybe if she at least got the chance to say whatever she felt compelled to say, she'd go and leave him alone.

"I didn't tell Billy yet," she said, rushing along. "I told my mother, but I didn't tell Billy. He doesn't have a clue—about any of this. I know you're angry, and I know you have a right to be, but I had to ask that you give this some time before you tell him—if you want to tell him, that is."

"I'm not going to tell him anything tonight, okay? Will you please go now?"

She stood, still in the shadows. He couldn't see her face or anything of her expression, but he felt some hope that this would soon be over.

"Billy's very upset right now," she continued. "My father... his father... He thinks his father just died a few months ago, and now my mother's ill. He's frightened. It's going to take some time. If you could just give it some time..."

She took three steps across the room toward him. He counted them. Mentally he judged the distance left between them, and saw that it wasn't enough. With his mind, he willed her to cut to the left, to walk around him and keep on going to the door, through it and into the night, so that he could be alone. But, of course, she didn't.

She put her hand on his arm, and he couldn't help himself. He flinched, then threw out his hand in an effort to tell her without words to get the hell away from him.

And, dammit, he'd frightened her. Hell, he was frightening himself tonight, and that was one reason he didn't want her anywhere near him.

This kind of rage, this out-of-control feeling was one he'd never experienced so sharply. He wasn't afraid that he'd hurt her physically; he wasn't that far-gone. But he couldn't be sure of what he might say to her right now. Some things couldn't be taken back.

"Please," he said, wondering how long it had been since he'd actually begged anyone for anything. "Please, just go."

"I'm sorry," she said, sounding as miserable as he felt.

Drew closed his eyes, willing himself not to look at her, not to stop her, not to explain. Not tonight.

She turned abruptly in the direction of the door. He was aware of every move she made, and he probably knew before she did that she'd thrown herself off-balance on the claw foot of the ottoman. He whirled and caught her as she pitched forward, saving her from hitting the floor and putting her squarely in his arms.

Helplessly he looked over her face. It was stamped with tension, weariness, pride, all mingling with some emotion that he couldn't begin to read.

He pushed her away from him, putting some distance between their bodies, but hanging on to her with two hands that remained on her upper arms, not letting her go at all, but not allowing her any closer.

"You understand, don't you?" He held her still, this old familiar power humming between them now. It was like a tangible force, something that bound them together, yet wasn't powerful enough to negate all the other influences that seemed determined to tear them apart.

She understood that. He would have sworn that she must, because it was so clear to him. That was what was making him so crazy tonight.

"It's right here," he said to her. "Everything I've been missing all these years, everything I've wanted. Everything I threw away—it's right here, no more than an arm's length away from me. It's so close, I can touch it, but I can't hang on to it. I can't figure out how to push everything else out of the way and make you mine. Forever."

The last part was the stickler. He wanted forever—with Carolyn.

And Billy and Annie and her mother—they were all standing here between them. He could have handled her mother's objections. He was working to somehow assuage the guilt that would always be associated with Annie. But Billy?

He had to take a very deep, slow breath and try to hold it for a minute in order to steady himself.

Billy was the immovable object now. And Carolyn wanted Drew to leave the boy alone. She wanted him to be content just to know him in some small way, but to leave him with the woman he believed to be his mother and to let him think his father was dead and buried. She didn't want him to tear apart everything Billy believed to be true about his life and his family.

He couldn't have said that he didn't understand her wanting that. God knew he'd seen enough families torn apart to realize what it did to the kids.

But he didn't see how he could walk away from the boy, either. And he didn't see how he could build a life with Carolyn and not have Billy planted firmly between them in the process. He saw more than enough anger and resentment between him and Carolyn to rip them apart all over again.

That was why he was angry tonight. He didn't see any way to fix the situation they were in. And he wanted her so badly; he'd wanted her like this for years.

What in the world was he going to do about that? It would only end up causing them even more pain than before.

"It's hopeless, Carolyn," he finally told her. "It's absolutely hopeless."

"Don't say that."

"Nothing's changed between us. Nothing," he repeated. "I still want you. I still need you. The feelings I have for you haven't changed. If anything, they've gotten stronger. And it's still absolutely hopeless. You understand that, don't you?"

But he didn't think she did. Carolyn looked as dazed as he felt, and he couldn't take the misunderstandings and half-truths and evasions between them any longer.

"I'm still in love with you." He blurted out the words, not afraid of letting her see the anger that went along with them, even as he pulled her a little bit closer to him, even as he came a little bit closer to the point of madness.

He wanted her. Ten years' worth of longing had simmered inside him for too long. Now it threatened to explode around them.

Heedless of that, he settled her trembling body against his, noted in some corner of his mind that she made no objections to her position.

Oh, he wanted her. He had no business feeling that way right now, but it was another of the things that were driving him crazy tonight.

He had to make her understand that. He had to explain it to her, because he couldn't be the only one to feel this way.

"I could take you in my arms right now and make you mine again, but it wouldn't last. No matter how hard I tried, it wouldn't last," he said, feeling his body harden at the thought of finally being with her again.

"I feel like someone's playing a vicious game with us. Like he brought us back here, let us remember how this felt, let us ache for each other all over again, only to yank it away."

She didn't say anything. Her lower lip trembled, but she didn't cry, didn't try to escape from his embrace.

"Explain it to me," he demanded, getting right up in her face. He was scaring himself now. "Tell me why it all happened this way. Tell me why it had to end this way."

"I don't know," she said, so close he could see the little green flecks in her dark eyes. "I know you're mad at me—"

"Carolyn, I'm mad at the whole world tonight. Everyone and everything under the sun. Tonight I'm downright dangerous."

Disgusted with himself and the whole situation, he dropped his arms down to his sides and turned his back to her.

When she didn't move, he added, "You need to go home. Right now."

Carolyn swallowed hard and stood her ground. She was still caught up in a whirlwind of emotions, back at the point where she could have sworn he'd said he still loved her.

How in the world could he still love her?

Of course, in the same breath, he'd told her that this whole thing between them would never work, that it was hopeless.

She could understand his thinking it would never work, but she had a hard time with the hopeless part. True, one seemed to be much the same as the other, but she needed the fine luxury of hope, especially since she didn't see any reason for that hope.

Until he said he still loved her.

No one had loved her in years. No one had ever wanted her the way Drew did. No one had ever made her feel the way he did. She hadn't wanted to fight for anyone else the way she was ready to fight for him.

And where there was love, she wouldn't give up. He couldn't, either. Surely the worst was over between them now. He knew what she'd done. She knew why he'd left her. It was all out in the open now, and they couldn't give up.

She wished she had the courage to tell him. If he still thought he loved her, if he still wanted her, after all this, he couldn't give up now.

Just as he'd said, it was all within their reach. He was right here beside her, and she had to make him understand that it wasn't hopeless at all.

Not if he loved her.

Not if she loved him—and she most certainly did.

He was downright dangerous, he'd warned her. Mad at everyone and everything, and downright dangerous.

Well, if that was what he felt tonight, they'd just have to work with it. She'd just have to show him that nothing was impossible.

Afraid to breathe, afraid to even think farther ahead than her next move, she inched closer to face him. Unable to meet his eyes at the moment, Carolyn concentrated on the hard set of his jaw and what she knew was the softness of his lips.

And, in an instant, the tension, the outpouring of emotion, the danger he'd warned her about, turned sexual. She watched as the awareness shot through him, as the temperature in the room skyrocketed.

"Go away," he said, catching her where she stood to keep her from getting too close. Then, as if through sheer force of will, he pried his fingers off her again. "Go right now."

"I can't," she told him. "I'm scared that if I do, I won't ever get this close to you again. I'm scared that you'll put up a wall between us that I'll never break through."

"Carolyn, there's a bed over there. I can't remember the last time I had sex with a woman, and I've never in my life needed or wanted a woman more than I want you right now. I want to lose myself in you. I want to forget everything standing between us, and fool myself for a little while into thinking this is going to work out."

"And there's a problem there?" she said, marveling at her own nerve. "Because I didn't pick up on it."

Drew swore softly, but stayed where he was. His hand settled against the side of her face. The pad of one thumb traced its way across her bottom lip, sending her pulse into overdrive, and her self-confidence threatened to desert her here and now.

"You're playing with fire," he warned her, probably as much as he was warning himself.

"I don't care anymore," she replied, feeling as reckless as he claimed to be, realizing in some elemental way that she'd pushed him right to the edge, that any second he was going to topple over it with her. "Don't you see? I don't have anything to lose anymore. I haven't since I watched you walk away from me, then walked away from here myself, without my baby. My life is... it's so empty, so lonely. And I can't stand it anymore. I just don't have anything or anyone, so if there's a chance for us, I'm not going to walk away from it without a fight."

"It's only going to complicate matters," he said. "They're complicated enough as it is, and our being together won't solve anything."

"Does that mean you don't want me?"

"It means I feel reckless tonight. I feel cheated and lied to, and I think I'm entitled to a hell of a lot more than one night with you."

He kissed her once then, kissed her hard and fast, his touch rougher than any she'd ever known from him, his strength barely contained.

"Don't you understand?" he said. "I don't want you to be hurt any more by this than you already have been. And I don't want to hurt any more, either."

He wanted to leave his mark on this woman, to take her so hard and so fast, to get so far inside her, that nothing could ever tear them apart again. He wanted to brand her as his, to so clearly imprint his possession of her on her body and her mind that she would never forget him, never stop missing him, never stop wanting him.

And even that wouldn't be enough.

She would do the exact same thing to him. He would never touch another woman intimately without thinking of Carolyn and wishing he could be with her instead. He would be ruined, forever.

"We had everything," he told her. "We had it all, and we lost it all. And that's making me a little crazy tonight."

When she didn't leave this time, he kissed her again. When she didn't protest, he did it once more. He simply couldn't get enough of her, couldn't get close enough, couldn't hold her tightly enough.

Somehow, they made it to the bed without him having to let go of her or break off the kiss. He could barely breathe then, as he quickly shed his clothes and followed her down. He'd never turned on the lights, so he couldn't see her as clearly as he would have liked, but the picture of her was so clearly etched on his mind that it didn't matter. And her body, beneath his hands, was nearly as familiar as his own. After all, a man didn't forget the feel of a woman who'd lived in his dreams for years.

With the last of his self-control, he slowed down long enough to undo the buttons of the shiny pink blouse she wore, to undo the snap of her bra and to pull down her slacks. He slid them off and threw them somewhere, pulled and tugged and flung at the rest of her clothes until neither of them had a stitch of clothing left.

"Don't be frightened of me," he said, looking down at her through the darkness.

"I'm not." Though she didn't sound convinced, her hand came up to caress his chest.

He let his mouth settle over the delicate skin at the base of her neck, searching for that ultrasensitive spot that he remembered so well. Pleasure shot through her, bringing her whole body up off the bed as she gasped his name. Tremors of pleasure shot through his body, as well, because he got absolutely high off the idea of pleasing her this way again.

He thought of all the little things he used to do that turned her on, thought again about how much he simply needed to join his body with hers in this instant, before he lost the chance at all.

This moment, this link between them, was so fragile, so tenuous, that he felt certain someone or something was going to snatch her away from him again, that they were going to be denied even this one moment in time.

It drove him on, even though he badly needed to prolong this, because he knew very well there might not be a next time.

She was writhing beneath him, struggling to somehow get closer to him. Her legs parted easily for him, and the heat of her was nearly his undoing.

As he settled himself on top of her, as he felt her arms close around him, her nails biting into his back and urging him on, he remembered that they had to be careful this time. And that made him mad. That made him think of what had happened before and of why he thought this was all so hopeless. And, irrationally, he didn't want anything between them right now. Nothing.

Still, he managed to grab a condom from the wallet in his pants on the floor beside the bed, managed to rip the packet open and put it on.

The process cleared his head for a moment, and he tried to squelch the feeling of desperation that had been driving him on.

"There has to be more than tonight," he told her, kissing again and again and again. "There has to be."

He put one hand on her pretty little breasts while he drank from her mouth. Then he let the hand go lower, testing to see if she was ready for him, finding that she was.

There would be other nights, he promised himself, positioning himself above her, tensing for the heat and the pressure inside her.

"I love you," he told her, tensing the muscles in his thighs and his buttocks, moving slowly inside her, when all he wanted was to quickly bury himself there. "I never stopped loving you."

The pressure gave way as she finally relaxed, letting him inside, and then, in the same instant, it started building all over again. She was so tight, so hot, so familiar. He was sweating and fighting for all he was worth to slow down, but it was too late.

''Don't stop,'' she told him, her nails digging into his back. ''Don't you dare stop now.''

He ground his hips against hers, once, twice. And then she splintered beneath him, coming apart in his arms, only moments before he did the same. Wave after wave of pleasure rocked him. He couldn't get close enough to her, couldn't hold her tightly enough, couldn't hang on to this moment that he wanted never to end.

''Mine,'' he told her, resting heavily on top of her. ''You were meant to be mine.''

And there would be other nights.

He'd fight the devil himself, if that was what it took, but there would be other nights for them.

They hadn't even made it under the covers, and when the heat finally subsided and the chill set in, he pulled the covers off the other side of the bed and threw them over top of them both. He adjusted their positions, so that she was lying on top of him, then pushed her head down to his chest.

Reality was slowly closing in on Drew, though he didn't want it to. He wanted to stay like this, with her body draped over his and his mind blessedly blank to everything but his blinding need to take possession of her.

He thought, disgusted with himself, that he'd taken her virginity with more finesse than this, with more patience and more concern for her pleasure.

And even now he felt this near-violent desire to have her again. This urgent coupling had done little, if anything, to blunt that blinding need. He wasn't sure anything would, except making love to her morning, noon and night for the next decade or so.

Drew closed his hand around a tangle of Carolyn's hair that was now draped across his chest. He liked the feel of it in his hands, hadn't had time before to experience that particular pleasure. It gave him something to hang on to. He needed desperately to hang on to her.

"Are you all right?" he asked, the words coming out almost as a growl.

She tensed above him, the sweet aftermath of lethargy gone in an instant, giving him yet one more reason to curse himself.

"I meant…" He backed up and tried again. "Did I hurt you?"

"No."

But he didn't quite believe her. "I begged you to go," he said, though he blamed himself for this.

"I know."

He tugged a little harder on that handful of hair, because he had to see her face. It was dark, so he had to trust his hand, as well. He found the tears on her cheeks. "I did hurt you."

"No… I just… I haven't done this… in forever."

He bit back the obvious question—how long it had been—because he didn't want to know. No matter how long it was, it hadn't been long enough. Because he didn't want anyone else ever to have been inside her the way he had.

"I'm a little overwhelmed," she said. "I'd forgotten how… personal it is. How you can't hold back… anything… or hide anything."

And he thought that if he let her, she'd be off him, off this bed, into every stitch of clothes she had and out of this room so fast it would make his head spin.

He held her even tighter. "I'm sorry. I'm not usually so…" He couldn't think of any word to describe the myriad things he had felt. *Desperate? Impatient as hell? Scared? Frustrated?* He could have gone on all night and not covered them all. "I don't know how I'm ever going to let you go, sweetheart."

Carolyn shivered, and he held her closer. She closed her eyes and knew she'd finally figured out what he was trying to tell her. That he loved her, that he didn't want her to ever forget about him. But that this was goodbye.

"You can't do this," she told him, feeling desperate now. "You can't tell me one minute that you love me and then tell me goodbye. You can't."

It took a while for her words to sink in. She hadn't been sure what to make of all of this. She'd only known that if she let him go tonight, he was going to put up all these walls between them, ones that she might never break down.

And then the whole thing had exploded on them. She still had the feeling of being sucked down into a whirlwind, into a flash of need and passion over which she had no control. Blindly, eagerly, she'd followed where he led. And the only thing she regretted was the fact that it was over.

She didn't want it to be. And he'd better not dare try to tell her this was goodbye, because for the first time in years she felt alive. She felt loved and wanted and needed again.

"I begged you to go," he said.

"And you wanted me to stay."

"But I didn't want to hurt you."

"Well, then, don't hurt me now, by trying to tell me this didn't mean anything to you."

"It didn't solve anything," he told her. "And it will only make it harder, in the end, when I go."

She thought about telling him, in no uncertain terms, that he wasn't going anywhere, because she wasn't going to let him. But she wasn't sure he was ready to hear that.

Instead, she asked him a question she'd already answered for herself. "Could it get any harder than it already will be to let each other go a second time?"

He swore, then rolled with her, so that she was lying with her back on the bed. For a second, she thought he was going to kiss her again, but he didn't. He rolled back over, leaving her there while he threw off the covers, sat up and started putting his clothes on.

"It's not hopeless," she told him as he put on his pants. She'd do anything to prove that to him.

So what if there was yet another mountain between them, another river to cross? This time, they'd cross them all. They weren't running away anymore, and they weren't lying to each other.

And surely it had to be easier at twenty-seven and twenty-nine than it had been at seventeen and nineteen. Surely they could handle things now. She knew she'd certainly work harder at it, because she realized now how rare and how precious this thing between them was.

She had tonight to convince him that it wasn't hopeless at all.

"Make love to me again," she said, sitting up in the bed and dragging the covers with her.

He swore.

Carolyn smiled. Clearly, she'd thrown him off-balance, and it gave her hope.

"Make love to me again. Tell me you love me again. Tell me I'm yours, and that you're never going to let another man touch me again, and then tell me goodbye—again. I dare you."

He bent over, picked up her bra and shirt and threw them at her. "Put your clothes on, Carolyn," he said, and she knew he'd shut her out.

Tears flooded her eyes. She stared up at the ceiling and tried to blink them back.

"I don't know how to fix this," he said. "It's always going to be between us, Carolyn. And I don't see how we'll fix it."

"Maybe not tonight, but someday we will. Give it some time, at least. You just found out, for God's sake. We can take a little time now to try to figure it all out, can't we?"

"Your mother hates me. She has for years, long before Billy became the issue."

"So? It didn't stop us from being together ten years ago. It certainly won't stop us now," she said. The cold was starting to sink in, now that he was all the way across the room.

"What about the guilt?"

"What about it?" She pulled on her shirt and held the ends closed around her. It hung to her knees, covering everything that had to be covered, but there was no way she could manage the buttons right now.

"It's still there between us."

"But it doesn't have to tear us apart this time."

"What about Billy?" That was his trump card, the one she couldn't explain away. "You want me to stay away from him, don't you? You don't want him to ever know the truth."

"I don't want him hurt, and I don't want you to take him away from the only mother he's ever known."

"Which is another way of saying leave him alone. Well, I don't know if I can live with that. And if I could, I'd sure as hell resent it. I'd resent you because of it. I see it eating away at us forever, like some poison in our relationship. Tell me what to do about that."

"I don't know," she said. "But I—"

What could she say after that?

She loved him.

He'd told her he loved her. He'd said she was meant to be his, and she wanted to belong to him, just as she wanted him to belong to her.

Surely that had to count for something, didn't it?

Carolyn was no longer naive enough to believe that love conquered all, but dammit, it had to count for something.

"I don't want to lose you again," she said, with as much pride as she could muster when all she really wanted to do was latch on to him and never let go. She couldn't stand to lose him again. That was what she meant, what her pride wouldn't let herself tell him.

And then she was all out of arguments, and he still hadn't budged. Feeling more miserable than she'd been in years, Carolyn struggled back into her underwear and her slacks, found her shoes, her purse, her keys, and went to stand by the door with her back to him.

Don't let me go, she prayed, but she got no answer from him. She risked one glance back at the bed they'd shared not more than five minutes ago. It seemed impossible to go from that to this so quickly.

Don't let me go.

But he did.

Hastily she swiped the tears off her cheeks, then held her head high. "What are you going to do now?" she asked.

"About Billy?"

Carolyn nodded.

"I don't know."

She didn't even bother to ask what, if anything, he planned to do about her.

Chapter 11

Carolyn didn't want to get out of bed the next morning. She'd arrived home around two-thirty that morning, feeling like a teenager trying to sneak in after curfew.

She'd brought her mother home from the hospital yesterday afternoon, and she was sure Grace had heard her come in last night. Her mother certainly didn't have to ask where she'd been or who she'd been with. Though, no doubt, she was waiting for some explanation.

For some reason, when Carolyn had just turned seventeen, a rebel of a boy named Drew Delaney had caught her attention, and she'd never managed to forget him. He'd worn his brown hair long—to his collar, he'd had a full beard and ridden a motorcycle. Her straitlaced parents had been horrified that their little girl, an honor student, a volunteer at the local hospital, head of the debate team, had wanted to go out with such a boy.

He'd graduated from high school the year before, but he hadn't gone on to college. He'd worked at Eddie's Garage instead, living with his grandmother. And he'd been well-known as the son of one of the town's loudest drunks.

Carolyn had met him when her car broke down one day and Drew pulled his motorcycle off to the side of the road and volunteered to help. When he couldn't get the car running, he'd offered to give her a lift back to town, then invited her to hop on the back of his bike.

Remembering the way he'd looked that day, his hair tied back carelessly in a loose ponytail, the front of it blown every which way by the wind, she was still amazed she'd ever gotten on that bike. He'd worn a black leather jacket, boots, and a killer grin. And something absolutely wicked had been lurking in those nearly black eyes of his.

He'd been the most dangerous man she'd ever seen, and riding to town with him had been the most reckless thing she'd ever done.

She'd been fascinated with him from the start, and she'd probably been half in love with him by the time he pulled to a stop in front of her house, the bike roaring on the otherwise quiet street, her parents both coming outside to see what in the world had happened to their poor little girl.

They'd disliked him on sight, her mother especially. They'd worried about his drunk of a father, wondered what someone like Drew could have to offer their daughter.

Carolyn had talked a mile a minute for months, trying to make them see that Drew wasn't anything like his father, that he drove the bike because it had come cheap, that he wore his hair long these days because he'd decided that if the town had already pegged him as a no-good trouble-maker like his father, then he'd hate to disappoint them.

But he hadn't been bad. Or dangerous. Or reckless. He hadn't been like that at all.

Maybe, if she had more time, she would have been able to convince her parents of that.

But Annie had disappeared not long after they forbade her to see Drew anymore. And in that instant, when all their lives changed forever, she'd been with Drew.

Irrationally, her parents had blamed him. In that same irrational manner, she'd blamed herself and her love for Drew Delaney. And once he was gone, she'd often rationalized that she'd deserved to lose him, that she didn't have any right to be happy with him when Annie was gone.

Carolyn rolled over in the little twin bed she'd slept in as a girl and listened for the sounds of the house coming to life again. Surely her mother couldn't hate Drew to this day. Surely she saw now how irrational their feelings about him had been.

But now her mother had even more reason to dislike him, even to fear him. Grace McKay worried that Drew was going to take Billy away from her. And as long as she saw Drew as a threat, she was bound to be upset about Carolyn having anything to do with him—particularly if she stayed out till nearly three in the morning with him.

Nervously Carolyn wondered if her mother would figure out what else they'd done last night.

Carolyn could hardly believe it herself. It had been a disaster, and yet it been like nothing she'd ever experienced before—at least not since Drew had left, nearly ten years ago.

Over the years, she'd lied to herself. She'd told herself the memories she had of the two of them together couldn't possibly be accurate, that it couldn't have been as wonderful as she remembered.

But it was.

He'd been lying there on top of her, his eyes boring down into hers, swearing that she was meant to be his, and she'd thought that settled it. She felt the same way—as if they belonged together and nothing could tear them apart.

But that wasn't what he had been telling her. The frustration must have been eating away at him at that point. That was what he'd wanted her to see.

She was meant to be his, but she wouldn't be.

Carolyn nearly jumped off the bed when someone knocked. Aunt Ellen called her name.

"Yes?" Carolyn replied, clutching the covers to her, wondering guiltily if he'd left some mark on her, either physical or emotional, that everyone would see.

"Phone's for you, dear," her aunt said, walking into the room and handing Carolyn the cordless phone.

She was afraid to take it. Carolyn was sure it was Drew, and she hadn't begun to figure out what to say to him this morning.

Finally, she forced herself to grab hold of the phone, then press the palm of her hand over the mouthpiece. "Is Mom up yet?"

Aunt Ellen was studying her too closely for comfort. "She's awake, but still in bed."

"And Billy?"

"He's having breakfast."

"What about school?" They hadn't discussed what to do about that. Billy was feeling much better now that her mother was home from the hospital, but he was still a little unsettled. "Does he want to go to school? Do you think he should?"

"If he goes, your mother will probably get more rest. And the doctor wants her to take it easy the next few days."

"Okay," Carolyn said, figuring she'd stalled as long as she reasonably could. "I'll be down in just a minute to talk to him. And thanks, Aunt Ellen. I don't know what we would have done without your help."

She waited until her aunt backed out of the room and closed the door behind her before forcing herself to put the phone to her ear.

Closing her eyes, she tried not to picture Drew in the darkness of his room last night. The lines in his face had been etched deeply, the despair clearly readable for anyone to see.

"Drew," she said into the phone.

"No, Carolyn, it's Brian." Brian, from Hope House. She clasped a hand over her mouth to stifle any involuntary sound she might make. "I've been here for almost twenty hours straight staring at my computer screen, and I've found three other possibilities."

"What?" It was all she could manage.

Yesterday she'd called her colleague Brian Wilson, a man who could do extraordinary things with a computer, and told him about Annie and Sara Parker. She'd asked for some information on other unsolved child abductions that might be connected with the two girls.

And now he had three—three other families whose lives had been ripped apart, just like hers.

It sickened her.

"Carolyn?" Brian asked. "You okay?"

"Yes," she fibbed.

"I can go over this with Drew, if you'd rather."

"He'll probably want to talk to you," she managed to get out. "But go ahead and tell me what you've got."

"A little girl, age ten, taken six years ago from a suburb of Louisville, Kentucky. Another one, age nine, taken three years ago from Cincinnati. A third, age seven, taken a year and a half ago from her aunt's, near Fort Wayne, Indiana."

Carolyn closed her eyes and tried not to put faces to the statistics he rattled off. "None of them were ever found?"

"No. All of them snatched off the sidewalk or the streets of their own neighborhoods and never seen again."

And then she didn't say anything. What else was there to say?

"Listen," Brian said finally, "why don't I print all this stuff out and express-mail it to you? You can have it tomorrow morning."

"Thank you." She gave him her mother's address.

"Carolyn, if you need anything else—and I mean anything—you'll call me, right?"

"I will. Thanks again."

Carolyn was simply numb for the next two or three hours. She tried to call Drew at the bed-and-breakfast, but he was out, and she didn't know how else to reach him.

She showered, dressed, walked Billy to the bus stop and waited there with him until he was safely on the bus, then made a point of avoiding her mother's room altogether.

She just couldn't stop thinking about those three other girls.

Around ten-thirty, as she was pacing the floor, wondering where Drew could have gone and what he could be doing, the phone finally rang, and Carolyn grabbed it. "Hello?"

"Carolyn?" a familiar female voice said. "I'd heard you were back in town. This is Emily. Emily Forrester."

The name meant nothing to Carolyn. "I'm sorry..." she began.

"Emily Bradshaw, I should say. I've been married for so long now, sometimes I forget I ever had a maiden name."

"Oh, of course," Carolyn said. Emily had lived just down the street. "How are you?"

"I'm fine, and I don't want to alarm you, but I thought you should know. I work at the elementary school, and—"

Carolyn jumped in. "Billy? He's all right?"

"He's fine," Emily assured her. "But his class is outside on the playground right now, and his teacher thought you should know—there's a man across the street who's just sitting there watching them play. His teacher swears the man hasn't taken his eyes off Billy the whole time they've been outside. And we're probably being silly even worrying about it, but you know how things are these days. You can't be too careful, so we thought you or your mother should know.''

Carolyn panicked at first. After all, the man who'd taken her sister had probably watched her for a long time first. Child kidnappers often did. They picked their victims, then watched and waited for the right opportunity to snatch them.

And if Brian Wilson was right, that man had taken three other little children, as well.

Of course, that was crazy—thinking that the man who'd taken Annie would ever come back and take Billy from them, as well. But so was the idea of a stranger grabbing a child and vanishing into thin air, and that happened. So this—

"Drew," she said, when the idea hit her, cutting off the wild turn her thoughts had taken. "Emily, is it Drew?"

"Drew Delaney?" The way the name had obviously popped into the woman's head, when he'd been gone for ten years, told Carolyn that the gossip was moving through the community at lightning speed, just as she had suspected. "I didn't get a good look at him, but now that you mention it...he's got that deep brown hair, the beard, the mustache, that dark, kind of dangerous look. Yes, it could be Drew."

Carolyn was sure it was. "I'll be right there, Emily."

"Should we call the children inside? Do you think Billy's in danger?"

"No." Carolyn tried to calm herself long enough to reassure her old friend. "Drew would never hurt Billy."

And all the way to the school, she prayed that she was right.

* * *

The school wasn't five minutes away. Carolyn parked in front of the building, then walked to the side where the playground faced Chestnut Street. That was where she found him.

There was a chain-link fence, there more to keep the kids off the street than to keep strangers out, and Drew was standing against the fence, his forearms resting on top of it, his chin on top of his folded arms.

He didn't seem to care that more than a few of the people who worked at the school had gathered in the corner by the lunchroom to stare at him, just as he was staring so intently at Billy.

He surprised her now, looking like the Drew she'd known so long ago, rather than the government agent in a subdued suit and tie.

He had on an old pair of jeans, a button-down shirt and a buttery-soft-looking brown bomber jacket. She wouldn't have been surprised to look around and find that old motorcycle of his somewhere nearby.

Dark and dangerous, her old friend Emily had said, and he definitely looked it today.

A part of her wished he had the old bike, wished they could just hop on the back and roar right out of town, at least for a little while. She used to fantasize about that— about him just taking her away from anything and everything that stood in the way of the two of them being together.

Carolyn was reminded of an old bluesy rock-and-roll song about a man picking up this woman and taking her off into the night, where nothing could come between them. That was the stuff her dreams had been made of, back when she still believed that dreams could come true.

Well, they definitely couldn't run away from this, not anymore. Resigned to that, she crossed the fifty yards or so between them and went to stand beside Drew at the fence.

He turned to stare at her, his eyes dark and brooding, his face seemingly etched in stone, as if nothing could touch him anymore, nothing could hurt him.

Just then the wind kicked up and a few strands of hair escaped from the clasp at the back of her head and flew across her face.

Drew reached out and brushed them away before she could, then stared down at her for a moment, before the hair flew back across her eyes. Carefully, gently, he tucked the strands behind her right ear.

A long, slow tremor passed through her, and the next thing she knew, he was slipping out of the brown leather jacket and wrapping it around her shoulders.

"It's damn near freezing out here this morning," he said. "Where's your coat?"

"I . . . I didn't realize it was so cold."

He appeared puzzled for a second. Obviously, it was hard to miss the cold on a morning like this. Then he looked around, as if to take their surroundings in for the first time. The kids were playing some kind of dodgeball game, and their teachers were gathered in a cluster in the corner outside the cafeteria, all staring at the two of them.

"They called you," he said.

She shrugged her shoulders and breathed in the warm, leathery scent that clung to his jacket—his scent. "The teachers didn't recognize you. They saw someone watching Billy, and got a little nervous."

"That's good," he said. "They should be watching out for anyone who stands here in the cold, staring at these kids."

She nodded and closed her eyes, trying not to think that a mere ten hours ago she'd been in bed with him.

"I just needed to see him, Carolyn. That's all."

"It's all right," she replied, wishing she could sink down inside his jacket—it was still warm from his body—and hide from all her problems for a little while. "I understand that, but...you're not going to tell him, are you? Not now, not right here?"

He looked absolutely murderous for a moment. Leaning heavily into the fence, laying his forehead on the top of it and staring down at the ground, he let out a soft string of expletives. She flinched at the thinly veiled anger evident in the words.

Turning her back to him, she stared across the playground to the spot in the corner where Billy was laughing and chasing a ball, his legs getting tangled up in another boy's, sending them both to the ground. They rolled over and came up laughing, still trying to beat each other to the ball.

"He's happy," she said. "I know you're hurt and you're angry, but look at him. He's happy. And he's had a good life, Drew. I know you want to be a part of his life now, and God knows, I do, too. I've always wanted to be more to him than just his sister, but I don't see how to make that happen. I don't want to hurt him."

"Neither do I," he said.

She closed her eyes and thanked God for that.

Then he added, "But I can't just walk away."

"Oh," she said, then felt compelled, in the name of honesty at last, to say, "You know, if you tried, you might be able to win custody away from my mother."

He shot her a purely incredulous look that was enough to cut off the very air she breathed.

"What?" he asked.

She was actually relieved to realize that he hadn't already been thinking along those lines, even if she had brought up the idea. It would have occurred to him eventually, and she didn't want to wait that long to see how he would react to it. So she forced herself to go on.

"You have legal rights that you've never signed away, and more and more the courts are recognizing the rights of birth fathers in adoption cases. If you wanted to take him, legally, you might be able to, but I'd beg you not to try to do that. The legal battle could go on for years, and you know it would only upset Billy—"

"Carolyn?" He took her by the arms and turned her to face him. "What in hell are you talking about?"

"The courts?" She shook her head, not sure what he was getting at. "Your rights, legally."

"Carolyn." It was a warning, and she heeded it.

The bottom line was so simple for her, and that was what he was asking for here. "Don't take him away from us. Please don't do that."

"Aw, dammit..." he said, turning away again and letting her go. He walked five steps in the other direction, nervous energy radiating from him.

"I don't know how my mother would handle it," she called after him. "I don't know how I'd handle it, and Billy... Think about what it would do to Billy."

"What do you think I am?" he yelled back. "Some kind of monster?"

"No." Anything but that, in fact, she acknowledged to herself. She'd seen the edge to him when they were teenagers, that attitude he'd adopted because he was sick of being compared to his drunken father and sick of knowing that the whole town didn't expect any more from him than to follow in his old man's footsteps. And, yes, he might have looked a little dangerous, a bit of a rebel. But that wasn't who he was.

The real man was—always had been—incredibly gentle. He was intelligent, hardworking, determined, and she'd depended on him so much back then—maybe too much. She'd thought after Annie died that he could somehow make everything better for her again, and he couldn't. No one could have.

"I'm sorry, Drew," she said. It was too little, too late. "I'm . . . I'm just so scared. I don't know what's going to happen next, and I'm worried about Billy and about you and my mother and . . . Annie. I don't know that I really want to know anymore what really happened to her. I think it's just going to cause us all a lot of pain."

"Are you asking me to drop this case?" he asked.

"No."

"Because I can't."

Their conversation all ran together, and it took a minute for him to realize that she wasn't asking him to do that.

"The man's still out there," he said. "He grabbed Sara Parker five days ago, and if we don't catch him, he'll grab someone else's little girl."

"I know that."

"So I can't stop."

"I know."

"And whatever's between us is just going to have to take a back seat to this case, at least for now. I don't have any answers for you, anyway. I don't know what to do about Billy. I don't have any idea."

She believed he was telling her the truth. He hadn't had time to get used to the idea, much less figure out what he was going to do about it.

In the distance, a bell rang out, and she flinched at the unexpected sound. The kids on the playground grumbled as their teachers started getting them lined up to go inside.

Billy and his friend got in line, pushing each other good-naturedly. He had a big smile on his face, which brought tears to Carolyn's eyes as she watched him go inside and bade him a silent goodbye.

This goodbye reminded her of all the others. Sometimes it seemed as if she'd spent her whole life either saying goodbye to him or trying to push him over into some small, carefully regimented corner of her heart, where she could love him and miss him and at the same time maintain some control over those feelings. She couldn't let loose and love him in the all-consuming, lavishly encompassing way she would have liked. She couldn't throw open her arms and latch on to him, because she'd never be able to let go.

"Carolyn?" Drew said her name softly. He was closer to her than she'd realized. She looked up and found herself nearly nose to nose with him. The wind cut through his hair, and his long, dark lashes came down, keeping her from seeing anything she might have been able to read in his eyes.

But in the next instant, his gloved hands were on her face, the leather cool and supple against her skin until he pulled off one glove and wiped the back of his thumb across her cheek. She blinked back the next tear before it had a chance to fall, but before he could pull away from her, she caught his hand and held it against her face.

"Last night..." She had to rush ahead before she lost her nerve. "Last night you said you still loved me."

He looked bleak. She thought he might kiss her, but then he seemed to change his mind. Pulling his hand from beneath hers, he backed slightly away.

"Drew?"

"But I didn't say it made a difference about anything," he said bitterly. "Tell me what, if anything, changes because of that."

"I don't..." she began, then faltered. What could she say? That it mattered to her? That a few men had claimed to love her over the years, but she either hadn't believed them or hadn't felt as if they were capable of loving anyone? That none of them had come close to mattering as much to her as Drew did, that no one ever would?

She was sure of that now. No one's love would ever mean as much to her as his did.

"Drew?" She put her hand on his arm, but he shrugged it off and held up a hand to keep her from coming any closer.

"Dammit, Carolyn, why do you think I'm so mad? Loving you just doesn't change anything."

She was quiet for a moment, and when she looked up, she saw that he'd put on his glove and pulled out his car keys. Obviously, he was ready to leave.

"Wait," she said. "With all this, I forgot to tell you. Brian Wilson called me this morning. You remember, he's the computer expert I was telling you about. He went digging through ten years' worth of unsolved child-abduction cases, and he found three that he thought might be connected to Annie's and Sara Parker's disappearances."

That stopped him faster than anything else she could have said. "This guy did what?"

"He found three other cases."

"When?" Drew said.

"I called him yesterday morning. He's been working on it all day and all night. Why? What's wrong?"

Drew shook his head. "I drove to the FBI office in Danville this morning to get on a secured line. I asked one of our data specialists to look through what we pulled from the computer banks when Sara Parker was kidnapped. He's searching for the same kind of information. I just don't understand how your friend could have accessed these resources so quickly."

"We have our own data banks, and we're linked to information clearinghouses maintained by each state."

"And what did this guy find out?"

"Three cases of missing girls, starting six years ago. One was near Louisville, one in Cincinnati and one near Fort Wayne."

He thought about the information for a minute, she could see the possibilities churning in his mind. "Picture that in your mind," he told her. Louisville, Cincinnati,

Fort Wayne, and where Sara was taken from, outside Chicago.''

"What?" she said.

"Come here and look at this."

He started walking toward his car—a dark brown sedan, no doubt something the government furnished him with. He opened the door and pulled an oversize book from the passenger side, a road atlas. He flipped it open to a map of the whole country, then, with a pen he'd taken from his pocket, made some dots on the cities they'd been talking about. He held up the marked map for her to see.

"It makes half of a circle," he said. "And look what's in the center of that circle. Or at least near the center. Hope, Illinois."

Carolyn went cold all over, and it had nothing to do with the temperature outside. She felt her stomach flip-flop inside her, and she thought for a moment she might be sick. She knew what was coming.

"He's right here, Carolyn. Or somewhere close by. He's been here the whole time, and we're going to find him."

Chapter 12

Carolyn didn't want to believe it, but the logic in it told her it was true. The man was probably right here—if not in Hope, at least within twenty or thirty miles of town.

It was so clear, once Drew plotted it on the map. Child molesters didn't just snatch one kid. That wasn't enough for them. In fact, as grim and as difficult as it was to believe, child molesters on average had more than a hundred victims before they were ever caught. So whoever had taken Annie had probably taken other children, as well.

Drew showed Carolyn the pattern, not only the locations where the children were taken, but the timing of the disappearances. Annie's ten years ago. Another six years ago, then one three years ago, then one a year and a half ago. Now Sara Parker. Either the man was getting more confident of his ability to get away with it, or whatever urges drove him on were getting stronger, because he was waiting less and less time between abductions. And that fit with what they knew about the kind of person who grabbed little kids off the streets. They grew more desperate as time went on and had less and less control over their urges.

She and Drew walked around downtown until they found a fax machine they could use, then called her friend Brian at Hope House and had him fax the most pertinent information on the other missing girls, so that Drew could have it right away.

He called the FBI office in Chicago and had someone there pick up the information from Brian and cross-check it with the FBI's own files. As big and as powerful as the FBI was, it was woefully behind in its efforts in computerization, and that was one place where Carolyn's organization could help.

As she and Drew sat in the back corner booth at the local coffee shop, scanning the records, he pointed out to her one other reason he believed the man who took Annie was nearby. The man had been careful. Before Sara Parker's disappearance, he'd snatched children from three different states—Illinois, Kentucky and Ohio—but still from within a relatively small area.

Drew thought he'd done that so that he didn't have to travel any farther than necessary with the children, because he was coming from somewhere nearby, either in Indiana or in Illinois. He'd wanted to cross state lines because, with children missing from four different states, it meant that initially four different state law-enforcement agencies, plus local sheriff's or city police departments, were looking for him.

Criminals were smart enough to know how piecemeal crime-fighting efforts could be. They knew, for instance, that they could use the same method of operation for a crime in one town, then the same one in three or four other towns or counties around it. Most likely, it would be a while before four separate law-enforcement agencies caught on to the fact that they were chasing the same crook.

''I can't believe he's been somewhere around here the whole time,'' she said. ''What do we do now?''

Drew put down his cup of coffee. ''We go over every bit of paperwork we can find on the cases, interview the people involved all over again, then try to find something that links these five kids together. Find out what they could have in common that would have brought this man into their lives. Then we find the bastard.''

And then what? she wanted to add. What happens once you do find him? But she wasn't sure she was up to hearing the answer.

''I need to go,'' he said. ''We've still got people wandering around in the woods near the place where Sara Parker was found, and one of them is my boss. I need to check in with him and tell him what we've found.''

He stood up, but she didn't. ''I think I'll have another cup of coffee, and then I have to check in with my aunt and make sure my mother's all right.''

''She's home from the hospital,'' he stated.

Carolyn nodded. ''Since yesterday afternoon.''

''She knows I'm here about Annie?''

''And that you know about Billy.''

He drummed his fingers on the edge of the table. ''I don't know what you can tell her.''

She didn't even look at him then. She couldn't. Not two days ago, he'd been telling her how much he'd missed her, how he wished he'd never left her. Last night...he thought last night was nothing but a mistake, that loving her didn't change anything. So she didn't even look at him now. She couldn't.

''Carolyn,'' he said. ''I know your mother's worried, and she's probably looking for some kind of answers. But I'm looking for them, too, and I haven't come up with any yet. So she'll just have to wait.''

''The doctors...'' Carolyn began. ''They're worried about her emotional state right now.''

"And what about Billy? Grace is mothering our son, too. And as far as he's concerned, his father died six months ago, and she's all he's got left. Have you thought about that?"

"Yes."

"How do you think that makes him feel?" Drew asked. "I saw him after Grace collapsed, and he was scared to death. He thought he was going to lose her, and he didn't think he'd have anyone else to take care of him if that happened."

"I talked with him. I told him he'd have me, and he understands."

"But he doesn't know he'd still have his real mother *and* father. Maybe he needs to know. Have you ever thought about it that way?"

"Yes, I have." She tried to keep her voice down, but it was difficult. She knew very well what he was getting at. "I've thought about it a lot since my father died, and even more so since my mother was taken to the hospital. But what can I do? Billy thinks she's his mother, and I've trained myself to think of her that way, too. I can't just ask her to give him back to me."

Drew kept silent.

"Please sit down, Drew. Just for a minute." Even though they'd been quiet, they were attracting more attention than she'd have liked. And she had to make him understand this one point, at least.

He had his back to the rest of the place, but now he turned and looked around. People quickly turned away, but it was clear that they had been the center of attention. Carolyn felt her cheeks burn at the idea. Soon the whole town would know that she and Drew had been arguing over coffee this morning.

"Let's get out of here," he offered.

Carolyn thought it a much better suggestion than hers. She grabbed her purse while he threw a dollar on the table for the waitress, then hurried to the door, trying not to meet anyone's eyes as they left.

On the street, she didn't know where to turn. She couldn't take him to her mother's house, because there was no telling what Grace would say to him. And she wasn't going back to his room at the bed-and-breakfast, not after last night.

"In the car," he said, a hand on her back guiding her to it. He opened the passenger door and urged her inside. He moved to the other side and got in, as well. Carolyn could almost feel Drew's warmth as he sat beside her.

This was impossible. And, unfortunately for her, this was what her life had become—one impossible situation after another.

They drove for almost fifteen minutes, ending up at one of their old hideouts, a deserted country road that came to a dead end at the river.

"Sorry," he said. "I didn't know where else to go."

She couldn't have begun to count the number of times they'd either sat near the shore or sat here in a car, watching the water rushing by. Sometimes, she would wish they could just jump in and let the current take them somewhere—anywhere except this impossible town, where they wouldn't have to face her parents' disapproval of Drew, where no one knew his father was a bad-tempered drunk or judged Drew based solely on that fact.

"Okay." He put the car in park and pulled the emergency brake on, but left the motor running. It was getting colder by the minute. "Tell me whatever you think you have to tell me about your mother and our son."

"He's not *ours* anymore." She figured that was as good a place to start as any. She could have come at it from a much less confrontational position, but they would have ended up at this point sooner or later, anyway. And he'd given her the perfect opening.

"All right," he said. "If you want to look at it that way, he never was *our* son."

She chose to ignore that and focus on what she had to say. "I mean, my mother's raised him from the time he came home from the hospital, when he was three days old, and I can't just go to her and tell her I want Billy back, like he was some piece of property that belonged to me. He's a little boy, and he loves her. She's the only mother he's ever known."

Drew tensed beside her. She could tell that he was working hard not to let this turn into a full-blown argument.

"Believe me," he said, "I understand that all too well. But you can't ask me to walk away and never see him again, never even know where he is or what he's doing or how he looks. You can't ask me to do that."

So there they were at another standoff. Carolyn wondered what she could do to make this situation better without hurting anyone. And it was clear that she couldn't. Either way, someone was going to be hurt.

She wanted out of the car, away from Drew, just for a moment. She was getting ready to go when his hand touched her arm, just enough to get her attention, then withdrew. Carolyn looked up into his face, saw his anguished expression, saw what could only be tears in his beautiful brown eyes.

"How could you give him up?" he asked.

In an instant, she was shaking. Tears filled her own eyes, and she had to hold her hand over her mouth to keep from crying out.

He hadn't asked in anger, hadn't accused her of anything. Maybe she could have handled either of those easier than his calmly voiced question.

"Make me understand that," he said huskily. "Because I need to understand. How in the world could you give him up?"

She swallowed hard and took her hand away. Somewhere deep inside, the door she'd forced shut years ago, the one that protected the most vulnerable part of her, was opening again. The pain she'd stored there was as fresh and as strong as it had been that day she first held Billy in her arms, the day she said her goodbyes to him and handed him over to her mother. She'd known she could never go back on that decision, that once it was made, she couldn't second-guess herself or try to change the situation.

She'd held that pain inside all these years, only to have him ask her to unleash it again. True, she owed him that much. But still, the pain was staggering.

Where could she start? How could she explain? How would he understand, when she couldn't herself?

"I...I knew you weren't coming back. I knew how much you wanted to get out of this town, and I didn't think I'd ever see you again."

She risked one quick glance at his face. He'd lowered his eyes, shielding them from view, and she decided to do the same. It was easier not to look at him and see how much this hurt him, as well.

"I didn't even suspect I was pregnant for a long time, because...we were careful." She'd been on the Pill since right after their first time together. "But after Annie died, everything got crazy. I was so torn up. I had trouble keeping anything in my stomach for a few weeks, and I didn't even realize that if the food was coming back up, the pills were, too. And I didn't think..."

"You couldn't stand to have me touch you anymore," he finished for her.

"No, Drew, it was never that."

"It was that last time, wasn't it? Right before I left. I thought...I thought then we had a chance. We finally got to be together again, and then afterward...I don't know, Carolyn. What happened afterward?"

She'd just fallen apart. She'd cried until she thought she'd never be able to stop. She'd felt guilty about every bit of pleasure she'd found with him when her sister was out there somewhere, God-knew-what happening to her. The guilt had just been too much.

"I thought about Annie," she told him. "I thought that if I hadn't wanted so much to be with you that day, then Annie wouldn't have disappeared. I thought it was my fault, and that made it even worse, making love with you, when she was gone.

"I know it's not logical," she rushed on. "But that's how I felt. I thought I deserved to lose you. That I had no right to be happy with you, when that's what made us lose Annie. In a way, I thought I deserved to lose you, and to lose Billy, too."

"Aw, Carolyn..." he said.

"I did," she admitted. "And I was so scared to keep him. I thought that if I ever loved him, the way I'd loved Annie, and then lost him... How would I have handled that? I was scared to love him, Drew. I cut myself off from him and my whole family, went to school at Northwestern, and tried to pretend I hadn't left anything behind when I went to Chicago. I tried so hard not to think about him, not to see him, not to even look at the pictures of him that my mother sent.

"But I couldn't do that. I loved him from the very beginning, the first time I looked into that beautiful little face of his and saw so much of you there. It was so hard to look at him and see you and think about how much we'd lost."

She stopped for a minute to stare out the window at the water rushing by, and to think through the barrage of emotions this had set loose inside her. She wanted Drew to understand.

"I wanted him so badly," she said. "But at the same time, I was frightened of the responsibility. Someone had to keep him safe and happy, and I didn't think I could do that. After all, look what happened to Annie.

"But I couldn't let him totally go, either. I thought about adoption with some couple I'd never seen and would never know, but I couldn't bring myself to do that. It would have been too much like losing Annie.

"And then my mother started talking about having a baby in the house again. She was scared, too, but…it sort of brought her back to life again. She had a reason to go on, and she wanted him so badly.

"It seemed like the perfect solution for all of us. I'd still get to see him. I could watch him grow up, and I'd always know that he was all right. And he's been happy here, Drew. My parents have done more to provide a good home for him than I ever could have."

She waited for some reaction from him, but he said nothing. There was nothing left to do to explain away what she'd done, except . . .

"Drew, I was seventeen years old, and I did the best thing I knew to do. You have to understand that."

He didn't say anything, and she was scared to even look at him, so she just kept talking. "I knew almost right away that I'd made a mistake in giving him up."

"Then why did you go through with it?" he asked.

"I knew it was a mistake for *me*—not for *him*. I think he had as much love and as much joy and security as a little boy could have. And I had to think about what was best for him, not what I wanted for myself."

"But it's different now," he said. "Your father's gone. Your mother… Can you imagine what it will do to her if we find Annie's body? Have you thought about that? And if anything happens to her, Billy's whole world falls apart. What about that?"

"I don't know. I don't have any answers. If I did, I would have told you. I'm worried. I have been ever since my father died. And I've tried to talk to my mother about it, but she won't listen. All we've done is argue about Billy. It got so bad a couple of months ago that she asked me to stay away until I got over this.''

Of course, she hadn't gotten over the need to be with her son, any more than Drew ever would.

And now he'd always blame her, or at least resent her, for what had happened. She could see that all too clearly.

That was the reason his loving her didn't solve anything. All it did was make this situation more difficult for both of them.

"I guess it is hopeless, after all," she said.

He didn't argue with her. They sat there in the car, watching the water roll by, and they didn't say anything. Finally, he backed up the car and headed for town.

Drew stood by the window of his room at the bed-and-breakfast watching the small downtown area empty of people as they left their jobs and made their way home. It was shortly after five o'clock and this late in the fall, the sky was starting to get dark earlier. Already the light was half-gone.

He turned away from the window for a moment, his eyes falling carelessly across the room, stumbling over the sight of the bed.

He didn't see how he could spend another night in this room, in that bed, in the same town with Carolyn, and yet not with her. He couldn't help but smile at the irony of how he'd wanted to leave his impression on her the night before, to reach down to her soul and mark her forever as his. Yet he'd done just the opposite. He'd forever imprinted the feel and the taste and the smell of her on his brain.

He'd taken the ten-year-old memories of a teenage boy, ones he'd tried so hard over the years to dismiss as adolescent fantasies that couldn't possibly have been as good as he remembered, and replaced them with the all-too-clear experiences of a man. The man who'd been obsessed with his recollections of a teenage girl for a decade now knew her as a woman, a beautiful, vulnerable, sensual woman.

She had branded him for life. He didn't have a chance in hell of forgetting her now. And he didn't see how he could ever have her.

If anything, the situation was getting worse. He saw nothing but the hopelessness of it now. They were going to clash over Billy sometime in the very near future, maybe forever. He didn't see how they could ever resolve the situation without ruining any chance they had of happiness.

Because he would not walk away from his son, and that was what she wanted him to do. He was sure that was what her mother wanted him to do, and he could see Carolyn caught in the middle. If her mother wanted to, she could poison Billy's mind against the two of them. Drew wasn't sure the woman was vindictive enough to do that, but it was possible.

After all, she was the person Billy knew and trusted above all others. If he asked Carolyn to take his side against her mother, he'd be asking her to risk losing what contact she had now with Billy. She'd never do that.

He could fight, in court, if he chose. He probably had some sort of legal right to the boy, but he wanted more than a piece of paper and some court-ordered visitation. He wanted Billy to know him and trust him, to depend upon him. He wanted his son.

No court could give him that, and he would never put Billy through the fight.

So they were at an impasse.

He had no idea what to do.

And he missed Carolyn already.

As always when he couldn't do anything else, Drew worked. It steadied him. It challenged him. It gave him an outlet for his energy, and something to occupy his mind.

He started searching through the faxed documents he'd received from Hope House and read summaries on the three missing girls.

It was possible, he decided, that these might be linked to Sara Parker's kidnapping—and to Annie's. He would have to wait until tomorrow to review all the documents, but it did seem possible.

He had to find a common link. What had connected the five little girls? If they'd all been taken by the same man, how had he come across them?

What could these five little girls have had in common?

His ruminations were interrupted by the ringing of the phone. He grabbed the receiver, his mind still looking for a connection between the girls, and answered absently, "Drew Delaney."

"Mr. Delaney?" a woman's voice asked tentatively. "This is Jill Parker...Sara's mother?"

"Yes," he said. The poor woman still sounded shell-shocked at all that had happened to her and her child.

"You said to call...if Sara remembered anything...or if anything out of the ordinary happened."

"Yes."

"Well, I wasn't sure if I should bother you. I mean, I'm not sure if it's important or not, but...Sara was just so upset today."

"It's no bother at all, Mrs. Parker," he said, his instincts telling him something significant had occurred. Maybe he was about to get a break for a change. "What happened to upset her?"

"She went back to school today. We weren't sure if she should go so soon, but the psychiatrist told us to try to make things as normal as possible for her. And it was class-picture day. We didn't want her to miss getting her picture taken with her classmates."

"Go on," Drew urged, the adrenaline starting to rush through his veins.

"She, uh... I don't know how else to put it—she just fell apart. Her class got in front of the camera, and the flash went off, and she just started screaming."

"Why?" he asked. "Did someone say something to her? Did she see someone she recognized?"

"I'm not sure. I stayed with her at school the first thirty minutes or so, and when she seemed fine, I left. So I wasn't there when it happened, and it took us forever to get her calmed down enough for her to talk about it."

"What did her teacher say? She was fine until the flash went off? Or was she edgy before that?"

"I'm not sure," Mrs. Parker replied.

"Think about it. It's important."

He thought back himself to when he'd arrived in Pritchard, Indiana. When he first saw Sara Parker, she'd been agitated, nervous, frightened, but quiet and composed. He'd thought at first it was shock, but after spending a couple of hours with her, trying to question her and waiting for her parents to arrive, he'd seen how much self-control the little girl had. She was one tough kid.

If she'd ended up screaming her head off at school, there was a reason.

And he would find the reason, because it could lead him to Sara's kidnapper—and Annie's.

"Think, Mrs. Parker. The man is still out there somewhere, and we have to find him. Was she all right in the classroom this morning, after you left?"

"Yes. Her teacher said she was a little quiet, but otherwise fine."

"Why don't you give me the teacher's name?" he said. "And her phone number, if you have it."

"Of course, if you think it's important."

"I definitely think it's important. How's Sara now?"

"She didn't move from my side all afternoon. She's asleep on the couch beside me right now."

Mrs. Parker gave him the teacher's name and number, and Drew assured her that she'd done the right thing by calling him. He told her that someone from the Bureau, and probably the psychiatrist who'd spoken with Sara before, would be returning to talk to her regarding the incident at school.

Impatient, he made a series of calls to make sure that happened, then got Sara's teacher on the phone. Someone else would most likely cover the same ground with her tomorrow, but he wasn't willing to wait that long. The woman was still shaken from what had happened that morning with Sara.

"Think carefully," he told her. "When did Sara start to get upset?"

"She screamed when the flash went off."

"And before that?"

"Well...now that you mention it, she wasn't sure if she wanted to have her picture taken. When she saw the camera, she held back a little, then came and stood by me. I told her she could be beside me in the picture, and that seemed to help. But when the photographer turned up the lights, that scared her, too. And then after that, when the flash went off, she was absolutely hysterical."

Drew took a moment to digest this information. He'd taken Sara's picture himself with an old Polaroid, right after he got to her that day. She'd definitely been upset when he photographed her, but he'd thought it was simply a delayed reaction, considering all she'd been through.

And now she'd done the same thing when someone else took her picture.

"Did she shy away from the photographer?" he asked.

"I don't know. I don't believe she got that close to him. It was a group picture, and there are twenty-two children in the class."

"Who was the photographer?"

"I don't know his name. It was one of those school-photography companies. They come to school every year in the fall."

"Sara was at your school last year?"

"Yes," she said.

"The same man came this year who took your school pictures last year?"

"I'm not sure, but it was the same company. It has some cutesy name, with a phonetic spelling. It's probably on the back of my copy of last year's class picture."

"Could you get it for me?" he asked.

"Of course. Just a minute."

It couldn't be that simple, he thought. A photographer would be in constant contact with children, and if he worked for a company that kept him on the road, shooting groups of schoolchildren, he'd be around thousands of kids each year.

Of course, if the man had just snatched Sara Parker last week, he'd be a fool to come to her school today and take her picture again.

Not that some criminals weren't fools, Drew reminded himself. But this didn't sound right to him—the guy coming back so soon. He would have known Sara went to school there. The odds were overwhelmingly against the man having picked her at random off the street. More than likely, he'd followed her, stalked her, before he grabbed her.

Still, his instincts told him this was important, that this was what would lead him to Sara Parker's kidnapper, and to Annie's.

"Mr. Delaney," the teacher said. "I have last year's photo right here. It was taken by a company called School Pix."

"Is there an address?"

"Chicago, Illinois. That's all."

He thanked the woman, assured her that she had been very helpful and made rash promises that he would definitely find the man who'd taken little Sara Parker. Then he was dialing Chicago Information. They had hundreds of agents in the city, and he should have sent one of them to this company in person, but he couldn't wait that long. Besides, it was nearly six, and there was no way he was going to wait until the place opened for business again tomorrow.

He was ready to bang his head against the wall when he got an answering machine telling him School Pix had indeed already closed.

Drew sat down and thought about what he'd learned. It didn't seem rational that the same man would abduct a little girl one week and show up at her school the next to photograph her. Besides, if he'd been there to take her picture, where had he come into contact with her before? When he'd taken pictures the year before? Drew supposed it was possible.

On the other hand, what if it wasn't that particular photographer who'd frightened Sara today? Her teacher said she'd freaked after the flashbulb went off, and that she'd seemed edgy from the time the class got to the room with the camera and the lights.

What if Sara had been upset not by that man in particular, but rather by the fact that he was a photographer?

Or simply because he wanted to take her picture? After all, she'd gotten upset when Drew took her picture, too.

Either explanation had possibilities. If the kidnapper just happened to be someone who got off by taking pictures of little kids he snatched from the streets, Drew had a long way to go. But if his man was a professional photographer, one who happened to take pictures of thousands of kids a year when he visited their schools, then Drew was on to something. He had a real lead, a fighting chance. Maybe his promise about finding Sara Parker's kidnapper hadn't been so rash, after all.

He started pacing the room then. At one point, he happened to glance out the window and across the street, to the school Billy attended, the same one Annie had gone to. Right next door to it was the junior high she'd attended. He wondered who'd taken her picture when she was there.

Drew was out the door in seconds. It was almost six, probably too late to get into the building, but there were still a few cars in the school's parking lot.

He found one of the doors at the junior high's main entrance still open, followed the signs directing him to the office. Luck was with him. A woman was still inside.

Drew introduced himself, and discovered she was the principal. He told her he was with the Bureau and showed her his credentials.

"I just need a moment of your time," he promised her when she informed him she was just about to leave. "Someone comes into the school every year to photograph the children?"

"Yes," she said. She was a matronly-looking woman in her fifties with salt-and-pepper hair.

"What's the name of the company?" he asked, having trouble getting out the words. This case meant too much to him, and he shouldn't be working on it. An agent needed a clear head to do his job, and this kind of emotional attachment only interfered with that. No way should he be working this one. No way was he going to let it go.

"Off the top of my head, I'm not sure," the woman said. "I could check for you."

"School Pix?" he asked. "Does that sound familiar?"

"Oh, yes," she replied. "We've used them for years."

It might not mean anything, he told himself. If the company did indeed do business all over the Midwest, then it wouldn't be all that surprising to find that all the little girls on his list had had their picture taken by that same company at one time or another. Still, it was the only link he had so far.

"Is there anything else I can do for you?" the woman said.

"I'm sorry." He'd been lost in thought. "Do you know how long you've done business with that company? Would they have been coming here ten or eleven years ago?"

"Maybe," the woman said. "I've only been the principal here for six, and I think we've been using them the whole time I've been here. I could have someone check for you, in the morning. Honestly, I wouldn't know where to begin to look up that information."

He was disappointed for a moment. Then he remembered. There was a much simpler way for him to check this out, and an agent always had to remember to take the simplest, quickest path to the information he needed.

He remembered sitting in Carolyn's childhood home, with those pictures of their son on the walls—and next to them, what he'd bet were school pictures of Annie.

Chapter 13

He hadn't expected it to take a confrontation with Grace McKay to get him inside the door that evening. Maybe he'd been hoping for one, eventually, but he hadn't visualized dealing with her so soon—not at that moment, when his mind was racing ninety miles a minute with all the things he needed to do to check out his lead.

Mrs. McKay opened the door, looking much better than when he'd seen her in the hospital the day before—looking, in fact, like a woman ready to do battle.

He didn't even get the first word out of his mouth before she came at him. With a look that could have turned water to ice, she told him, "You're not welcome in this house."

From behind her, he heard Carolyn telling her mother to stay put, that she'd get the door. She'd find out soon enough that it was too late.

And then he heard Billy calling to her. Was the boy coming to the door, as well?

Drew didn't know, and he couldn't risk that. He was mad enough about the injustices of ten long years to grab Grace McKay by the arm, pull her out the door and close it behind her.

"Don't you dare," he said to her, his manner as menacing as any he'd used on crooks from coast to coast. "Don't you dare try to make my son think I'm not welcome here, or that he has any reason to be afraid of me or to dislike me."

"You are not—"

"Don't you dare."

She glared at him, and he glared right back. This woman who, from the start, had never liked him. This woman who had judged him solely on the fact that his father was a loud, no-good drunk, who had once, in the midst of the madness after Annie disappeared, pointed her finger at him and told him and half the town that it was all his fault.

He had never come so close to wanting to hit a woman. Never. He didn't even like admitting that ugly truth to himself, didn't like seeing how low he'd sunk in the midst of this mess. But he would not allow her to poison Billy's mind against him. That was his bottom line, and she was going to have to live with it.

As for Grace McKay, she seemed to have been running on bravado alone. He watched as it all deserted her, leaving her once again looking older than her forty-seven years, more tired than he remembered, more vulnerable.

He had the impression then that she wasn't the monster he liked to paint her as, that she was nothing but a mother who, long ago, had lost the most precious thing a parent has to lose—her child.

And that, for now, she was doing what any mother would do—fiercely trying to protect another child. He couldn't fault her for that instinct, and he felt more than a little ashamed of himself for coming on like a steamroller. And he had to admit that he'd want the mother of his child to react in just this way if anyone ever threatened that child.

Clearly, she saw him as a threat. That was what he had to change. Raving at her like a madman wasn't going to do him any good at all.

"Look," he said, backing up a step or two, "I'm not going to hurt him."

He would have gone over the whole thing with her—the whole directionless mishmash of feelings threatening to choke him at any moment—but he was certain it was pointless. He was sure Carolyn had told her everything already, and he doubted the woman would believe anything he said, anyway.

"I'm not even here about Billy right now," he said. Surely that was something Grace McKay could understand. "It's about Annie."

Quickly, remembering what had happened the last time he told her that, he braced himself to catch her in case she swooned. But the woman stood her ground. She was a shade paler in the glow of the porch light, and she froze for a moment, but then she nodded as she tried to take in the news.

She didn't say anything, didn't ask anything. He didn't see the point in making any explanations at this point. Most likely, she didn't want to know the details. And maybe that was for the best, given what he knew about the woman's emotional state.

"I just need to see some of your old pictures of her," he said. "That's all."

Her eyes dropped to the floor, and then she hung her head and brushed a hand across her cheeks. When she looked up at him again, she was composed, almost resigned.

"Come inside. I'll get them."

She pulled the door open and left him to follow her inside. He stood in the entranceway, feeling as awkward as he had the first time he came to pick up Carolyn for a date.

Grace McKay walked to the doorway that led to the kitchen, and he heard her asking Billy to go to the next-door neighbor's and get some eggs the woman had promised to lend them.

Carolyn stood in the hallway to the right, watching them, not saying a word.

The back door closed with a thud. Mrs. McKay turned to him. "Billy doesn't need to hear this," she said, and he couldn't argue with that.

"What is it?" Carolyn asked.

"It's about Annie." He rushed on when he realized that would be just as upsetting to her as the thought of him coming here about Billy. "I just need to check out something—some old pictures."

"What kind?" her mother said.

"School pictures, the latest ones you have that were taken at her school."

Carolyn walked across the room to him. "You found something."

"Maybe. I'll know in a minute."

Her mother returned with a gold-framed photo of a beautiful blond-haired child. "This was taken in the fall, about nine months before she disappeared."

Drew pulled the cardboard backing off it and carefully extracted the photo from the frame. The light in the hallway was weak, and the print on the back was faint with age.

He walked farther into the room and held it under the light of the lamp. It was faint, but it was there.

School Pix.

He'd been an agent for four years now, he'd done six years in the army before that, and he'd seen things that

horrified him. But he'd never had such an emotional reaction to a piece of evidence before.

It sent chills through him, and waves of revulsion and
nausea, as well. He didn't want to touch the photo, didn't
want to turn it over and see Annie's smiling face, didn't
want to think about what this monster had done to her.

He had the definite impression of evil encompassed in
this mix of paper and chemicals that he held in his hand.
He could feel its presence, as clearly as he'd felt the cold air
outside.

He'd found something. Every instinct he possessed told
him so. But could he stand to follow this lead where it took
him? He'd known from the start of this that there wouldn't
be a happy ending for Annie. Not after ten years.

And he wasn't sure what he'd hoped to accomplish in
taking this on. Oh, there was the job, and it was important to him. There was the need to get this pervert off the
streets. But surely he'd been looking to ease something
within himself, as well, and to give something back to
Carolyn and her family.

He wanted to bring Annie back to them. He wanted to
absolve himself of some of that irrational guilt he'd carried around all these years. He wanted this to be his gift to
the McKays, wanted it to buy him something precious and
rare—another chance with Carolyn. And, now, a chance
with Billy, as well.

But now that the moment was right here—the beginning of the end of the mystery of Annie McKay's disappearance, for he was sure it was within his reach—he didn't
see what finding Annie's body would accomplish now.

He could only imagine what it would cost them all, the
pain it would bring back, the anguish of likely finding out
in grim detail exactly how she'd died.

Why? he thought. Why had he started this in the first
place?

"What is it, Drew?" Carolyn asked.

He dropped the picture, and the revulsion that he'd felt, that sickening impression of pure evil, began to dissipate. "It may be nothing," he cautioned. "Maybe just coincidence."

"You don't believe that," Mrs. McKay said, coming to stand beside Carolyn.

"It's the photo company—this one that specializes in school photos. The same company that took that photo of Annie also took one of Sara Parker."

He watched as the two women moved closer together, as Carolyn put her arm around her mother. Maybe the rift between them wasn't as big as she'd feared. Or maybe this would bring them closer again.

"It may be nothing," he repeated. "Supposedly this company takes photos all over the Midwest."

"What are you going to do now?" Carolyn asked.

"I'm going to Chicago in the morning, to see if they photographed any of those missing girls who showed up on the search your friend did for us."

He thought about all the other things that the three of them needed to say to one another, thought about how impossible it still seemed to be, then became even more determined to stick to business. For now, he had to. It just might be the thing that kept him sane.

"I have to go," he said, before he could change his mind. "I'll let you know as soon as I find out anything."

And then he turned around and left.

He was just letting down his guard, letting the fatigue get to him, letting the adrenaline run down, when he stepped onto the front porch and found Billy heading up the steps.

"Ah, dammit..." he muttered in an aside. Not tonight. Not now. He'd been through too much already.

"Hi," the boy said hesitantly, then smiled tentatively.

This close to him now, Drew saw in an instant what he couldn't believe he'd missed earlier. The shape of his face, the jawline in particular, the eyes, even the way he walked—the kid was him all over again. It was amazing he hadn't seen it before, even if he hadn't been looking.

"Hey, Billy," he said, "whatcha doing?"

"I had to go get some eggs from next door." He held them up for Drew to see, then stood there waiting—for what, Drew couldn't imagine.

"I just had to talk to your mother for a minute," he said.

"About Annie?"

"Yes."

Billy smiled then. "Carolyn said you're gonna find her."

"I'm looking for her." He wasn't going to start making this kid promises he couldn't keep.

"Here?" he said. "'Cause my mama says she's in heaven with my dad. And we can't go there. Not yet. So I don't know how you can look for her. If she's in heaven."

Oh, great, Drew thought. His first real conversation with his son, and the kid wanted to debate philosophy and logic with him. He didn't stand a chance.

Drew shook his head, feeling at a total loss as to how to handle the situation. "We just want to find out for sure what happened to her when she disappeared."

Billy nodded, looking a little sad, a little lost, seeming to be waiting for something from Drew that he didn't even understand.

All the while, Drew was battling with himself. More than anything, he wanted to hold this little boy in his arms and promise to keep him safe from anything and everything that would ever try to hurt him.

It was such a crazy damned world these days, especially if you were a kid. He was beginning to understand the enormity of that task—keeping him safe—and to see what Carolyn had meant about worrying over the staggering responsibility of making sure Billy was indeed safe.

Surely that would have scared him to death ten years ago; it frightened him even today, when the responsibility wasn't his, but Carolyn's and her mother's.

Billy, he wondered, what in the world is going to happen to us?

"Drew?" the kid asked.

"Yes."

"Are you going to catch the man who took her?"

"Yes." He had more reason now to do that than he'd ever had before. He had a child of his own to keep safe.

"Carolyn said you catch all sorts of bad guys." Billy seemed to like that idea. "Do you have a gun? A real one?"

Drew actually laughed then. He'd never thought he'd resort to using the fact that he carried a weapon to impress a child.

"Billy," Carolyn said from behind him. Drew hadn't even known she was there. "That's enough for tonight. And we need those eggs in the kitchen."

Billy turned back to Drew. "Will you show it to me someday?"

"Someday," he promised.

"Cool." He headed for the door.

"Careful of the eggs," Carolyn said, holding the door open for him.

Drew watched him disappear into the kitchen, hating to see the little guy go. He was hungry for the sight of him and the sound of his voice. He had years to catch up on.

"He likes you," Carolyn said, and he wondered if she knew how much he needed to believe that.

"Because I carry a gun and chase bad guys?"

"No, he liked you before he even knew that." She folded her arms in front of her in a vain effort to ward off the cold.

"I want more than that," he said, fighting the urge to draw her against him and let her warm herself with his body heat.

"So do I," she replied.

Did she think she wasn't going to get it? Was that the message? That he wasn't the only one unhappy with this situation? He thought again about how pointless arguing about this was, how pointless it was to yearn for things he couldn't have. It hadn't been twenty-four hours since he and Carolyn had been together, finally, after all this time. Less than a day since that all-consuming need had driven him on to have her, blinding him to all the reasons he should resist her. And that had only made things even more complicated than they already were.

It had made it nearly impossible just to be here with her in the darkness and the semiprivacy of the porch and not take her in his arms. It had made him more frustrated than he'd ever been in his life, because he, who made a living solving puzzles and finding solutions to seemingly impossible things, couldn't solve this—the thing that meant more to him than anything.

He'd paused there at the top of the steps, and she'd stopped about five feet away. Even from that distance, he felt the pull that urged him closer. And he couldn't give in to it.

He knew too well that, barring a miracle, he would be forced to give her up. He didn't need one more embrace, one more kiss, one more stolen hour of the night with Carolyn, to remind him of her. As it was, he'd never be able to forget her.

"I have work to do," he said, forcing himself away from her. "I'll call you tomorrow, as soon as I know anything."

And once again he turned and walked away.

Carolyn watched him go down the steps and out the front gate. She fought the urge to call out to him, to reach out her hand and hang on to him for dear life. Once, he had been her whole life.

And she wasn't going to lose him again.

He could go on and on about how impossible this whole mess was, about how they'd never find a solution that all of them could live with, one that wouldn't hurt Billy but would still let them all take a part in raising him. He could throw up as many roadblocks as he could think of, and it wouldn't matter to her.

She'd found her bottom line, and it was very simple.

She wasn't going to lose him again.

Her mother was waiting for her when she came inside. Carolyn glanced to the left, to the open doorway to the kitchen, and saw Billy sitting at the table, talking excitedly with her Aunt Ellen. They were making cookies— their excuse for needing him to leave the house earlier to get eggs from next door. Warily Carolyn turned back to her mother.

"Is he gone?" Grace said, in a tone that left Carolyn feeling utterly weary.

"What do you mean, is he gone? He's not the enemy, Mother."

"He wants to take Billy away from us," she said.

"Did he tell you that?"

"He threatened me."

That Carolyn absolutely couldn't believe. "How?"

"He grabbed me, pulled me outside, and told me I'd better not ever say one word against him to Billy. Or else."

Trouble was, Carolyn didn't think she could trust her mother not to bad-mouth Drew to Billy. It would be totally unfair, both to Drew and to Billy, and her mother was normally a fair-minded woman. But she was scared now, and desperate. Desperate people, especially mothers guarding their children, would do anything.

But then, Carolyn was a mother, too. And she, too, was guarding her own child.

"I'm so sick of this," she said. "I would have told you the same thing. You'd better not ever say anything to make Billy dislike Drew. Not ever. I won't let you do that. And you know Drew won't."

Her mother backed down a fraction. "I knew that boy would be nothing but trouble from the minute you first brought him home. I knew it."

Carolyn tried to hold it in. She loved her mother, honestly she did. And her mother loved her. They seldom fought. But she couldn't let that go unanswered.

"You'd better be thankful I did bring Drew home that first time. Otherwise, you wouldn't have a son right now. Did you ever think of that, Mother?"

"Carolyn—"

"No," she said. "You listen to me for a change. You were never fair to him, not from the start. And it wasn't like you and Daddy to judge people because of where they came from or how much money their parents made. So I don't know why you were ever so hard on Drew, or so unfair."

"He wasn't right for you," her mother said.

"How did you know? And how could you know better than I did who was right for me?"

"He was trouble right from the start."

Carolyn shook her head, the frustration eating at her, the unfairness making her want to scream. "He was good to me. He was kind and caring and loving. And if he seemed a little hard-edged to you, it's because this town, and you along with it, couldn't quite forgive him for being his father's son."

She was burning now. Only the fact that Billy was in the other room kept her under some semblance of control. "And if you're going to judge someone by his father, and Drew's no good, then what do you think that makes Billy?"

"Don't be ridiculous," her mother said. "I didn't mean that at all. I just ... I knew he wasn't right for you. I knew that from the start."

Carolyn figured it was hopeless then. She might as well get this all out in the open. "Drew wasn't right for me?" she said. "That's funny. I've been looking for someone to take his place for almost ten years now, and in all that time, no one's come close. I love him, Mother. I've missed him. I've needed him. I'm not going to lose him again."

"You can't do that," her mother said. "If the two of you get together again, if he's always around here..." She turned and looked back at Billy, who was still sitting at the table. "You can't do that to me. Or to Billy."

"I can't give him up again, not if he'll still have me, after the way I lied to him and the way I robbed him of his son."

Her mother looked honestly shocked. "And you think, if the two of you get back together again, things will change?" she said to Carolyn. "You think you're going to come back and take Billy away from me then? Is that what you think?"

"No, Mother, that's not what I think at all. But you need to understand, I'm not giving Drew up. He's going to be a part of this family, and you might as well get used to it."

"I won't," she said. "I can't do that."

"He doesn't want to hurt Billy. I trust him not to do that, but don't push him. If you make him mad enough, if you try to keep him away from Billy, or if he finds out you've said anything to Billy about him that makes the boy mistrust him, then I don't know what Drew will do."

Her mother looked stunned at the ugly tone this argument had taken. Carolyn was just as surprised, just as upset. But this argument had been brewing for days, and all these things had to be said. They all had to know where they stood.

"Remember what I told you about the courts," she told her mother. "Drew is Billy's biological father. He has a legal right to Billy, and if he goes to court, there's no telling what would happen."

"You said he wouldn't do that." Her mother's voice cracked, and Carolyn waited for the tears.

"I said I asked him not to do that, and he told me he understood that it would only hurt Billy in the end, and he doesn't want to do that. But if you push him, if you try to close him out of Billy's life totally, I can't tell you what he'll do."

"And you'd take his side, against your own mother?"

"Who said anything about taking sides?" Carolyn asked. "You make it sound like you two are enemies fighting a war, and if it ends up that way, we're all going to get hurt. Billy most of all."

"I won't let that happen," her mother said.

"Then you're going to have to stop thinking of Drew as the enemy. You're going to have to accept him as a part of our lives, and you can't growl at him every time he shows up at the door."

"I don't... I don't see how I can do that."

"You have to," Carolyn said. "For Billy's sake."

Carolyn sat up late that night. Eventually, she ended up in Annie's old room, talking to her sister. She held one of her favorite old pictures of Annie in front of her, held Annie's old stuffed dog in her lap and sat cross-legged on Annie's bed, with her back in the corner, so that she could see the whole room.

She did this in her apartment in Chicago at times, when she was feeling so depressed she couldn't get the words to come out. She stared at Annie's picture and had conversations with her little sister inside her head.

She did believe Annie was dead, and most of the time she believed there was more to this world than the things people on earth could see or touch or hear. If there was a better place somewhere, Annie was there.

Who knew? Maybe she was listening. Maybe she could help.

Drew said this whole thing was hopeless, and after talking with her mother tonight, Carolyn knew she was being naive in thinking that it wasn't.

She loved Drew and Billy and her mother. Why should it be so hard for her to love them all? It wasn't as if love were some finite quantity—that once you used yours, it was all gone. And she understood her mother's feeling threatened by Drew and his need to be a part of Billy's life. Carolyn had felt threatened by that, as well.

But if love was an infinite thing, then Billy had an endless supply. Loving Drew, letting him be a part of Billy's life, didn't have to take anything away from the woman he believed to be his mother. There was plenty of time and plenty of love inside that little boy for them all to share.

Why was that so hard for Drew and her mother to understand? Where had they gotten this idea that Billy could have one of them or the other, but not both?

It didn't have to be that way at all.

She explained it all to Annie—the whole sordid mess. And she cried a little bit more.

There had to be a way to convince her mother that Drew was a good person, that he wasn't going to take anything away from them, that he'd only add to Billy's life.

She had to find a way to do that. She—

The phone rang, sounding absurdly loud in the stillness of the house, where everyone but Carolyn had gone to bed hours ago.

She put down the photo of Annie and jumped off the bed, running for the nearest phone, the one in the hallway.

It was nearly eleven, and no one called here this late.

It must be Drew, she thought, and he must have some news. Otherwise, he wouldn't have called so late.

She managed to grab the phone in the middle of the second ring. "Hello."

"Carolyn."

It was him. She closed her eyes. "Where are you? You sound so far away. And what's wrong?"

He didn't ask how she knew anything was wrong, didn't pretend nothing was. "I couldn't stand to sleep on this before I found out anything else, so I drove to Chicago. I picked up those files your friend Brian had from Hope House, then came into the office," he said, plunging right in without giving her time to prepare at all. And she needed time to prepare for this. "I looked over the complete files on those other three missing kids, and they look like good leads. So I sent agents to see the kids' parents."

He sounded awful, his voice flat and devoid of all emotion. She knew the news was bad.

"They pulled their kids' pictures off the walls," he told her. "I can't imagine how the parents handled that."

But he could. He'd watched her mother do the very same thing, and it had hurt him just to watch it. She'd seen it so clearly. The work that he did had to nearly kill him at times. It was too important to him, the children were too important, for it not to haunt him.

"One of them was a match," he said. "Right there on the back of the photo—School Pix. But the other two hadn't ever had their pictures taken by that company, at least not recently, while they were at school."

"The company doesn't do anything but schools?" Carolyn said.

"I don't know. I still haven't talked with anyone from the company, but apparently, from what a couple of school people told me today, it's very specialized work. And the other two girls had pictures from a company called Watson's."

"But you still have something to link Sara Parker with Annie and another little girl who disappeared. Don't discount the importance of that," Carolyn said, hating to hear what this was doing to him, as well as the rest of her family.

"It's coincidence," he said. "I checked out these companies. They're huge. Three-quarters of the schoolkids in this state had their picture taken by one or the other in the past year alone."

She could hear his frustration so clearly, and she wished he could have come over, instead of calling. "That doesn't mean you're not on to something with the photographs, Drew."

He paused for a minute, and she knew he had to be at least considering what she said. She thought about it herself.

There had to be something to this.

So what if it wasn't the same company? Companies changed, merged, expanded, bought out other companies. People . . . the people staffing them changed, as well.

"Wait a minute, Drew," she said. "Just because it wasn't the same photo company producing the pictures, that doesn't mean the same man didn't take all the girls' pictures."

He swore softly. "Of course. I can't believe I didn't see that right away. I don't . . . This thing is turning me inside out. I can't even think straight anymore. I want to solve this. I want that so bad, and I'm not even sure why it's so important to me anymore. But it is."

"I know."

And then he didn't say anything for the longest time. She heard the hum of the phone between them, felt as if she could hear the sound traveling across the distance separating them, and she hated knowing that he wasn't right down the street from her anymore.

''Well,'' he said self-consciously, ''it's late. I probably shouldn't have called you, but...''

''I miss you, Drew.'' She wasn't ashamed at all to say it. He might not know it yet, but he would soon—she wasn't going to give up on him without a fight. And he might as well get used to it.

''Carolyn, don't,'' he said.

She blinked back fresh tears. ''What are you going to do tomorrow? And when will you be back?''

''I'm going to the photography company, hopefully both of them, and find out who took the pictures of those girls. After that...I don't know. It depends on what I find out.''

''Call me when you know something?'' she said.

''Of course. How's your mother? I...I forgot for a minute that she just got out of the hospital.''

''She's all right. We talked after you left.'' Carolyn had talked. Her mother was the one who had argued. ''I told her that she was going to have to get used to having you around—for Billy's sake at least.''

''I bet that went over real well.''

''Give it time, Drew. Nobody ever said it was going to be easy, but it's not—'' She wanted to say that it wasn't as hopeless as he believed it was, but she didn't think this was the moment to get into that with him. ''Just give it some time. And call me tomorrow, as soon as you know something about the photographer.''

''I will.''

Did he sound strangely reluctant to let the conversation wind down? Or was that just wishful thinking on her part?

''Good night,'' she said.

He hung up the phone without a word.

Chapter 14

Drew was at the offices of School Pix before they opened. He followed the first employee, a secretary, in the door at 8:10, and started brushing past every reason she could come up with on why she should wait before showing him what he wanted to see.

Two phone calls later, to both the company's owner and its manager, Drew was sifting through records showing where the company took pictures and which of the company's two hundred employees had actually snapped them. He also had to think that it might be someone who worked processing or printing the photographs, and he knew it was going to be impossible to trace any lab employee to any individual picture. But he would tackle that problem when he came to it. First, he had to know about the photographers.

The company truly did work all over the Midwest, and that had him feeling foolish for being so confident he'd found something significant the day before.

He'd found out the name of the man who'd been at Sara Parker's school yesterday. He had two agents checking him out, but they didn't think he was their man. For one thing, he was too young. He would have been in school himself the last time anyone took a picture of Annie McKay. But they had to check.

And even if that didn't pan out, it shouldn't worry Drew. He hadn't thought the man would actually be so stupid as to come back to Sara's school so soon after snatching her.

Still, he was worried. His instincts had told him yesterday that he was on to something. They were distressingly silent today. Unless, of course, he considered the possibility that he was actually scared to solve this case.

It was too personal, too much a part of his life. It had cost him much too much. And if he found this guy, he might well kill the man himself.

A trial, some slick defense attorney somehow painting the animal as a victim, forcing Sara Parker to see the man again, to tell some more strangers what he had done to her—it seemed like too much for everyone involved to handle. Drew couldn't be sure of what he might do to the man if he found him first, and if he found him alone.

Just to be safe, he'd called for help this morning. Two other agents had joined him in the search. They were in the basement, digging through faded, dust-covered records from as far back as ten years ago.

He was upstairs in the main offices, looking through the more recent records for those on Sara Parker's school, thinking they would be the easiest to find. According to the paper he now held in his hand, the man who had photographed her last at her elementary school was named Ray Williams.

He took the piece of paper into the office of the company owner. "What can you tell me about this guy?" he asked.

"Not much," the man replied. "He used to work for us years ago, before I bought the company. Apparently he wasn't too reliable. We fired him. Still use him on occasion, but only when we're in a bind. Someone gets sick, they hit some bad weather and can't travel the way they're supposed to, some equipment problems slow them down, whatever. When we can't cover a scheduled shoot with someone on staff, we call somebody like Ray."

"You must have some records on him." Drew said. "His phone number? His address? You'd have to have that, at least, and a social security number, to pay him. That would help."

"Sure, I have that."

"One more thing— Would you know whether he ever worked for a photography company called Watson's, based in Chicago?"

"Not offhand, but I'll check."

"Thanks," Drew said, turning around when one of the agents he'd left in the basement called his name. "What have you got?"

"Hope Junior High School, eleven years ago." He handed Drew a sheet of paper.

Drew looked down at the paper in his hand, searching for the name, needing to see it there to be sure. He found the date—it checked out—found the name of the school. And then, on the bottom of the form . . . There had to be thousands of them in that basement, and he couldn't believe he was fortunate enough that the company had kept them all. There was the name.

Ray Williams.

He tried to speak, but couldn't. And he needed to find a way to get rid of the other agent, a man he'd never met before this morning, a man who had no idea how much this meant to him.

"Is that what you needed?" the man said.

Drew nodded. That wasn't so hard. He could nod his head. "Give me a minute," he said, not caring what anyone would make of his request.

The guy hesitated, then glanced at the open doorway, as if to ask if what he wanted was for him to leave.

Drew nodded again and turned his back, not caring how that looked or how rude it was. Thankfully, the next sound he heard was that of the door clicking shut.

There was a desk in front of him, and he put his trembling hands down on the surface, spaced them farther than shoulder-width apart and leaned into the solid mass of the desk. Somehow, he was still standing.

The coveted paper landed faceup on the desk in front of him, and as he hung his head, he found himself staring straight at it, straight at that name.

Ray Williams.

Eleven years ago, that man had been in Hope, Illinois. He'd taken one of those cherished final pictures of Annie McKay. His work still hung on the walls of her mother's house.

How could her mother stand to look at those pictures after this? Drew wondered.

Annie had sat in front of that man, smiling and carefree, a normal, happy twelve-year-old at the time. And a year later, she'd been gone.

He'd taken her. God knew what he'd done with her then. Drew wasn't sure he could handle knowing, but soon... He could feel it in his bones now. He knew that soon he would know. He would catch this man. Hopefully, someone would hold him back, and he wouldn't kill him. And then he would know for certain what that man had done with Annie McKay.

After that... he couldn't begin to imagine what would happen after that. And he couldn't think of that now. He had a job to do. He was going to go get the man who'd kidnapped Annie McKay, the man who, ten years ago, had irrevocably altered the course of his life, and Carolyn's, and their son's.

And the man was going to pay.

It wouldn't solve anything. It would in no way undo what the man had done. Drew saw that so clearly now, and it only made him all the more furious. But if it was possible to punish someone adequately for taking a human life, especially the life of an innocent child, the man would pay.

"Mr. Delaney?"

It was the photography company's owner. With some effort, Drew managed to stand upright and turn around. His stomach was churning; he might well throw up, something he hadn't done on the job since he'd watched someone fish what was left of a corpse out of the ocean after it had spent two months there. And he had developed this strange tunnel vision that was making it hard to see. All he could manage to focus on was the man's face.

Drew swallowed hard, willing whatever was inside his stomach to stay there, and said, "What have you got?"

"Everything I have on the guy."

Drew took the paper. He had an age—thirty-six—a social security number that would buy him all sorts of information, and an address, somewhere in Indiana. He pointed it out to the owner. "Any idea where that is?"

"Not off the top of my head, but there's a map on the wall behind you."

Drew walked across the room to it. The town was called Riverdale, and it sounded vaguely familiar. He scanned the area in the middle of the state, from Bloomington west, and he found it right away.

It was just across the border from Illinois, fifteen, maybe twenty minutes from Hope.

Drew phoned Carolyn as soon as he thought he could talk to her about this without scaring her to death simply with the sound of his voice.

There were a half-dozen people he should have called right away, but he had a duty to protect someone else now. And right this minute, that person came first with him.

"Where's Billy?" he asked when Carolyn answered the phone. Irrational as it was, the boy was his first concern.

"He's at school. Why? What's wrong?"

"You don't have to be scared, all right? I'm being absolutely illogical about this, and you need to understand that up front. But I want you to get Billy and not let him out of your sight until I call you back. Will you do that for me?"

"Of course, but what's going on?"

"I found the man." He almost choked on the words. "I don't have proof yet. I haven't even checked the photography records on all the girls, but I found the ones on Annie and Sara Parker. I'm certain I found the man who took them."

He heard nothing but the sound of her breathing. He gave her a moment, needing one himself. "Carolyn? Are you still there?"

"Uh-huh."

"He's maybe twenty minutes away from you. Dammit, I bet he's been there the whole time."

"I don't... Oh, Drew."

"Don't cry, sweetheart. We're going to get him. We'll find him tonight. I promise you that."

"And you think Billy's in some kind of danger? You think he could somehow connect Annie to Billy?"

"Not in a million years," he said. "But I can't stand the idea of that man being loose and being that close to the two of you. I... if anything ever happened to Billy... I don't know what I'd do."

"I'll go get him," she said.

"Wait a minute. Carolyn?"

"Yes."

"This is how you felt, isn't it?" he said, truly understanding for the first time. "When you were pregnant? When you thought about Annie? About losing her? About how you could possibly keep a child safe in this crazy world? When you were too scared to keep Billy yourself. This was how you felt."

It was staggering. It was a paralyzing fear, the kind he'd never faced in all his years with the Bureau and in the army. He'd done incredibly risky, frightening things, and none of them had left him like this. None had left him feeling powerless, even with all the strength and skills he possessed, to protect one innocent little boy.

If he could simply grab him and hold on to him, if he could never let him get more than an arm's length away for his whole life, he would do it. He would never let the kid out of his sight, and even then it might not be enough to protect him.

The reality of that, the responsibility of keeping a child safe in these crazy times, was staggering.

Carolyn was crying, and she couldn't answer him.

"I understand now," he told her. "I didn't before. I couldn't imagine, but now I do. And...I'm so sorry, baby. I'm so damned sorry you had to go through that all by yourself.

"Look," he said after a minute when neither one of them could manage to speak. "I've got to go. Get Billy and keep him there. I'll come to the house as soon as it's over."

Funny, Drew thought, Ray Williams didn't look like a monster. He looked like a little wimp of a man. He had one of those short, slightly rounded bodies, the shoulders hunched in, the head eternally pointed downward, the muscles soft and mushy. He was the kind of person you could walk past on the street and never think a thing about, the kind who blended in with the landscape as if he were nothing at all, a totally unremarkable-looking man.

His manner was mild and meek, though a bit agitated. They'd lain in wait for him at the little house on a quiet, tree-lined street near the center of the tiny town.

He would never have brought the children here. Drew was certain of that. So it shouldn't have been that hard for him to look at the house, but it was.

Two hours into their surveillance, this meek-looking little man had driven into the driveway in an old pickup. He'd gotten out of the truck, looked around as if he sensed he was being watched, then headed for the house. When he turned the key in the front door and stepped over the threshold, the agents had moved in.

Drew hadn't been one of them. His boss, Bob Rossi, knew the whole story about Annie McKay, and he'd decided right away that there was no way he was letting Drew near the guy. Rossi had held him back himself, physically restraining Drew when the man pulled into the driveway at the house.

"It's him," Drew had said. They'd found the records at both photography companies. Ray Williams had photographed all five girls in the months before they disappeared. "I know it's him."

The man had let the agents in willingly. He hadn't tried to resist in any way. He'd voluntarily let them search his house, and the search was continuing even now.

Drew couldn't be still, and they wouldn't let him go in. He paced. Bob Rossi allowed that, and no more.

"I want to kill him," he said. "I want to do it with my bare hands, and I want it to take one hell of a long time before he dies."

"I know," his friend said, putting himself between Drew and the house.

"He's got to tell us what happened to those girls. We've got to make him crack. Ten damned years we've been waiting, and that bastard's got to tell us. Did you tell the guys inside? Do they understand that?"

"I told them."

"He had to take them somewhere. There's no way he could have kept them in that house. Too many people close by."

"I know, Drew."

"He's got to take us there. We've got to make him crack, then make him take us there."

"We will. I promise."

They stood in the dark for hours, waiting. As the information filtered out, they heard that the man sat in a chair in the kitchen, drumming his fingers nervously on the table as the agents searched his house. He'd shown no resistance to that, and the first thing he'd said was enough to make Drew sick.

"It's about that girl," he'd told them.

Finally, at dawn, the first team was ready to concede defeat. They hadn't found anything. Another team, the real experts in evidence-gathering, was coming in this morning.

Ray Williams was on his way to jail.

Someone had snapped his picture there, then rushed it through developing and faxed a copy to a town about a hundred and eighty miles away. When they showed it to Sara Parker the next morning, she screamed.

But they still had no idea what the man had done to Annie McKay or any of the other girls.

Carolyn waited all night and into the next day for him to call. Finally, around eight o'clock the next evening, she answered the phone and found Drew on the other end of the line.

"I'm in Hope," he said. "I'm at the bed-and-breakfast, and . . . I need you, Carolyn."

"What about Billy?" she asked. "It's safe? I can leave him here?"

"Yes."

She got there in minutes. Drew looked awful, as if he'd been beaten but the bruises hadn't yet begun to show. She was afraid to even ask what he'd found out or what had happened in the thirty-six hours since he'd last called.

He was sitting on the bed, his legs stretched out in front of him, his back propped up against the headboard. The look in his eyes frightened her.

"C'mere," he said, motioning her over to the bed, then pulling her into his arms. They locked around her, nearly cutting off her breath.

He was trembling badly, and she was surprised he had the strength to hold her as tightly as he did.

"You got him?" she asked, thinking she was going to have to do most of the talking tonight.

He nodded.

"He's the one?"

"No question in my mind. Of course, a jury may have different ideas."

"What about Annie?"

She felt the breath leave his lungs in a whoosh, felt his arms tighten around her even more.

"I can't breathe, Drew." Even when he released her a bit, she still couldn't seem to draw a breath.

She'd waited for this moment for years, prepared herself as best she could. And it shouldn't be this hard. After all, she'd accepted Annie's death long ago.

"What did he do to her?" she said, before she had time to think about whether she wanted to know.

"I don't know."

"But he had her?"

"At one point. He recognized her picture. He recognized that the clothes he gave Sara Parker to wear were Annie's. And Sara Parker finally told us why she was so upset the other day, when I showed her Annie's picture in the red suit. It was because she'd seen it before, at that place where the man took her."

"He had pictures of Annie?" The thought had Carolyn's stomach lurching.

"Yeah. Pictures of her and the others. Sara couldn't say how many different girls."

"So what did he do to my little sister?"

Drew pushed her face down into the hollow between his shoulder and his chin, holding her there. She knew that, if he could, he would draw this pain of hers down inside him, feel it for her, absorb it into his own body, despite all the pain he felt himself.

"He won't say, or maybe he doesn't know anymore himself." He swore before he went on. "He's crazy, Carolyn. He says that he lost Annie. He says he lost all of them. Four little girls. Sara's the only one who was ever seen again, and he says he just lost them."

They sat on the bed, Drew holding her tightly. She would have simply come apart if he hadn't.

"Lost," she managed to say, incredulous and infuriated at the enormous number of possibilities that term implied.

"Lost. I'm telling you, the guy's insane. I'd never admit it to anyone but you, anywhere outside this room, because we'll never get him convicted that way. But the man's a nut case."

"We've got to know what happened," she said. "After all this time, you can't find him and not figure out what happened to Annie."

"I'm not giving up yet. Not by a long shot."

"I know. I didn't mean to sound ungrateful. I am grateful, Drew. And I'm so proud of you and the work you've done. I—"

"It's not done yet, Carolyn."

"But you'll finish it."

He gave a sound of disgust. "Even if I do. . ."

"What?"

"Don't go making me out to be some kind of hero here," he said.

"What do you mean?"

"You know why I did this, don't you? You know why it means so much to me to find her? Don't get me wrong— Annie was a great kid. I hated what had happened to her, but she's not the only reason I'm doing this. She's not the reason this case has haunted me all these years.

"I wanted to make another chance for us, Carolyn. I wanted to somehow undo what I'd done, to ease some of the guilt. I felt it, too, irrational as it is. And I couldn't make it go away. You need to understand that—that a part of me understands why your mother needed to blame me and to blame us."

Carolyn could understand that all too well. She still had hope that once this was all resolved, she and Drew would be together. She listened as he continued.

"I thought if I could find the man who did this to Annie, if I could find out what happened to her, that it might somehow buy me another chance—for us. I thought maybe we could finally put everything behind us and start over. I thought. . . Aw, hell, what does it matter, anyway? It's not working out that way. And now there's Billy. . ."

"Drew, I know you don't see how it's going to work out, but you haven't given it any time. It's only been a few days. Maybe we don't see the answer now, but that doesn't mean there isn't one. It doesn't mean we'll never find it. Couldn't you just have a little faith?"

"Faith? I think I lost the last of mine years ago."

Fine. She had enough for the two of them. For the three of them, even. And she was ready to fight for this man.

"How about this, then?" she said. "I live in Chicago. You're in Chicago now. Maybe you don't see how we can be together, but tell me, how are you going to manage to stay away from me?''

Drew pulled away from her then, though he hated the idea of letting her go.

He hadn't even thought about that, because this whole thing had happened so fast. She lived in Chicago, too. They were going to have to share the same city. She'd be only minutes away. He might only be a few blocks from her, and every day he'd have to fight to keep himself away.

How in hell was he ever going to manage that?

He backed away from her totally, then got up off the bed.

She'd frightened him. In an instant, he saw that she was going to ruin any hope he had of finding some peace of mind once this was all over.

She would haunt him.

"Come on," he said. "I'll take you home."

She looked surprised at that, and she glanced around the room, as if she meant to stay. As if she were going to make him pick her up and throw her out of his room.

He'd never manage to do that.

Thankfully, she came willingly, but not quietly.

"I still love you," she said, looking him right in the eye as she pulled on her coat.

He swayed on his feet, felt himself leaning toward her, then fighting to bring himself upright again.

"You love me, too," she said. "You told me so right here in this room, so don't even try to deny it."

He certainly didn't need to be reminded of that, either. In this room, in this bed, in that instant he'd joined his body with hers, he hadn't been able to hold the words back. And he'd never be able to take them back, or to discount his confession in any way.

He still loved her. He'd meant it with every bit of his heart and his soul. He still loved her. He always would.

"You don't have to say anything," she said, at the door now. "I just had to tell you. I wanted to make sure you understood how I feel about you, and that I'm not going to give up on us. Not ever. You can try to deny it or try to ignore it, but I'm going to fight you every step of the way."

Chapter 15

Ray Williams didn't crack. For three days, they questioned him. For three days, he couldn't come up with anything more plausible than the statement that he'd somehow lost those five little girls.

A thorough search of his house yielded nothing but a fetish for nude photos of little children—none of them showing the missing girls, however. He did happen to wear a size twelve-and-a-half-wide shoe—the same size as the footprint found in the woods the day Annie was taken. Of course, many men wore that size shoe. His record showed an arrest for exposing himself to a young woman twelve years ago, then nothing.

His neighbors described him as a quiet man who kept to himself. They'd never seen any children around his house, never seen him take any undue interest in them.

He did like to fish, they thought, and he had a cabin somewhere in the woods nearby. No one was sure where. He'd never taken anyone there, but at times they saw him leave with his fishing gear.

He lived quietly, taking odd photography jobs here and there, drawing on the small estate left to him by his mother, who'd died six years before. No one knew of any other relatives he had. No property showed up as being registered in his name or his late mother's.

The authorities were sure the cabin was the key to unlocking the mystery of the missing girls, and they had no idea where it was.

Sara Parker, as a witness in court, would be awfully shaky. Simply looking at a photo of the man had frightened her so badly that her parents now said they'd never be able to let her go through a trial. Drew couldn't have said that he blamed them, and Sara's parents were counting on him and the Bureau to find the evidence they needed to convict the man without Sara's testimony.

Ray Williams was being held on a kidnapping charge, but they'd never be able to make it stick with what they had. They had nothing but circumstantial evidence that linked the man to the other girls' disappearance.

And they were nowhere near finding out what he'd done with Annie McKay.

Drew wished he'd strangled the man that first night, before the legal system ever got ahold of him. If he had to listen, one more time, to the public defender assigned to the case talking about his client's rights and his client's needs, he was going to put his fist through a brick wall.

He was exhausted, more frustrated than he'd ever been in his life, and he needed answers. He'd promised them to Carolyn and her mother. He needed them for Billy, as well.

He had failed. It tore at him, night and day, until he couldn't eat or sleep or do anything except think about it. In this, the most important case he'd ever worked on, he had failed.

He still needed answers that he didn't think he was going to find. That was why he went to Carolyn.

"I hate asking you to do this," he said when he called her from Chicago. "But I don't see any other way."

"I'll do anything to help you find out where that man took the girls and what he did with them," she said, sounding invincible in that moment. But he knew she wasn't.

"It's going to hurt," he warned.

"So does not knowing."

"Okay. I want you to come to Chicago. We're having a press conference tomorrow afternoon. We've managed to keep the lid on this arrest so far, but it's not going to last. We're losing control of it even now, and if the word's going to get out, we want to pick the time and the place."

"What do you want me to do, Drew?"

"I want you to tell every TV-station reporter who will listen all about Annie. It's going to be hard, I know. But you have to make it personal for them. Let them see how badly this hurt you. Talk about what it did to your family. Bawl your pretty eyes out—whatever it takes. TV producers eat that sort of stuff up. I need you to catch their attention and hold it. Make them remember you and what you said. Make them remember Annie, and this monster we've got sitting in jail."

"Why?" she asked.

"Because somebody knows something. Somebody heard something or saw something. Someone has to be able to lead us to this man's hideout, and we've got to find that person. The bigger the impression you can make, the more people will remember. I want it to haunt them, Carolyn. I want people on the street talking about it the next day. Can you do that for me? Can you do it for Annie?"

"Of course," she said. "I meant it. I'll do anything I can."

"Good." He told her where to meet him, then was ready to hang up. He had a million things to do. And he thought maybe, if he just never stopped moving, never stopped working, he'd forget how impossible this whole situation seemed to be.

So far, that wasn't working as well as he'd hoped. Hearing her voice again wasn't helping. Knowing he hadn't seen her in three days, that he would see her this afternoon, wasn't helping, either.

"Drew?" she said. "It's going to work out. You'll see."

The case? Or them and Billy? He wasn't holding out much hope about either situation.

"I've missed you," she said. "Have you thought about what I said?"

"I have, but I've got to go," he said, like a coward. "We can talk tomorrow, after you get here."

Drew was about to leave his office late the next night when the phone rang one last time. It was nearly midnight, and he'd been here most of the night. The press conference had gone well. All the major networks in Chicago had carried portions of it live. All had rerun some of the footage on the evening and nighttime newscasts. They'd gotten some footage on the national newscasts, as well, plus additional coverage in many of the major markets in Indiana, Illinois, Kentucky and Ohio, because of the connections to the other missing girls.

As he'd suspected they would, the cameras had eaten up the image of Carolyn, a beautiful woman tearfully relating the long years she'd spent trying to come to terms with the loss of her sister. She'd been wonderful, but he knew how much it had cost her.

He felt guilty about putting her through the media hype, but he was desperate. He needed evidence that he didn't yet have.

They'd gotten lots of crank calls, lots of information that hadn't led anywhere except to frustration. If nothing panned out from this, they'd take their show on the road tomorrow, to the area where Sara Parker had been found, in southern Indiana. There had to be someone there who'd seen Ray Williams heading for that fishing shack of his.

Drew looked up at the clock, then thought of Carolyn alone in her apartment. Her place wasn't that far away, and he wanted to check on her to make sure she was okay.

And hell, who was he kidding? He'd take any excuse he could to see her again.

He hadn't actually thought about it until she told him the other night, but they were both going to be in the same city. He knew where she lived, not that far from his own apartment, and it would be sheer torture knowing she was close and forcing himself to stay away from her.

He'd said he didn't know how they could be together, how things could ever work out between them. And she'd said she didn't know how they could be so close, could need each other so much, and still stay away from each other.

He was just beginning to see how hard that was going to be.

"Drew?" someone called from across the room.

"Yeah?" He turned in the direction of the voice.

"Line three, asking for you by name. He doesn't even sound like a crackpot."

Drew didn't get excited about it, after the night he'd spent on the phone. He just picked up the receiver.

"Drew?" the voice on the other end asked. "I knew you'd still be there. This is Nick. Nick Garrett."

The psychiatrist who'd questioned Sara Parker. "How are you, Nick?"

"Confused. I saw you on TV tonight, and this is going to sound wild, okay, but hear me out."

"Sure." Drew had met Nick a couple of times since moving to Chicago. He respected him, and if he had a story to tell, Drew would listen, even if it was almost midnight and Carolyn was waiting.

"I don't know why I didn't put this together when I talked to Sara, but I didn't have any connection to the name Annie. Didn't even know her last name. It was seeing Carolyn on TV tonight that made it all click for me. Before that, I had no idea that one of the missing girls was Carolyn's little sister."

"Go on," Drew said, totally baffled by what the man was trying to say. From what he'd seen and heard, Dr. Nicholas Garrett was a very methodical, logical man.

"You don't have anything to indicate that this little girl, Carolyn's sister, is dead, do you?"

Drew tried not to sound sarcastic, but it was hard. "Other than the fact that no one's seen her for the past ten years, no, we don't."

"Okay, hear me out. It's a long shot, but I couldn't go to bed for thinking about it. I just had to tell you."

"Take all the time you need, Nick."

"First, you need to understand that this conversation never took place. My license is on the line here. This is all caught up in that heavy doctor-patient confidentiality stuff that would get my license pulled in a minute if it came out."

He had Drew's full attention now. This was serious stuff. "Sure you want to tell me this?"

"I have to. I couldn't live with myself if I didn't."

"Okay, shoot."

"Right after I came to Chicago, six years ago, I worked at this runaway shelter on the South Side called the Gate House. I did some group sessions there with the kids, when we could get any of them to sit still for one.

"This girl shows up, says she's seventeen or so, and she's different from the rest of them, somehow. She's angry, but it's that fresh, raw kind that you rarely see in a runaway. Usually, by the time they run, they've been angry and abused or neglected for years. And they don't care that much about anyone, especially not themselves.

"Anyway, this girl is eaten up with it. She's furious, and the wound's still fresh. She hadn't learned to hide it yet, or to keep it all locked inside her.

"She hadn't been on the streets long, and you could tell. She wasn't doing drugs, hadn't found a pimp. We still had a shot with her. I just couldn't write her off as one of those lost causes, like you can with so many of the rest of them.

"So, we got her into the shelter, started talking to her about going home, but didn't get anywhere with that. She said her home was gone, that she'd never really had one. I kept pushing her—couldn't we call someone, anyone, just to let them know she was okay? Couldn't she go to someone, anyone, she trusted? Wouldn't anyone make room for her in their home?

"She tells me this bizarre story about the people who raised her all these years, who died a few months back. She'd found out, after they died, that she's not who she thought she was. She's not their daughter. And now she has no idea who she is.

"She tells me that she had some accident when she was eleven—at least, the people who'd raised her told her she was eleven. And she doesn't remember anything before that, except what these people told her about her past. Except it wasn't her past at all.

"Anyway, I keep working on her. I tell her she has to try to find out who she is. She says she doesn't care. I finally talk her into letting me try some hypnosis, and I try to take her back to this time when she was eleven.

"It was awful. The kid was terrified. She was screaming. I can still hear her. You can't imagine what it was like to listen to that. She wanted her mother and her father to come and save her from someone, and when that didn't work, she started calling for someone else, some older person, someone she obviously saw as a sort of protector.

"The name she was calling . . . it was Carolyn."

Drew's pen slid out of his hand and clattered down onto the top of the desk when he heard the name. He'd been taking notes while Nick talked. It was an automatic action for him to jot down notes when he talked to people, particularly over the phone.

He couldn't believe the clatter the dropped pen made, but it served some purpose. It had brought him out of this tunnel vision he'd developed, all his concentration focusing on the story being told through the phone, and made him realize where he was. He was in his office. It was late, and he'd been on the phone all day.

He'd heard hundreds of stories by now, and none of them had made a damn bit of difference.

And then he'd heard this one.

"Nick," he began.

"I know. It's crazy. I realize that. But I saw Carolyn telling this awful story about her little sister on TV, and I couldn't stop thinking about A.J. That's what she calls herself—A.J. But it's not her real name. She doesn't have any idea what her real name is."

"It's—" Drew couldn't even talk. This had thrown him that badly. "I never even thought about finding her, Nick—at least not alive."

"I know, man."

"What are the odds? Hell, it's been ten years."

"I had to tell you."

"Is that all you've got?" Drew asked, starting to remember his job here.

"She's the right age. A.J. thought she was seventeen when she wound up at the shelter, which would make her twenty-three or so now. How old would Annie be?"

"Twenty-three." Drew had never been able to picture Annie at that age.

"She's maybe five-three, and slight. Still looks like a kid. Has this white-blond hair that I'd bet didn't come from a bottle, and dark blue eyes."

"That's it?" Drew asked, eager for more now.

"What do you want? Her blood type? Her finger-prints? Maybe something you could lift some DNA from?"

"It would be nice." Drew decided to go for broke. Before he got too excited about this, he needed a reason more. Because it had been so long since he'd even allowed himself to hope like this. "Why did you call me tonight, Nick?"

"You'll think I'm crazy."

"I already do. Tell me why you called."

"I couldn't get A.J. out of my mind. Not ever. She pulled her life together. I knew she would, because she was such a bright kid. Got a scholarship, got a degree in counseling, and she works at one of the runaway shelters in the city now. I still see her every now and then, and I can't forget how frightened she was that afternoon when I hypnotized her. I can't forget the way she begged for these people to come and get her.

"I was thinking about her the whole time I was watching the piece on TV, and then at the end, when they went to Carolyn, I put the names together. Right before the segment was over, they flashed the pictures of those little girls, and Annie's picture...it's A.J. ten years ago. I can see it in her eyes, in her smile. It's my A.J."

Drew still wasn't letting himself get excited. It was too farfetched to think that Annie had somehow gotten away from that monster, and that all this time she'd been in Chicago, with Carolyn and now with him.

What were the odds?

A million to one?

A billion?

"I've got a picture of A.J.," Nick told him. "If you've got a fax machine, you can see it tonight."

It was an offer Drew couldn't refuse.

* * *

He couldn't help but remember, as he sat at his desk in the still-crowded, still-noisy office, that night not so long ago, when he'd waited in the police department in that tiny Indiana town where Sara Parker had turned up. He'd been waiting for another picture of Annie to come over the fax machine.

Drew'd had no idea then that he'd be sitting here, now, waiting for a picture of a young woman someone thought was a grown-up Annie.

Just as it had been that night, his hand was shaking when he took the photo from a fellow agent a few moments later.

Just as he had then, he turned his chair around and put his back to the room, then took a minute to try to prepare himself to flip over the sheet of paper and look at the image it contained.

He'd had the presence of mind to get the case files, to pull out his own old pictures of Annie and spread them out on the desk behind him. Not that he'd ever forget how she looked. Not that her image would ever be erased from his mind.

But he didn't trust himself to make the comparison, because he wanted too badly to believe it could be her.

Four years on the job with the Bureau, four years of the cynicism and occasional horror that had jaded his senses, yet he still wanted to hope.

Maybe Carolyn was right. Maybe there was always room to hope. Maybe it was always the last thing to die, and his had one last gasp of life left in it.

He couldn't imagine how Annie could have escaped dying.

He flipped over the flimsy sheet of fax paper in his hands and closed his eyes. Annie's image, smiling, laughing, looking like an angel with the sun shining on her hair was in his mind's eye.

He finally found the courage to look down at the paper in front of him.

"Carolyn?"

She was sleeping. At least she was trying to, and someone wouldn't let her. She was exhausted, both physically and emotionally, after driving to Chicago earlier for the press conference, and she'd taken a painkiller for her head that had a little something in it to help her sleep, as well.

"Carolyn?"

"What?" she asked, blinking hard against the brightness of the light in the room, which had been dark only moments before. "Drew?"

"Who else would be here this time of night?" he said, holding up the key she'd given him when she hoped he'd come over tonight, no matter how late it was when he finished his work.

And now he was here, in her apartment, but she must be dreaming. It was the only thing that could explain the almost teasing quality in his voice. She hadn't heard that in forever. And he had nothing to smile about, and no reason to tease her.

"Well? I'm waiting."

Same voice, same man. She must still be dreaming. "Why are you smiling like that?"

That seemed the easiest thing to do, just to ask him and to watch it fade away, maybe watch him fade, as well.

"I'm happy for a change."

"Oh."

"Are you awake yet?"

"Obviously not."

"Take something to help you sleep?"

She nodded. That explained it, of course. She was drugged. But then...she hadn't thought the stuff was that strong.

"You have to wake up for this. It's important, and you'll want to remember it."

She buried her face in her hands to block out the offending light, rubbed her eyes, then sat up all the way. She was on the couch. She'd fallen asleep, and now Drew was here.

Finally, she remembered what he'd been doing tonight—trying to follow up leads on the kidnapping. She'd wanted to be there, but this afternoon's activities, all those lights for the cameras, all those questions, all those memories. She hadn't been able to take any more after that.

"You found something?" she asked suddenly.

"You woke up." He was still smiling.

Why would finding something have made him happy? How could he tease her this way?

It was as if the old Drew were back. With her.

To see him that way again, now…she was baffled.

Carolyn glanced over at the clock on the mantel. It was nearly two in the morning. Why was he here at this hour?

"You found the cabin where he took the girls?" she asked. But that wouldn't have made him happy.

"Better than that." He moved her a bit, half lifting her, to make room for himself on the end of the couch, then settled her in beside him. "Are you ready to hear what I have to tell you?"

"No. You're scaring me, Drew."

"Don't be scared. Not anymore. Hold out your hands and close your eyes."

She trusted him, so she did as he asked. He dropped something into her hands. A sheet of paper? No, it was too thick.

"Open up," he said, his tone coaxing.

There were tears in her eyes, and she didn't know why. She was close enough to Drew to feel the nervous energy radiating from him, and she couldn't imagine what could have caused it. This thing in her hands?

"What do you see, Carolyn?"

She looked down.

It was a picture of a girl with white-blond hair and blue eyes, a picture of a smile nearly as familiar as her own.

"Is it—?" She searched her mind for some explanation, then latched on to the only reasonable one she could find. "Is this one of those computerized age-progression photos?"

She knew about them. Hope House had the technology to produce them, but why would Drew need one of those?

"What is it?" she asked.

He smiled. The man had such a beautiful smile, and she'd missed it all these years. She had missed so very much about him.

He pulled her closer, held her tighter. "It's just a picture, Carolyn. A plain old picture, taken about six months ago."

"Then it's . . . I don't understand."

"Who's in the picture, sweetheart? Tell me who you see."

"Annie."

Carolyn was certain. She'd have known that face anywhere, except . . . this girl wasn't thirteen. And Annie had never gotten past thirteen. Unless . . .

Drew pulled Carolyn over onto his lap and held on. "She's right here." He started to laugh. "She's in Chicago. She has been for years."

Carolyn wasn't sure what had happened next. At least she couldn't have put any order to it. She'd laughed. She'd cried. She'd been in Drew's arms. They'd been exhausted and excited, and they'd needed each other.

One kiss had led to another, and another. She couldn't stop crying, but at the same time she was smiling. There'd been so many times when she didn't think she'd smile again.

"I love you, Drew," she told him again and again as he kissed her mouth, then went after the spot at the base of her neck that had always made her a little crazy when he so much as touched it.

She held him as tightly as she could, determined that she'd never let him go again, that she wouldn't let anything come between them now.

Let him try to leave her. Let him try to forget her. He'd have to forget this, as well. Let him try to tell her this was impossible—she'd dare him to do that right now, dare him to do it afterward, too.

His arms came around her, the muscles straining to hold her closer. Their bodies strained toward each other, with much too much between them.

She tugged at his already loosened tie, then started working on the buttons of his shirt. His jacket fell to the floor. She pulled the ends of his shirt from his pants, then found warm flesh beneath it. She pressed her face against his chest, nuzzled her nose against the fine, curling hairs sprinkled across it and drew in the scent of him.

He had his hands on her hips, pulling her against his body. The hardness there left her with no doubts as to how much he wanted her now, when anything in the world seemed possible for the two of them.

"I can't stop," he said, working furiously on the buttons on her blouse.

"I didn't hear anyone ask you to stop," she said as her shirt finally came undone and he threw it to the floor, as well.

It wasn't long before all their clothing was lying in a heap in the middle of her living room. She stood in the middle of the room, her body lit by the lamp and what was left of the fire. She stood trembling in front of him while he looked at her, as if memorizing her with his eyes, then with his hands, as he touched her face, her shoulders, her breasts, her hips.

He didn't need to store up memories of her, she wanted to tell him. Because he was going to have her, forever. She was going to find a way to make that happen.

"You are so beautiful," Drew said. "Even more beautiful than I remembered, if that's possible."

Then he picked her up in his arms and carried her to bed.

They went to tell her mother early the next morning, because Carolyn couldn't wait for her to hear the good news. It was also a good excuse for not having to hang around in her own bed, listening to the man she loved tell her what a mistake they'd just made, and that finding Annie hadn't solved the problems between them.

Instead of slugging Drew right then and there, instead of getting angry at him for his lack of faith—even now, after an absolute miracle had happened and he'd found Annie for her—Carolyn made him get in the car and drive.

Let him say he was sorry for making love to her, if he absolutely had to do so. He could say it, but she wasn't going to believe it. He couldn't make her believe it was true, no matter how hard he tried.

It was only a matter of time, she told herself, before she'd finally convince him otherwise. Her little sister was alive and well and living in Chicago. It was an absolute miracle. How could he tell her everything was hopeless after that?

The lights were on at the house when they arrived, shortly after dawn, and they didn't have a lot of time to waste. Billy got up at seven to catch the school bus, and they wanted to be able to tell her mother privately, because they weren't sure what her reaction might be.

Grace McKay surprised them by being amazingly calm about the whole thing. She cried a little over the picture and held it against her heart.

Drew tried not to look at Carolyn during this. He was still a bit dazed that this whole situation had gotten so far out of his control and that he didn't seem capable of keeping his hands off her anymore.

Everything was happening so fast, he was having trouble keeping up with all the changes. He was, however, able to think clearly enough to warn Grace McKay about some simple, basic facts that seemed to have gotten lost in this celebration they were having.

They hadn't proved anything yet, he told her. All they had was a picture and a long-buried memory of a little girl calling out for her older sister.

But Mrs. McKay was as certain as Carolyn had been. The girl in the picture that she refused to let go of was her Annie.

The older woman looked at him with absolute awe, as if he were some sort of angel come down from heaven to grant her most sacred prayer. Drew would never forget the feeling of having her look at him this way, of having redeemed himself in this woman's eyes. She didn't care who his father was anymore, or what gutter his drunken old man had landed in.

She'd misjudged Drew all those years ago, and though she might never come right out and say so, that look did it for her.

That, together with the early-morning hours he'd spent with Carolyn, had him feeling like a million dollars. It was as if a weight he'd carried all these years had simply been lifted off his shoulders.

He felt amazingly free, felt something that vaguely resembled happiness on this cold October morning in Hope, Illinois.

"You brought my baby home to me," Mrs. McKay said, still hugging the picture to her chest. "I just can't believe it."

She took one of his hands in hers and squeezed it tight. The gesture surprised him. And he thought she was asking for forgiveness in a way. He hoped he had it in him to forgive her.

"When can we see her?" Mrs. McKay asked, turning to Carolyn. "She's in Chicago? We could go today. I can't . . . I can't wait to see her."

"Wait a minute," Drew said. "We have to give this some time. This source of ours . . . he's told us things he had no right to tell us. We can't just barge into this woman's life, and tell her she's Annie McKay and her whole family's waiting to see her again."

"We can't see her?" Mrs. McKay looked crushed.

"It's a delicate situation, and we have to be cautious," Drew said. "Also, we've got to think about this woman's emotional state. From what she told our source a few years back, she has no memory of her childhood beyond nine or ten years ago. Springing a whole family on her without any warning or any preparation would likely be very difficult for her."

"You expect me to stay away from her?" the older woman asked.

"For the moment, at least."

Carolyn came to stand beside him. "What's Nick going to do, Drew?"

"He's going to try to talk to her today, to tell her that he thinks he knows who she is. Then he's going to try to talk her into meeting with the two of you. And we'll want to do a DNA test, to check her blood against your mother's, to be sure of who she is."

"So we can go this afternoon," Mrs. McKay said.

"No, not until we hear from someone in Chicago that this woman's agreed to all this," Drew said.

"But she's my little girl. She's my Annie. How can you expect me to stay away from my own child? To be two and a half hours away from her, finally, after all these years, and not see her?''

Drew backed up a step. He had a million things he could have said right then. Uppermost in his mind was his son, and the fact that he was in the identical position when it came to Billy. He hadn't recognized the irony in that until just now.

That particularly generous mood he'd been in all morning was gone in an instant. Still, knowing that this wasn't the time or the place to get into the subject with Grace McKay, he held his tongue.

And that was when Billy walked into the room. Still rubbing the sleep from his eyes, still in his pajamas, he came padding into the room in his bare feet. "Is it time to go to school yet?"

Drew couldn't hold back any longer. He wasn't so much angry as frustrated as hell. He turned to Grace McKay, his back to Billy, and, in a voice only she could hear, said, "Yeah, that's what I'm telling you. Your kid is right there, and you can't just go and see her. You can't reach out and touch her, hold her. You might not be able to tell her for a while that you're her mother. And I don't know how long it will be before any of that changes."

"Drew." Carolyn tried to stop him, but it was too late.

"I've got to get back to Chicago," he said. "You all stay put. I'll call you as soon as I know something for sure. I can't promise anything, but I'm going to try to at least get to see the woman today, even if I can't talk to her or tell her what's going on."

He turned and said goodbye to Billy, who had just realized he was there and still remembered Drew's promise to show him his gun.

"Maybe this weekend," he said, daring Carolyn's mother to say anything different.

It made him absolutely ache inside, but he didn't touch the boy at all, didn't even ruffle his hair, which stuck up every which way on his head.

And he didn't have it in him to say anything to Carolyn. She'd thought all their problems were going to magically dissolve, now that they'd found the woman who might be Annie. But they weren't just going to disappear, and he had to find a way to live with that.

Still, the irony was almost too much for him. He'd found Annie.

It was an absolute miracle.

Yet in an instant, back there in that room, he'd seen that it wasn't enough. He still needed another miracle to make things right between him and Carolyn and Billy.

Chapter 16

Her name was Allison Jennings, but everyone called her A.J. She had short, sassy, almost white hair, the same color eyes as the little girl in the red suit in that picture that had haunted Drew for ten years, the same smile as the woman Drew loved.

Maybe he even saw a little of Billy in her.

Unfortunately, she didn't want to see him. The only reason he'd gotten into the same room with her was that he'd flashed his credentials to the man at the shelter's front desk and strolled on through like he owned the place, allegedly looking for some missing kid from Peoria. But all he'd really been doing was checking A.J. out.

He hadn't gotten to talk to her. He'd only seen her from across the room, as she gave some kid hell for coming into her shelter with fresh needle tracks in his arm. Apparently she knew the kid, because she'd taken it quite personally, and in this business you couldn't afford to take every kid's troubles that personally. Otherwise, you'd never last.

Of course, he was a fine one to talk. Look what he'd done with her case.

Before he got a chance to talk to her, Nick Garrett had walked in and spotted him. If looks could kill, he'd have been six feet under by suppertime, and he'd known it. He'd left.

"You promised me," Nick roared at him later that evening.

"I'm sorry. I wasn't going to say anything to her. I just had to get a look at her."

"And you will, when she's ready. But until then, remember, you promised me we'd take this all in good time, when she can handle it."

"I'm sorry, Nick. But it's been ten days."

"And she was out of town for the first seven of those."

"Well, how long is it going to take?"

"I don't know. I'm trying to talk to her, but she doesn't want to have anything to do with this so-called family of hers. For one thing, she doesn't believe for a minute that she's related to these people. For another, she claims she doesn't want to know anything about her past. She says she's made her peace with it, and wants to leave it alone."

"Let me get this straight," Drew said. "She knows she has a mother and a sister a couple of hours from here, people who'd given her up for dead ten years ago, and now she doesn't even want to see them?"

"She's been hurt, Drew. Badly. She won't even tell me how, exactly, but I can promise you, it was bad. And she's not ready to face all that yet."

"When is she going to be ready?"

"I'm working on her, but you've got to back off. Remember, she has a choice in this. We can't force her to let these people into her life."

True enough. They couldn't force her into doing anything, but Drew still had to try. "Just a meeting, Nick. A quick one. Surely you could get her to agree to see them.

After all, they've waited ten years. In the last ten days, they found out that by some miracle, she might still be alive, and now they're caught in this limbo. They're afraid to hope that it's true, but it's impossible not to at least hope. She's got to understand that.''

''She's scared, Drew. It's as simple and as complex as that. She's scared. She had a family once—at least she thought she did—and it all turned out to be a big lie. Now she's decided she's better off alone. Believe me, I know all about this. I'd like to be much more than a friend and a sometime therapist for this woman, but she won't even consider it.''

''Oh.'' So it was like that? ''Sorry, buddy. I didn't realize. I'll stay away until I hear otherwise.''

''And I'll try to arrange something. It may not be what Carolyn and her mother would like, but I'll give it a shot.''

Drew was more than a little nervous later that day, as he stood at the door to Carolyn's apartment. He'd been sitting at his desk not twenty minutes ago, when Carolyn's mother called from Carolyn's place and asked to speak to him.

He was sure it was about Annie, and he didn't have any answers for her. He also didn't want to fight with her anymore, about anything.

Determined not to do so, he knocked on the door. Mrs. McKay must have been waiting for him, because she answered right away. He noted first that she seemed nervous, and that made him curious. Quite formally, she offered him a seat. He sat. She offered tea or coffee. Even more intrigued by this attempt at civility where he was concerned, he declined.

''I don't know where to start,'' Grace said. ''This…it's going to be harder than I thought. Billy and I have talked about it, and we're thinking about moving to Chicago.''

Drew was speechless, and suddenly hopeful. Hadn't Carolyn told him there was always a reason to be hopeful?

"Carolyn's here, and she loves the area. Annie's here, and even if she isn't ready to get to know us yet, I want to be here when she is. I know that someday she'll want her family around her, and I ... uh ..."

"Go on," Drew urged.

"Billy and I have been lonely in Hope without his— without my husband. And it's difficult to think about that awful man living right down the road from us all these years. I've driven down that road where he lived so many times. My husband used to work not far from there, and ... it's hard. I think we're ready for a change, and we want to be closer to our family again."

"That's it?" he asked.

"No." She shook her head. "I did a lot of thinking about what you said ... when you were telling me that Annie was here and I couldn't see her, that you didn't know when I could see her, if ever. Knowing that she was here, knowing that I had to stay away ... it was one of the hardest things I've ever dealt with. And at least I can hope that it won't last for long. Ten days has already seemed like an eternity.

"And then I realized I've been doing the same to you where Billy's concerned, and I was ashamed of myself. It's hard for me to imagine being so cruel to anyone."

That was one admission Drew hadn't thought he'd ever hear.

"I want you to understand," she continued, "or to try to understand, that I love Billy. I couldn't love him any more than I already do, and I was so frightened at the idea of losing him. These last few months, since my husband died, he's become my whole world. But then, I didn't come here to make excuses for myself. I just wanted you to know that he's been loved and wanted and needed throughout the years.

"And when you came back, I was sure you were going to take him away from me. But Carolyn's assured me that you wouldn't do that."

"I wouldn't hurt *Billy* that way," he explained.

"I understand. I don't want to hurt him, either, and I think some of the things Carolyn's been telling me are finally sinking in. She says there's more than enough love in that little boy for all of us, and she's right. She said that letting him get to know you and to love you wouldn't in any way take away from the love that Billy and I share. I know now, in my heart, he'll always be my son, and I'll always love him. But that doesn't mean he can't ever be your son and Carolyn's, as well.

"I think little boys need lots of people to love and trust and share their lives with, and I think we can find a way to do that for Billy's sake."

"What are you saying? You're going to give him up?"

"I don't think I have to give him up, any more than you have to take him away from me."

"You're willing to let him know that I'm his father?"

"Someday, I think he'll be ready to know that. I think he'll need to know that. And whatever he decides to do then will be his choice. I won't stand in his way if he wants to live with the two of you, but I was hoping that it wouldn't matter so much where he lived or who he called his mother or his father. I'd hoped we could all come together in a big extended family where we all took care of each other. Do you think we could do that?"

"I don't know." It sounded too good to be true. And he still wasn't sure what this woman was asking of him.

"I've misjudged you, from the very start, and I've been unkind. I'm sorry for that. I think I knew from the start how strong Carolyn's feelings for you were, and I worried that you were going to take her away from us, especially after Annie died. Still, that's no excuse for what I've done."

Drew didn't know what to say or where this was going, and it must have shown on his face, because Grace McKay smiled at him then. She reminded him of Carolyn and of Annie in that moment. He didn't think she'd ever smiled at him before.

"My daughter would like very much to marry you," she said.

That floored him. He supposed he'd known it already, but hadn't allowed himself to even think about it. He tried to pull himself together and contribute something to this conversation. "And how do you feel about that?"

"I could tell you that it would solve a lot of our problems quite neatly. If you married Carolyn, you'd be Billy's brother-in-law, at least to start with. You'd be part of the family. You'd see him on a regular basis. He'd get a chance to know you. It would be a good start. But, of course, that's no reason to marry someone."

Not that he needed any other reason.

"Carolyn loves you," her mother told him. "She's been lonely all these years, and she needs you."

"I need her, too. And I love her."

"I know." She stood then, and picked up her coat. "I'll let you think about it. Maybe talk to her about it. She's right across the street, playing in the park with Billy. I'll send her up."

Carolyn couldn't get to her apartment fast enough. Her mother looked... She wasn't sure she could have described it. *Five years younger* came to mind, but that didn't do justice to the change in Grace. She seemed ... hopeful.

And she'd been talking to Drew?

That part didn't fit at all.

"Drew," Carolyn called out when she opened the door. Walking into the empty apartment, she threw down her coat on the living room sofa.

"Out here." She followed the sound of his voice to the narrow balcony that ran along the far side of the apartment.

She walked outside and saw him leaning over the railing. "What in the world are you doing out here?"

"Watching you and Billy in the park." He smiled.

"Oh," she said, nervous about that smile. "My mother told me that you two had a talk."

"We did."

"Well?" Was she going to have to drag it out of him? She hadn't been able to get anything out of her mother at all. "What did she say?"

"Your mother told me that *you* wanted to marry *me*."

"What?"

"That's what she said."

Carolyn stood there with her mouth open. He was teasing her.

"You do want to marry me, don't you?"

"Drew Delaney, that is absolutely the most arrogant thing you have ever said to me."

"I'm handling this badly."

"Yes, you are."

He had the nerve to laugh then, and take her by the arms. "I'm sorry. She just threw me. Carolyn, she...gave us her blessing. That's the only way I can think to describe it."

"*My* mother?"

"Yes. She wants us to be one big happy family. You, me, her, Billy and Annie. And...you do want to marry me, don't you?"

"You call that a proposal?"

"I'm handling this badly," he said again.

She nodded, the enormous implications of her mother's turnaround just now starting to seep in.

The next thing she knew, Drew was down on one knee, smiling from ear to ear. "I love you, Carolyn McKay. I always have. I always will. And I'd be the happiest man in the world if you'd marry me."

She backed up a step and sat down hard on the edge of the chaise longue. "My knees," she said by way of explanation. They'd simply given out.

She had the strangest impression that she'd just finished an incredible journey, one that she'd been sure she'd never be able to endure. It had taken forever. It had taken all her strength, all her faith. It had taken a miracle. Actually, two of them.

They'd gotten a miracle—again.

It had seemed like too much even to hope for, but they had.

She reached out her hand, and he caught it. His fingers laced their way through hers, his other hand closing over the back of hers to hold it in his grasp.

He was real. She could feel him touching her.

"I love you, too, Drew."

"Then say yes," he said teasingly.

"Yes."

Epilogue

Carolyn sat in her office at Hope House two weeks later, amazed at how rapidly her life had changed in so short a time.

She had Drew's engagement ring on her finger now. They would be married soon.

They were traveling to Hope this weekend to help her mother and Billy pack their things and move into the city. The two would be staying at Carolyn's apartment temporarily, until the four of them found someplace else to live. Carolyn thought a duplex in one of the suburbs would be perfect for starters.

All she needed now was her little sister, who still expressed a strange reluctance to meet with them or even to consider the possibility that she might be Annie McKay.

But Nicholas Garrett was working on her, and he'd said the strangest thing yesterday, something about sending Annie to her, to be ready and be prepared not to give herself away.

A brief knock sounded at her door, and Carolyn looked up, expecting to find her secretary, but saw Drew standing in the doorway instead. "Hi. I wasn't expecting you until lunchtime. What's up?"

He leaned across the desk and kissed her. "Nick told me to get over here."

"Why?" She got up from her chair and went to give him a real kiss.

"He didn't say. Are you expecting him?"

"I'm not expecting anyone but you."

He laughed. God, she loved to hear him laugh.

"That sounds promising," he said, kissing her again.

And then she heard her secretary buzz her. "Carolyn?"

"Yes, Julie."

"There's someone here to see you about the in-house director's job at the runaway shelter."

"We haven't even advertised it yet, have we?" Her live-in director was leaving to take a year's fellowship to study in Boston, and she was happy for him, but dreading the task of filling that job, particularly on a temporary basis. Rick had done wonders at the shelter.

"The ad should come out tomorrow," Julie explained. "But this woman says Dr. Garrett sent her over."

Carolyn wasn't smiling anymore. She grabbed Drew's hand. They looked at each other, no doubt both thinking the same thing.

Nick had said he would send Annie to them.

"He wouldn't," she said. "Not like this."

"He told me she had a degree in counseling, and that she worked at one of the shelters in the city."

"I'm not.... It sounds crazy to say I'm not ready, when we've been hounding Nick to let us see her. But I'm not ready."

"Sit down," he said, guiding her back to the chair behind the desk, then sitting down on the edge of it. "You can do this. Last night you told me you couldn't stand to wait another day to finally see her."

"Carolyn?" her secretary repeated. "What do you want me to do?"

Drew leaned over and pressed the intercom button on the phone to answer for her. "Send her in, Julie."

Carolyn gasped.

"You can do this," he assured her.

"I know, but...we don't have any proof, not really. And we both know that nothing short of a miracle could ever bring Annie back to us."

A knock sounded on the door. "I can't help it, Drew. What if it *isn't* her?"

"Come in," he said to the woman behind the closed door, and then there was no time left to worry.

Carolyn was glad she was sitting down, glad that Drew was here beside her holding her hand. She watched the door swing open, watched as this girl—she definitely looked more like a girl than a young woman—walked into the room, stood directly in front of her and held out her hand.

"Hi, I'm A.J."

Carolyn looked at the white-blond hair, hair that reminded her of Billy's when he was a baby, looked at the deep blue eyes, the smile that held for an instant, then started to falter when Carolyn didn't respond.

Drew responded first. He shook the hand she'd offered. "Drew Delaney. It's nice to meet you."

The young woman shook his hand, then, clearly puzzled, turned back to Carolyn. "I'm sorry about the mix-up with the appointment. Nick told me he'd arranged everything, but your secretary didn't have any idea I was coming, so I guess you didn't, either. I can come back...if this isn't a good time.''

''No, don't go.'' Carolyn wasn't about to let her go anywhere. And she finally managed to get to her feet and extend her hand. In a way, she was afraid to touch her, afraid that this was all some impossible dream that could never come true.

Carolyn watched as, seemingly in slow motion, Annie's hand came out to meet hers. Drew's arm closed around her back, holding her up when she wouldn't have been able to manage on her own.

Their palms met. Annie's fingers clasped hers. Something burst open inside Carolyn, some wellspring of emotion that threatened to choke her all over again. Tears filled her eyes, and she had to take back her hand to brush them away.

''Is this a bad time?'' the girl asked. ''I can come back. It's no trouble.''

''I'll be fine,'' Carolyn said, looking to Drew for help. She didn't think she could pull this off. She was too overwhelmed. This young woman . . . she would swear this was her sister.

''We just got some news,'' he said. ''Family things . . .''

''I hope nothing's wrong.''

''No,'' Carolyn said, desperate to make her stay. ''Everything's fine. I'm just relieved. And...I'm so happy, I've forgotten all my manners. Please sit down.''

The young woman sat. Carolyn was grateful to be able to sit, as well. ''So,'' she said, happy just to be in the same room with her. ''Nick sent you?''

''He said your shelter director was leaving.''

Thankfully, that was true. Carolyn couldn't believe her luck on that point. She couldn't believe she was sitting here in this room talking to her little sister.

"And you'd like to work at Hope House?"

"Yes."

Drew placed his hand on Carolyn's shoulder and gave it a gentle squeeze. She caught his eye, returned his smile, and read his mind.

Miracles did happen.

* * * * *

And look for Annie's story, HOMECOMING, coming in 1996—only from Silhouette Intimate Moments.

COMING NEXT MONTH

Take 4 bestselling love stories FREE

Plus get a FREE surprise gift!